the Snake God

the Snake God

Ashok Singh

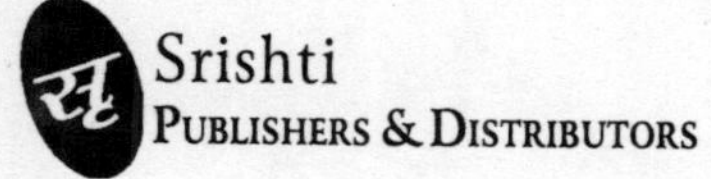

SRISHTI PUBLISHERS & DISTRIBUTORS
64-A, Adhchini
Sri Aurobindo Marg
New Delhi 110017
First published by SRISHTI PUBLISHERS & DISTRIBUTORS in 2001

Rs. 195.00
ISBN 81-87075-71-6

Cover Design by Arrt Creations
45 Nehru Apartment, Kalkaji, New Delhi 110 019
e-mail: arrt@vsnl.com

Printed and bound in India by
Saurabh Print-O-Pack, Noida

Contents

Freedom

The man was standing in the square or a dusty little village in the cool shade of a Peepal tree. He was dark in complexion, thin, tall, with a longish face, protruding nose, curly hair and an unnaturally looking large Adam's apple protruding from his throat. He was dressed in a filthy white dhoti and an equally dirty green kurta while his right hand held a flute which he called a 'Bean'. Placed on the ground near his feet was a five foot long stick with cloth slings attached to both the ends. In front of him were two round little brown baskets woven out of dried feeds. They were of the same size and were covered with little lids made from the same material. The local people called the baskets Pitaras since they contained snakes. The man standing was a snake charmer.

The snake charmer put the bean to his mouth. It was an

odd looking flute which was one inch in diameter and had a round wooden bulb in the middle. Blowing into it he made a weird shrill noise which was supposed to sound exotic to snakes and literally charmed them into a dance. The snake charmer was surrounded by a crowd so he stopped blowing and shouted, "ladies and gentlemen, I have come to your village to give you an opportunity to behold with your own eyes your beloved snake lord, the Nagraj."

People in the crowd shuffled their feet as they waited patiently for the man to show the snake. They were villagers and were illiterate and believed in the snake god. The men wore dhotis and kurtas while the women wore sari's of assorted colors. The children were mostly naked.

Ladies and Gentlemen, continued the snake charmer, You will soon behold the snake lord, so dig into your pockets and pull out what ever you can offer."

"First show us the snakes", said in elderly looking man who sported white hair.

"Thank you sir", replied the snake charmer who lowered himself and sat on his haunches. "Come on snake lord come out of your dwelling. Your subjects want to see you," he goaded.

"Do you have a cobra", asked the old man, "A Nagraj".

The snake charmer nodded his thin head as he proceeded to open a string which was tied around one of the baskets. He placed the basket on the ground before him and changed his sitting mode by cross legging himself. Lifting the flute to his mouth he blew into it as his fingers played over little holes that had been drilled into the instrument. "Aah ladies and gentlemen, behold the snake god". He cried as he lifted the lid off the top of the Pitaara with a flourish.

The crowd bent forward to have a proper look. People standing behind the first rung of spectators looked over shoulders. What they saw was a dark brown snake wrapped in coils in the basket. The head rested on the top coil and there was a black shade on the neck.

"Behold the snake lord, the snake charmer shouted again. 'Behold the Nagraj'.

"Make it stand up", requested a little pot bellied naked boy who was clinging to his mother's green saree.

The snake charmers left hand touched the snake and gave the head a slight poush, but the snake did not move. So the man gave the groggy creature a couple of jabs. The reptile lazily raised its head and put it down again so the snake charmer gave it another push.

"Can't you let me rest", the irritated snake thought as it lifted it's head six inches above the topmost coil and spread its long thin neck ribs to tighten loose skin into a beautiful hood with the markings of a spectacle clearly visible on the back. The sight caused some of the spectators to shudder and others to exclaim in "ooh's" and "aah's", as the snake looked at them with its glazed eyes. It did not like what it saw and hated the crowd. Oh how it would have loved to dig its fangs into their dark brown skins. But only if it did have fangs. They had been tonsoured with the help of a pair of plyers by the snake charmer. He had in fact pulled out the venom bags so the snake was now a harmless, fang less, play thing to be cajoled and made fun of by the humans at will.

"Make it dance", ordered a spectator.

The snake charmer looked up and smiled. "Won't you first pay your respects to the lord?", he asked.

Some people in the crowd mumbled a silent prayer.

"Make it dance", cried the little pot bellied child who was holding onto his mother's saree.

"Of course, of course", replied the snake charmer, "it will, but first you will have to give the lord an offering. After all it sis the snake which resides around Lord Shiva's neck, and it needs money to drink milk. I think you know little boy that milk its expensive now-a-days".

Some of the onlookers dug into their kurta pockets and pulled out coins which they threw on the ground in front of the snake. The snake charmer shook his head. "This won't do", he said. "Here is lord Shiva's snake who has the power to fulfill all your wishes. Ask for a child and he will give you one, ask for filled coffers and he will fill them. As for anything and he will grant it to you, and all you care to give him in return are a few measly coins. Shame, shame, shame. It is a shame on us humans."

The crowd laughed and people dug into their pickets for

more coins which they threw at the snake, causing the creature to turn and look at them as it occasionally flicked out its forked tongue. It's gaze rested on the little pot bellied boy who was holding onto his mother's green saree. The shout and head looked horrible covered in large scales and caused the child to wince and hold tighter to the cloth. The broad ventral scales and the belly plates made the reptile look uglier still.

"Aaah, don't be afraid little child", exclaimed the snake charmer. "He can do no harm to you. He is under my power and he will do as I say."

The child wasn't impressed as it clung tightly to the saree so the snake charmer tapped the snake on the hood just as a master taps the head of a naughty boy. The reptile instantly turned around and hissed menacingly at the hand and lunged forward in an attempt to bite it.

"Hah", said the snake charmer, "you still think you have your teeth do you?" Then folding his hands in mocked prayer he continued. "Look snake lord if you stare menacingly at our bread givers, they will all run away, then you and me will have to go hungry."

This brought another round of laughter from the crowd. Pleased with the result of his little act the snake charmer continued. He slapped the snake on the hood causing the creature to immediately bark out a loud hiss. The sound was mid way between a bark and a hiss, it was a loud "Khaaa", which the creature emanated by opening its mouth and letting out a burst of air. The sound caused some of the spectators to shudder.

"Now everyone", shouted the snake charmer, "together in one loud voice shout with me. Nagraj Ki Jai".

"Nagraj Ki Jai", bellowed the crowd.

With a flourish the snake charmer picked up the bulbous looking flute, and placing an end to his lips he blew into it as his body swayed to the rhythm of the weird wound that emanated from the instrument. The irritated snake looked on and did not move. The snake charmer continued swaying as he blew and soon stopped swaying but swiveled his head from left to right and vice versa in half a semi circle. The snake end of the flute swung back and forth in a little arc missing the snake by a couple of inches.

The snake is not dancing, grumbled an old man.

The snake charmer continued his little act and abruptly shot his head forward causing the open end of the flute to hit the reptile's snout. The latter reacted and tried to bite the flute which instantly moved away. The instrument looked menacing with its long tube like structure and the bulb in between. It looked as though it would strike it again, so the snake marked it and decided to follow the latter's movements. The flute moved to the left so the snake swayed to its right. The flute moved in the opposite direction and the snake swayed to its left.

"Aah the snake is dancing", exclaimed a lady. "How horrible it looks.

The snake charmer continued blowing and swiveling his head from left to right and right to left. The snake continued swaying as it suspiciously marked the end of the instrument while the crowd continued emanating "oohs", and "aah's" as shudders continued climbing up some of their spines.

"There!, exclaimed the snake charmer," the snake lord is dancing. He is granting all your wishes, so please throw some more coins for his milk."

A few more coins pinged onto the ground while the man blew into his flute as the wretched creature continued swaying, goaded by an occasional jab from the instrument. The snake charmer soon realized that no more money was coming. He decided to pack up so he stopped blowing and put the flute into the filthy cloth sling which was attached to an end of the stick that was lying on the ground.

"Does the snake have a name?", asked the little pot bellied boy.

"Yes it has".

"What do you call it?"

"Fangs".

"What a weird name!", retorted the boys mother, "What does it mean?"

"It does not mean anything. It is the English name for a snake's poisonous teeth."

"How did you think or such a name?"

I did not think of the name", it was an English sahib, the English inspector or police in Patna who gave it the name. I had the pleasure to make it dance before the sahib. He was pleased and gave me ten rupees and told me to call it Fangs. So that is the name".

"Couldn't you give it a better name?", asked the woman.

"What's in a name", replied the snake charmer, "the English sahib gave it the name, so the name will stay".

"Make it dance again", requested an old man.

"The Nagraj is tired", announced the snake charmer, "it is time for me to go back home. Saying this he took the Pitara's lid and placed it on the snakes head, gently forcing it down to rest on the lower basket. He then took a string and tied it around the Pitara and placed the basket in the cloth sling next to the flute. The other Pitara housed a green vine snake and a brown shield tail snake. The snake charmer lifted the basket and placed it in the cloth sling. He hadn't thought it necessary to take out the other snakes as it was getting late and he was in a hurry to get back home.

Collecting the last coin and putting it into his kurta pocket, the snake charmer picked up the stick, balanced it on his shoulder and hauled himself up. Namastaying and thanking the cowd, he walked towards the road which led to the railway station with the Pitara's safely in the cloth slings which hung from both ends of the stick.

Inside the Pitara, Fangs flicked his forked tongue. He did not enjoy the slight bobbing of the basket as his master walked towards the station. He hated the master and the latter's kind as much as he hated his present existence. He would now have to stay couped in the basket not able to move or flex his muscles till the snake charmer reached his home. Even there he would be lucky it the latter allowed him to leave the basket and stretch out on the floor to gobble down a mice or a frog which the masters wife would have caught and kept reserved for him. Fangs relished frogs or mice or lizards and hated milk which his master sometimes forcibly dipped his snout into when he tried to dupe his customers into believing that snakes drank milk. He hated the liquid and felt like vomiting when the saucer was placed in front of him.

The Pitara bobbed as it synchronized to the snake charmers walk. Once inside the railway station, it lay still on the platform as the snake charmer waited for the train that would take him to his village and his waiting wife. When the train arrived Fangs felt the thunderous rumbling of the wheels and felt the Pitara being lifted off the ground. In the train he recognized the clickety clack rhythm of the trains wheels on the tracks which he received from his sensory organs. He soon realized that the train had stopped and felt the slight tug as the Pitara was lifted off the ground followed by the same slight bobbing of the basket which told the reptile that the master was walking again.

The snake charmer walked into the darkness and soon

reached a little village and walked upto a single roomed hut which had a thatched roof and mud walls. There was a lantern inside whose yellow light seemed to filter through a tattered gunny sack which acted as a door. Pushing the gunny sack aside, the snake charmer entered the room and realized his wife was not there. He supposed that she would be in the neighboring hut so he put the stick with the two Pitara's on the ground in a corner of the room.

The room itself was a humble affair with mud walls, a dirt floor and a thatched roof made out of needs and palm leaves knitted together and covered with a layer of hay. The room was eight feet long and eight feet broad, and the floor and walls were plain and hard as they were regularly pasted with cow dung. The repeated dung pastings intact helped to thicken the walls and make them stronger, though the room smelt of the dung.

Along the southern wall as a cot and in the middle of the room was a chulha which held a pot. In the north western corner were arrayed a row of cheap battered aluminum utensils near which was an earthen pot that held water.

Filting the water pot the snake charmer washed his hands and sat cross legged near his Pitara's. "Malini", he bellowed as he took out a beedi and lit it.

"Yes", came the reply from an adjoining hut.

"I'm back".

"I'm coming".

The snake charmer continued putting at his beedi and a thin short bare footed woman wearing a worn out faded blue saree walked into the room. She was dark in complexion and had cheap aluminum trinkets hanging from her ears and nose. "How much did you earn today", she asked.

"Ten rupees".

The woman proceeded to a corner of the room where she sat down and picked up a place and scooped out rice from a bowl and put it in round balls in the plate. She then waddled over to the chulha and emptied the pot of red chilled curry on top of the rice after which she pushed the plate towards the snake charmer. "Here eat", she said.

"Water", ordered the husband.

Still sitting on her haunches the woman waddled back to the earthen pot and taking a glass, she filled it with water and getting up, walked over to her husband and placed it in front of him. The snake charmer took a palm full of the liquid and sprinkled it on the food after which he mixed the curry with the rice. He then scooped up a handfull of the mixture and stuffed it into his mouth, half chewing and half gobbling it down. "you're cooking hasn't improve", he complained as he gulped down water. "Where is the arrack?"

The woman got up and from under the cot pulled out a "lota". "Here", she said as she pushed the vessel towards her husband who was still eating. "Here drink this. You will enjoy it when your intestines rot".

The snake charmer smiled and belched loudly, "Woman, you are always complaining,", he said.

"Why shouldn't I, she replied, "you spend half your income on that horrible liquid."

"Horrible liquid?", replied the snake charmer, "who said it is horrible?" It is manna from heaven".

"Yuck".

The snake charmer finished eating so he picked up the glass containing water and washed his hands over his plate. "here take the plate", he ordered as he burped and put down the glass and lifted the lota to his mouth and took a gulp of the throat burning liquid.

"Where is the money", asked the wife.

The snake charmer fished out a fistfull of coins from his kurta pocket which he placed on the floor in front of him. "Here take them, he said.

The woman leant over and scooped up the coins from the ground and put them unter the mattress which was on the cot. The snake charmer went on drinking and was soon sozzled. "Wife", he drawled.

"Yes".

"You are my dear wife".

"Only when you are drunk".

"Don't speak back to me".

The woman shrugged.

"My loving wife".

"Drink the arrack fast", ordered the woman. "I will have to wash the lota and the other dishes".

"My dear wife", continued the drunk man. "My lolly pop, my dear rosogulla. You work so hard for me".

The woman shook her head.

"I will earn lots or money, my wife, and dress you up in diamonds and pearls".

"Only when you are drunk".

"I promise you my dear, I promise you".

"For now the ten rupees will suffice".

"You think I am telling you lies, my dear?" The drunk man turned to the little brown baskets and picked up the one which housed the cobra. Opening the string which was tied around the Pitara, he lifted the lid and released Fangs whose head rose up and spread his hood and flicked his forked tongue in anticipation of a dead rat.

"Now look at this stupid creature?" the snake charmer drawled as he slapped the cobra on the hood. The snake instantly lunged forward but the hand shot back to a safe distance. "This creature", the drunk continued, "will earn us a fortune. Its spectacled hood will dress you in satins and pearls".

"Stop illtreating the snake", the woman scolded.

"Who's irritating who?" drawled the snake charmer as his right hand shot around the snake and caught the neck. He lifted the reptile and kissed the nape.

"Put that snake back in the basket and go to bed", ordered the wife.

"Okay dear. Don't get angry".

The bewildered reptile was lowered into the basket and the head was pressed down. "There little one go to sleep. Close your eyes". Then giggling the drunk man remembered. "Oh, sorry", he said, "I forgot. You have no eye lids". Putting the lid safely on the basket, the man got up and staggered to the cot where he slumped down, lay back, and was soon snoring in a deep drunken sleep.

Inside the Pitara Fangs was again cramped and crouched in his colds. It seemed today he wouldn't receive his weekly quota of trapped Mice or Frog and he felt hungry. It wasn't that he wasn't used to this kind of existence. It was his daily routine to lie locked in the Pitara and he hated it. He longed to be back in the wild, in the grass, in the jungles and amongst shrubs, hiding from predators or tracking down a prey. He craved to once more have the re-assured feeling of a pair of fangs tucked neatly in his mouth. Many a times he had pushed up at the baskets lid with his head, but to no avail. The lid was always firmly in place. Being a reptile he never accepted defeat and regularly pushed up with his head since he had nothing else to do, only to find the lid still firmly in place.

Fangs decided to try again just for the sake of it. It would be something to do and was better than lying idle, so he pushed up knowing what the result would be. But lo, the lid moved, so the snake pushed harder and lifted the lid off its base. The lid was well balanced on the reptiles head who had spread its long thin neck ribs to tighten the loose neck skin into a hood.

The snake seemed to peep out from under the lid which was now balanced on its head like a straw hat. It peered towards the cot and realized the snake charmer and his wife were asleep. May be this was a chance to escape, a god sent opportunity to slither off. The drunk master in his stupor had lazily forgotten to tie the string around the Pitara. The lid had been left loosely on the basket and he had opened it.

Flexing his muscles, Fangs slithered out of the Pitara onto the dung pasted dry floor. His forked tongue flicked out, touched the ground and shot back into his mouth. In the process it picked up chemical signals or molecules from the air and the ground which were passed to a pair of Jacobson's organs which were situated in the roof of his mouth. This organ analyzed the signals to give him the information he needed to trail his prey, recognize a predator, find a mate, or run away from his captor which Fangs wanted to do just now, so he flexed his muscles and straightened his body. He thoroughly enjoyed the change in position and relaxed for a minute but kept a watchful eye on the snoring master. This was his chance to escape and he didn't want to botch it. He had a line of scutes along his long underbelly. When necessary these pushed back and moved forward alternately allowing him to move in a straight line which he did just now. The scutes moved back and forth and

Fangs slowly slid forward and seemed to tip-toe out of the room. He kept a cautious eye on the cot and the snoring master, since he did not want to get caught red-handed trying to escape and got a fright when the latter growled in his sleep and changed his position. The man had been sleeping on his back with his face upwards, now he was on his side and was facing the snake. The terrified cobra immediately pulled up its body in a couple of S shaped curves, pushed the hind part of each curve against small irregularities on the ground, pushed hard and was soon zipping across the surface towards the doorway where it did not stop but continued and was soon out with its head leading the S shaped curves as it rapidly move on.

Fangs was out of the room and was zipping through grass and shrubs and around trees desperate to be as far away from the little hut and the snake charmer as was possible. In his fright he did not realize he had knocked over a coiled Millipede. The creature was brown colored with black stripes and had coiled up into a round ball when it saw the snake approach. A part of the reptiles body hit it and sent it rolling two feet away.

Fangs continued his mad run as he zig-zagged through obstacles and unknowingly broke out of the grass scaring a purple black Centipede which scampered out of its path. The snake headed straight for a little pond. Pushing into the water it swam with the help of the same S shaped curves and disturbed a myriad of creatures living in the water. Water Boatmen and Back Swimmers swam away while a couple of water stick insects which hung from the surface film by their respiratory siphons' hastily slid away. Little fishes darted in different directions.

On the opposite bank, on seeing the snake shoot out of the water, a trap door spider disappeared into its burrow which was closed behind it with a hinged door. Fangs left the water and shot across the dank squelchy mud to again enter grass where he scared a group of black colored Dung Beetles who scampered out of its path. The snakes fright was too much for it to notice these creatures as it zipped on.

"It seems as though a dragon is chasing that reptile", thought a green colored Chameleon who was sitting on a branch of a small shrub like Magholia tree. Its turret like eyes moved forward as it watched the snake slip past.

Fangs zipped on with his head leading the S shaped curves and was unperturbed by the creatures he disturbed. Grasshoppers jumped to safety as bugs scampered away. Butterflies and moths flew over to a safer roosting spot.

Fatigue, soon overtook the snake causing it to slow down as it traversed a termite mound which rose up to form the silhouette or a tall mud chimney. On the other side of the chimney, Fangs slid into grass again. He was tired and wanted to rest so he headed towards the silhouette of a huge tree. Reaching it he stopped and saw a dead log at the base. He drew his body alongside the dead wood and lay his head on the ground. He lay there relaxing his tired snaky muscles and watched the night draw on. As he gained strength and his fright subsided, he noticed his surroundings. He didn't have ears so he could not hear the tick, tick, tick of a grasshopper or the mating call of a Cicada. Neither could he hear the hooting of a Great Horned owl or the distant lonely howl of a Jackal. He could however see hundreds of flashes around him. They were Fireflies who gave out a phosphorous glow from the tip of their abdomen which could be switched on and off to produce a regular series of synchronized flashes. These light signals were picked up by the females, the wingless larvae like glow worms who lovingly signaled back from the ground.

Fangs was now enjoying his surroundings as he found the flashes funny. His forked tongue picked up molecules of dank mud, dead wood, dirty water and chlorophyll from the various shades of green he had slid through. These were molecules of happiness, molecules of ecstasy and most important molecules of freedom.

The night drew on and the sky gradually took on a bluish tint. The snake watched the fireflies disappear as the blue tint turned crimson and deepened in texture till it turned orange, then yellow and soon it was a bright morning with a hot sun overhead.

Fangs pulled himself together and lifted his head and drew up his body onto the dead wood where he created two coils, one on top of the other over which he raised his hood. He couldn't blink in the hot glare of the sun as he did not have any eyelids. He however had a pair of colored lenses on his eyes to protect the retina from too much sunlight. The eyes were further covered by transparent windows called a bridle which gave him a glassy star.

Looking around Fangs could not see well as he was short sighted so he regularly flicked out his forked tongue to get the information he wanted. He enjoyed the fresh morning air and the slight pressure of a breeze on his hood and did not hear the squawk of a crow above him. "What's down there?", it seemed to ask.

The bird squawked its warning to the other crows and continued caw-cawling as more friends arrived. Soon there was a swarm flying around the tree creating a din which the poor snake could not hear.

A pair of Jungle Babbler's flew over. "What's the ruckus abouit", they seemed to ask as they flew with the crows.

"The egg thief is down there", was the reply.

The Babblers added their harsh chatter squeaking to the din and realized that they weren't the only one's helping the crows. There were a host of common Myna's, white chested Pied Common Babbler's all perched on the higher branches of the huge Fig tree and were chirping and chattering and squawking and squeaking their anger at the intruder.

Disturbed and irritated by the ruckus, a big Brown Spider who was sitting on a twig watching its web for food, decided to go down and investigate. It let out a silken thread and let itself down till it hung just two feet above the snakes hood. It studied the reptile with its ogre like eyes and decided that the former was dangerous, so it rolled up the silken thread and travelled all the way upto the twig it had been sitting on where it hid under a leaf. It didn't want to be eaten by one of the birds.

Down below Fangs looked up at the circling birds and realized that he was unwanted. He saw a few dive bomb him and pull away when they were still at a safe distance. He however lunged at the ones who came too close and barked out loud Khaa's at them.

He realized he was badly outnumber and decided that it would be a good idea to slither off to a place where there was more privacy so he uncurled himself, drew his body in S shaped curves, flicked out his forked tongue, pushed the hind part of each curve against small irregularities on the wood and slithered down to the ground and was soon cruising through thick grass. Working his way on, entering little troughs in the ground or sliding over little mounds, he stopped and lifted his head to look around to see if there was anything to eat. He was feeling hungry and desired to eat a frog or a field rat. Flicking his forked tongue he understood that none of these delicacies were available so he continued cruising through the grass till he reached the edge of a ploughed field, where he stopped and looked across the uneven ground and decided to continue on his way to the other side.

Unknown to the reptile a couple of Kilometer's away in eagle flapped its wings as it lifted its heavy body out of a nest, leaving behind a pair of nestlings who were demanding food. It was a Parian Kite which was flapping heavily into the sky and was soon soaring with its outspread wings, its eyes and acute vision concentrated on the ground below in search of prey. It was dark brown in color with a forked tail and a wing span of around four feet, with strong feet and a curved beak to tear at flesh. The feet ended in four sharply curved claws called talons.

The eagle soared higher and occasionally screeched at the ground or a friend predator. It was looking for mice, rats, frogs, lizards, and insects with which it would feed its young. It didn't mind tearing up and devouring a snake if it could find one.

Down below, oblivious of the danger, Fangs slithered on. He entered the field and his head seemed to bob as he crossed the uneven ground. He was half way across when he saw a shadow cross over hi so he stopped and thought. He remembered the shadow. He had seen it somewhere else and had an inkling it did not bode him well. Where had he seen it before?, and what did it mean? He did not hear the shrill call as the shadow once more passed over him. He remembered. It was the shadow of an eagle, a predator who was out to get him. The eagle was about to dive.

Lifting his head Fangs looked up and could make out the form of the bird that had been circling above him. He realized he was a sitting duck in the open field. He had been an idiot to come out into the open. The years in captivity had dulled his senses and slowed his reactions. He thought slowly and reacted sluggishly. He would have to learn the rules of the wild all over again. Or at least try to remember them.

The eagle screeched again as Fangs drew up his body into coils over which he lifted his hood. His belly plates and broad ventral scales shone in the sun as he looked up at the predator and hissed a warning.

"I'm coming for you", the eagle screeched.

"Come down", hissed back the snake, "and have a taste of my Fangs, Ooop's, he had no Fangs. They had been tonsured out by the horrible human he had left behind. Anyway Fangs or no Fangs, he was a cobra and like other cobra's he had the courage to fight. He would be ferocious and give the enemy all he had, even though it meant biting with a venom less mouth.

Fangs watched as the bird steadied itself and began its dive. It swooped down at a speed of a hundred and sixty miles an hour with outstretched talons and it" greedy eyes concentrated on the snake.

The snake watched the predator focus into his view as if came lower till it seemed it would slam into him. He reacted and lunged out and let out a loud "Khaa", from his mouth causing the eagle to swerve at the last minute and miss him. If flapped its mighty wings to gain height and prepare itself for another attack. The bird did not know that its prey was weapon less. It was Fangless. If it had known, it wouldn't have played safe and swerved at the last moment. It would have simply flown down to the reptile and wished it a "hello, I am taking you home for lunch. Any objections?" It wouldn't have mattered if the latter objected. The eagle would have simply pounced on it, held it with its claws as its beak gave the fussing thing a couple of blows after which it would rip open the head. It however did not know the snakes secret and was soaring once more in the sky as it took proper aim. It lifted its wings slightly and began to drop with its talons out stretched once more.

Down below on the ground Fangs felt how vulnerable he was as he saw the eagle swoop. He did not have his Fangs and he was furious. It was his anger that gave him the strength to face the bird. He saw the brute focus into view and timing himself perfectly, he lunged out at the last moment and let out a couple of vicious "Khaas", at the fast approaching bird. The eagle saw the lunge and tilted sideways to its right, breaking its fall as its talons slammed into the cobra's hood, slamming it against the hard ground as the bird zoomed by.

Fangs saw stars and birds twittered in his head. His hood had shrunk back into his neck so he raised his head and painfully re-opened the hood. He longed for his fangs, then he would have had a better chance against the eagle who was diving again." I am coming for you", the eagle screeched.

Fangs remembered. He had to save his tail or the eagle would snatch it and swoop it up with the rest of him following suite.

He hurriedly drew it up under the protective shadow of his hood.

The eagle came lower as it zoomed towards its prey at a speed of a hundred and sixty miles an hour. It saw the snake pull its tail up, and as it closed in, it saw the reptile lunge out with its open mouth. It tilted to avoid the mouth and swooped past as its talons once more slammed into the hood throwing the reptiles head back against the hard ground. Flapping it's wings heavily it once more lifted itself into the blue sky to turn around for a fourth attempt. What it saw raised its spirit. The cobra was slithering away as fast as it could with its neck leaving a thin trail of blood.

The eagle swooped down again, this time concentrating on the fast moving tail. It rapidly lost height and the snake grew larger in its sight. The talons shot forward and grabbed the tail after which the eagle flapped madly as it gained height with its captive writhing and hanging from its clasped claws.

Fangs felt the pain and the jerk as he was rudely snatched off the ground and lifted into the air as the eagle gained height. He reacted by lunging up at the eagles feet in an attempt to bite them, but soon realized that his bone structure wasn't strong enough to send half his body up alongside the other half which was hanging from the eagles claws. The snake however, continued in its attempts to bite the eagle but soon realized that it was useless since he couldn't reach the feet so its head fell back and it hung from its full three feet as the eagle flew on.

The snake felt weird and found it funny at the way the ground grew smaller and went out of focus as the eagle flew higher. He looked down and saw the blur down below. His eyes could not see well so he relied totally on his bifid tongue and his other sensory organs. He was frightened. What would happen now it the eagle let go and he was to fall all the way to the ground making impact with a sickening splat? Al his little bones would break, his single lung would puncture, his little heart would squash and he would certainly die.

The happy eagle flew on as it carried its heavy load causing the snake's body to slice through the air. This was a new experience for Fangs who partly grew out of his fright. He looked down and wondered at the blurred patches of different shades of green which were the fields, the blurred lines which were the roads and the railway line. He was curious and his forked tongue rapidly shot out of his mouth providing him with the information he wanted. He didn't hear the screech of his captor or the replying ones that was coming from a second eagle. Fangs looked up and was horrified to see a second eagle focus into view. It looked horrible and was flying straight for him.

The second eagle was flying a little higher than the first and was swooping down in a dive which was aimed at the snake. At the last moment, in a perfectly executed maneuver, Fangs captor lost height and the second eagle sped on three feet over head as it missed. The first eagle tilted slightly to the right and flapped its wings to gain lost height again.

Fangs felt his innards shoot up as he suddenly lost height and felt the rude tug as he gained height again.

The captor flew higher and higher and below it the second eagle flew around in an arc and screeching its challenge, it headed back towards the fleeing eagle. The first eagle increased speed and to Fangs horror, he realized the second eagle was closing in on him fast. He was desperate so he lunged up and hissed and squirmed and fell back and let out loud "Khaa's", at the wildly chasing bird. The snake understood that an aerial dogfight would ensue in which he would be badly mauled so he desperately twisted and squirmed and let out loud "Khaas" at his captor and the chasing eagle.

The second eagle was free with no weight to carry, enabling it to fly faster than Fangs captor so it soon caught up and was just five feet behind the snake when the first eagle suddenly lost height and fell with its load causing the chasing eagle to college smack into the fleeing one in a flurry of dark brown feathers. The impact caused the eagle to let go off the snake and turn to face the second eagle who seeing the snake fall swooped down and caught the tail in its talons, and was off with the previous captor giving chase.

The snake was terrified. It did not want to end its life as an eagles breakfast. The eagles however seemed madly in love with him and did not want to let him go.

"Let me go", hissed, Fangs.

The captor refused to let go and swerved to the right. The trailling eagle followed suite.

The captor eagle tilted to the left. The second eagle did the same.

The first eagle rapidly lost height. The second eagle swooped down, so the first eagle went down lower and Fangs realized he was flying at tree top level. His captor lost height again and headed straight towards a mango tree. The eagle swerved to the right and taking Fangs along skirted the tree and headed for a ten feet high boundary wall across which a group of humans were ploughing a field with the help of a wooden iron tipped plough and two bullocks. One of the men saw the first eagle approach with the snake hanging from its claws. Instinctly he picked up a stick and threw it at the bird who let go off its prey and flew on flapping its wings to gain height to get out of the human menace. The second eagle however made a last ditched attempt to retrieve its breakfast and swooped down and made a frantic attempt to grab the snake with it's talons. It missed and carried on as it desperately flapped its wings to gain height and get out of the place as fast as possible.

The humans saw the snake fall and the second eagle swoop down to grab it. The person holding the plough screamed and ran. The other peasants did the same and Fangs found himself alone in the field. He was desperate and was scared that the eagles might turn and take another shot at him so he hastily zipped towards the edge of the field where he had spotted some bushes in a bamboo grove.

Weaving in and out of stones and blocks of mud Fangs reached the edge of the field and entered thick grass. He continued through the grass and entered some bushes where he stopped to rest. He had had a harrowing time and a close shave. He lifted his head and peeped out towards the field he had just left. The humans were back and were holding sticks and were searching the ground for him. High up there were two blurs flying in the sky. They were circling the field. Fangs was thankful for his escape and lay his chin on the ground to relax. He felt scared and hungry and wondered where he was as he flicked out his forked tongue. He did not know that he had plopped into the compound of Zamindar Vikram Singh of Ramnagar.

Vikram Singh

Vikram Singh's haveli was a simple single storied whitewashed structure facing southwards. The building itself was square in shape and faced the fields with its back to the rutted road which led to the highway which in turn led to the district town of Monghyr. The heart of the building was a central square courtyard which was surrounded by a verandah which had rooms facing to it. This was the ladies section and was out of bounds for males who did not directly belong to the Zamindar's family.

The exterior of the building was as simple as the interior. The entrance was a rectangular verandah with square pillars holding up a gabled roof. The southern wall of the verandah boasted of a row of six windows which provided ventilation to three rooms. Next to the last window was a door which led into a passage which in turn ended in the verandah which surrounded the inner courtyard. The entrance verandah was furnished simply with a square table and two benches in a row along the northern wall. A reclining wooden chair faced the benches. The building however had no electrical fittings since electricity hadn't reached the village yet.

Behind the haveli was the boundary wall which ran alongside the rutted dirt track which was supposed to be a road. Next to the north eastern corner of the mansion the boundary wall was breached by a gate which boasted of two concrete yellow lions crouched with jaws wide open in a soundless roar at a scarecrow which stood in the paddy field across the road opposite to them. The scarecrow seemed to smile back as it stood lonely in the field with a crow perched defecating on its pot like head while it's hands were spread out like a traffic policeman's.

The double lioned gate led into a drive way with the haveli's western wall to the right and the Hathikhana and a couple of garages to the left. One of the garages was occupied by a sky blue Fordson Major tractor, and the other had the grill and headlights of battered 1930 model Buick peeping out. The garages themselves were a shabby affair with brick walls and tiled roofs. The walls were plastered with dung cakes which were also plastered on the tractor trolley's blue metal body which silently stood outside. The Hathikhana was a similar structure with dung cake spattered walls with a lone elephant residing inside it.

The driveway carried on past the garages and past the haveli to finally stop before a thatched roof which was supported by eight bamboo poles. The roof itself was square in shape measuring twenty feet by twenty feet, and was made out of hay and palm leaves and housed two benches, a cot and two old faded chairs. On three sides of this structure ran a two feet high mud and brick wall which had a two inch hole on the south eastern corner which led into the ground. It was presumed that the hole housed a field rat or a mole. The ground was smooth and plain and clean and was made up of hard earth. It was actually made up of layers of dung which was religiously plastered over it every second day. The dung paste was infact plastered over the acre of ground which separated the thatched roof from the Haveli. This plot of land should have been an exotic garden with beautiful plants and psychedelic flowers. Instead there were mounds of dung and heaps of hay for the bovines to eat. Along the southern boundary behind the thatched roof where the beautiful shrubs and trees should have been, were a row of twenty cows and buffaloes tethered to a row of troughs full of hay and green grass near a well which was used by the Zamindar to bath in . Along the eastern boundary of this supposed to be imposing garden plot was a row of twelve shacks in which the Zamindar's peasants and servants lived. These should have been neatly cut hedges and instead of giving out sweet smells of exotic flowers, gave out the obnoxious odor of shit and urine. The occupants had a habit of defecating in the fields ten feet away from the shacks. The Zamindar did not supply toilets to his subjects so the air in general smelt of a mixture of human defecate, cowdung and urine.

The British did find the place filthy. If they had owned the property there would have been a beautiful garden with patches for Snap Dragons, Begonias, Chrysanthemums, Daisies, Marigold, and Pansies. There would have been a riot of colors, a delight to the rural eye. A rock garden would have been thrown in with a fish pond with little lilly leaves floating on the water. The driveway would have been graveled, the lawns moed, the hedges cut and a long pole would have been installed in the middle flying the Union Jack.

A long pole was however installed in the middle of the empty plot. It stood proudly in the midday heat of summer time Bihar. The mighty hot wind called the Loo blew its hot breath over the burning land shooing the English sahibs to the high altitude hill resorts of Darjeeling, Shimla, and Mussourie, making the flagpole untouchably hot. The flag was unfazed by the heat and fluttered proudly over the haveli as though it was the latter's master.

It was the latter's master. It was the Union Jack. The Zamindar had installed it to please the English who were his master. His "Mai Baap". He had infact, requested them to allow him to fly the flag in his compound since he was a loyal subject of the crown. To the freedom fighters he was a traitor, a back stabber and a powerful rascal whom they stayed away from.

The British however felt that this most probably was the filthiest piece of territory over which the Union Jack proudly flew. They were sometimes appalled when they had to pass below it with their hands to their noses. They wanted the place cleaned, but did not pester the Zamindar. After all he was a faithful subject of the crown and provided them with vital information of the movements of the rascals who waged war with the King Emperor. That's why they humored the Zamindar and allowed him to fly the flag in his compound.

Vikram Singh was a huge pot bellied man with a little pigtail on the back of his bald head. His face was round with huge jowls and a double chin. Decorating the face was a thick gray mustache which seemed to flow to the ears and the head seemed to be perched on a short neck which itself was perched on a naked torso which sported a large paunch which hung over the dhoti which was tied around his midriff. Directly opposite to the bulge of the paunch was the bulge of the bottom protruding from below the midriff which could be sometimes seen through the thin fabric of the dhoti. This obese structure was supported by a pair of wobbly legs which had been weakened due to hours of sitting cross legged on the ground.

The Zamindar loved sitting cross legged on the dung pasted floor under the thatched roof. After all this was the way of his fathers and fore fathers. Tables and chairs were an unnecessary necessity which the English had brought along with them. He infact kept the English furniture for the English officers themselves when they came visiting him. Then he would himself sit on a chair and pray a silent prayer to his fore fathers to forgive him for elevating himself. After all this was done for the good of the family, for his sons and their sons. Good business couldn't be carried out with an irritated British officer sitting cross legged on the dirt floor with all sorts of little creatures crawling up his khaki half pants.

Sitting opposite to the Zamindar was his spiritual adviser, a thin hook beak nosed bearded Brahmin Priest. Panditjee was as tall as the Zamindar, dark in complexion with a long face, small ears and a large Adams apple protruding from a thin long neck. His eyes were sunk in deep sockets and his jaws and lips were hidden by an ill kept beard which flowed to the base of his neck. The rest of the body seemed to run parallel from the arms to the feet with hardly any protrusions and the ribs could be easily counted. Like the Zamindar he was also half naked and wore a simple saffron cloth around his abdomen as he sat cross legged on the ground opposite the landlord. Panditjee seemed to be perennially puffing at a mud chillum and puffing out smoke like one of those English railway engines. The result was a pair of glazed eyes. What was his name?, no body knew. The people simply called him Panditjee.

Vikram Singh was seated in the north eastern corner of the thatched shelter. He had braved the heat and instead of snoozing away the mid-day sun in one of the stuffy rooms of his haveli,he was chatting with a group of villagers who were petty Zamindars themselves and were sitting cross-legged behind the priest while two half naked moustachioed broad shouldered, tall Pehelwans massaged his back with mustard oil. The topic of discussion were the English and the quit India movement. Vikram Singh had his priorities clear. He favored the British. "The English will not go", he told the villagers, "they are too strong to be thrown out of the country".

"We will drive them out", said the headman. He was a short stocky person who had a pudgy nose, pudgy lips, round eyes and a face disfigured by small pox. "We will throw them out of this country".

"Impossible", replied Vikram.

"Vikramji, nothing is impossible", continued the headman.

"The brown man cannot fight the white man".

"That myth has been broken. The Russians have repeatedly lost battles against Japan".

"You are talking about Russians, and I am talking about the English. There is a vast difference between the two".

"There is no difference in quality. The Russian's are white and so are the English. If one white race can be defeated so can the other."

Vikram Singh looked at the village headman then at the other villagers. "Look we all are Brahmins", he continued, "We are all landlords. The only difference is the size of our land holdings. Some of us have got more and some have got less".

The village headman nodded his head.

"We are the product of the English. They created us Zamindars".

The villagers nodded their heads.

"I tell you", shouted Vikram, "If the British go, then Zamindari will also go".

"It will not", shouted back the headman.

"No shouting on my premises", retorted Vikram.

"Sorry".

"Now look", continued Vikram, "have sense. If the country gets independence, the first thing the Congress party will do is to abolish Zamindari. You people are playing with fire. You are hacking at your own feet".

"Zamindari will not be abolished," replied the headman, "it cannot be abolished. This is the only system that exists for the government to collect land revenue.

"See sense", continued Vikram, "I have no love for the white man and I too would prefer independence. But I know their strength. They have thousands of tanks and aircraft and guns and the Congress party has only their Gandhi caps. I personally would love to see them go. But they are too strong and they won't go, so I might as well remain their faithful servant. More over we Zamindars have a future under them".

"We have a future under any Government".

The little group stopped talking and turned around to look

towards the double lioned gate. A little olive green Jeep had entered, giving two sharp parps from its horns and was bouncing down the rutted driveway. The vehicle was hoodless with its windscreen lying neatly on the bonnet. Driving it was a short stocky Nepalese policeman, and sitting next to him was an English officer. In the rear sat two tall dark Khakhi clad policemen. The four seemed to do a jig as the springs of the vehicle winced at the shocks it received from the rutted road.

Vikram Singh motioned to the half naked Pehelwans and the villagers to go as he himself got up and pulled on his cream colored kurta which was lying on a nearby chair. The villagers quietly slunk off as Vikram moved towards the Jeep. It had a little Union Jack perched proudly on the tip of the bonnet.

"Namastay Sahib", Vikram greeted as a pair of Jackboots alighted from the vehicle and landed firmly on the ground. It was followed by the body. Out of the boots grew a pair of brown socks out of which shot up white legs into a pair of baggy khakhi half pants. The half pants were held tightly to the hips with the help of a brown buckled belt from which dangled a holster. Out of the belt grew a khakhi shirt with front pockets and topped with a khakhi collar. A white neck flowed into the collar with a pink face perched on it. The face was irritated with the summer's heat and wore a police officer's cap. It belonged to James Powell, the Superintendent of Police of Monghyr District.

"Namastay Sahib", Vikram Singh wished again as the

bearded priest hurriedly put off the chillum and hid it under his bottom as he picked himself up and seated himself on a bench. James Powell's right hand went up and a shiny baton touched the Englishman's cap in an acknowledgment to the Zamindar's namastay. "Hello Mr. Singh", Powell replied as he walked towards the thatched roof. "And how are you?"

"Very good sahib",

"And how are the villagers?"

"All right sahib, all right".

The officer proceeded to cover his nose with his right hand as he passed under the flag.

"It is very hot sahib", continued Vikram, "you shouldn't be moving around in this heat. It does not suit us Hindustanis. You could become very sick".

Powell walked on and removed his hand from his nose only when he reached the thatched roof. Vikram singh motioned to the priest to get up and hurriedly dusted a chair for the Englishman to sit down in. "Take your seat sahib, take your seat. What a pleasant surprise. I didn't expect you today".

Powell sat down. "Thank you", he said as a gust of wind blew from the shacks bringing with it the obnoxious smell. This resulted in the right hand flying back to the nose.

"I say old chap, can't you get this place cleaned. It stinks, this place does".

Vikram looked around and sniffed the air. "What smell sahib? There is no smell. The air is fresh as the lily in the pond and the duck in the river".

The bearded priest smiled as though he understood what was being said and nodded his head in approval.

"Cant you smell the shit?".

Vikram Singh went on sniffing at the air so the bearded Priest decided it was wise to do the same.

"You've got a jolly blunt nose Mr. Singh".

"What is smelling sahib?", Vikram asked innocently, "I can smell only cow dung".

"That's it", replied Powell, "Cowdung. Cant you smell the piss. I must say you Indians should be taught some hygiene".

"But Powell sahib, cow is our mother. Cowdung is very pure. We Hindustani's purify the ground by pasting it. Cows urine is also sacred. We drink it. If you drink cows urine, you are sure to go to heaven".

"Goodness gracious", retorted the Englishman, "what did you say"?

"We drink cows urine".

"Now that's a mighty dumb thing to do".

"And I pray to cow mother to save his majesty and give him a long life so that he and his sons and grandsons will rule India as long as possible".

"Thank you. I'm sure the King will appreciate that".

The bearded priest smiled and nodded as though he understood and approved of the conversation just as another gust of wind brought more smells to the thatched roof.

"And what about the stink coming from those shacks".

Vikram looked towards the shacks and shook his head in dismay. "Those shacks sahib. That smell also irritates me. I tell those miserable people to defecate further away in the fields. But what to do sahib. They are da- da–".

"Dumb".

"Yes sahib. They are dumb. They say that there are a lot of snakes in those fields. They are afraid that they will be bitten in the, in the ", then pointing a finger at his own bottom Vikram asked, "what do you English call the chuttar?"

"You mean the bottom".

"Yes sir. The bottom. You see to defecate you have to bare open your bottom and sit down with it close to the ground. It is in easy reach of even the smallest snake. But I tell these miserable people to take the risk and defecate further away". Shaking his head again he continued, "But what to do sahib. They refuse. They are sure that the snakes will bite them on the bottom. They aren't even bothered that the English sahib dislikes it".

"Okay, then lets get down to business", James Powell had decided to come to the point, the reason why he had come. "Do you have any knowledge of the Bengali who threw a bomb at the District Magistrate of Bhagalpur?.The damned fellow. Our intelligence report says that he is holed up somewhere in these parts".

"Aaah", exclaimed Vikram, "so that is why you have come.

To catch a Bengali. No problem sahib."

The bearded priest looked at Vikram and asked in chaste Hindi. "What does he want with a Bengali".

"The sahib wants the Bengali who killed the D.M. of Bhagalpur", explained Vikram.

The priest nodded his head.

Unknown to the three people under the thatched roof, a brown snake was making its way across the scorched, harvested wheat fields towards the row of shacks in which the three humans sat. It meandered through the dried stubs that were the cut paddy stalks. The ground was hot and parched and cracked in places and the snake wanted to reach a cooler spot. It was the same snake that had escaped the two eagles and had fallen from the sky. It was hungry and was in search of food.

Fangs stopped and lifted his head two inches above the ground to survey the area around him. There was nothing to eat so he lowered it and slithered on zigg-zagging into troughs and over little mounds, across cracks in the earth and over the hot baked soil. He was soon amongst the huts that bordered Vikram's compound and was slithering through little cracks, holes and partitions in the thatched walls in search of something to it. There was nothing and if a human had seen him, he would have screamed and yelled and would have proved that the fields beyond the huts were infested with snakes with one of them occasionally venturing into their domain for easy prey.

Infact fangs could easily bite anyone if he wanted with his fangless gums or with the bone that was supposed to be his teeth. He could bite the humans on their bottoms, legs, hands, inside the huts, outside the huts, in the fields, in the Zamindar's haveli, in his room, bedroom, sitting room, anywhere. So not defecating in the fields far away from the huts because the snakes would bite them on the bottom was a lame excuse. As lame as the sacred cow with a broken leg who saw the snake leave the shacks and slither on past it. It mooed its warning to the other bovines and pulled at the rope that tethered it to its lunch time feast.

Fangs passed the row of cows he had excited. Oneparticular long horned creature stamped her feet and brought her head down to show the snake her horns as she snorted a warning at the reptile. "If you come any nearer", she seemed to say, "you will get this".

Fangs stopped, looked at the irritated bovine and changed his direction. He passed the row of cows he had excited and stopped at a place sixty feet from the thatched roof under which the khakhi clad representative of the crown, dhoti clad representative of aristocratic Bihar and saffron clad representative of Hinduedom, with a chillum under his bottom, sat and chatted about the Bengali who had killed the D.M. of Bhagalpur. Fangs drew up his dark brown body behind the neck and proceeded to make a couple of coils over which he raised his neck. Opening his neck ribs to unfold the hood he elevated his head eight inches above the upper coil. His shiny scaly underbelly glistened in the sun as he surveyed the area around himself. The beady eyes scanned the field to the left, not perturbed by the cows behind it. There was nothing to eat so the head turned to the right, towards the distant fields but there was no rat or lizard or mice or frog there either.

Under the thatched roof the conversation continued. "It is very easy to catch a Bengali who is amongst Biharis," said Vikram. "His culture and language is different from ours. I could at a single glance spot a single Bengali standing amongst twenty lakh Biharis".

"I know where the Bengali is hiding", intruded the priest.

Vikram looked at the hook beak nosed gentleman and frowned. "Do you really know where the Bengali is hiding?"

"Yes".

"Then why didn't you tell me earlier?"

"I never thought it would interest you".

"What is the sadhu saying?" asked Powell.

"He says that he knows where the Bengali is hiding".

"Can you ask him where?"

"Where is he hiding?", asked Vikram.

The bearded gentleman spoke excitedly as he gesticulated with his hands. What he said was mumbo Jumbo to Powell who looked at Vikram for a translation. "What did the sadhu say?", he asked.

"He isn't a sadhu", retorted Vikram, "he is pundit, a priest and he says that the Bengali is hiding in a village called Khagaul in the Postman's house. The village is just three kilometer's down the road from here".

"But we raided that village last week", complained Powell. "We did have information about the postman but there was nothing in his house to vindicate him".

"What indicate him sahib?"

"Oh sorry, to vindicate means to find proof of some one's doings".

"Oh vindicate", continued Vikram, "it is nice word. A wise word". He then turned and told the pundit what the Englishman had said. The priest replied speaking and gesticulating excitedly. All these noises sounded gibberish to the Englishman.

"What did he say?", Powell asked again.

Vikram Singh smiled. "If you excuse my language sahib this pundit says that the English and freedom fighters are brainless. The English only have the brains to search the houses and garages and cowsheds and the terrorist only have the brains to hide in the haystack and nowhere else".

"But we searched the haystack. My men prodded it with their bayonets".

Vikram Singh conveyed this information to the priest who again spoke excitedly gesticulating with his hands as though he was jabbing at something.

"What did he say?", asked Powell.

"He says sahib that your policemen jabbed into the haystack with their bayonets. But their rifles are only four feet long and the haystacks are sometimes twelve feet deep."

"So that's it", Powell exclaimed as he smacked a fist into his palm. "I knew there was something wrong with that haystack. Something told me that the fellow was hiding in there".

"I told you sahib".

"Good show Mr. Singh, good show," continued Powell," and tell that priest of yours that I am grateful. He hit the nail right on the head".

Vikram Singh looked perplexed. "Have you gone crazy sahib?" he asked, " the pundit has no hammer and no nail and he never hit a nail on the head in his life. He is too lazy for that. He could never hit a nail on a head. Even if he tried, he would have hit his own fingers".

"You're taking my words literally", replied Powell, "hitting the nail on the head means to come to the point directly. You're priest told me precisely where to find the culprit. We will get the rascal this time". Then turning to the priest he exclaimed, "Thank you Mr. Pundit, it was a jolly good show. I am grateful to you".

The priest was not looking at the Englishman, but was looking past him. He was terrified and sat motionless with his mouth wide open. The only movement was a twitch in the right eye. He suddenly screamed "SNAKE", and jumped onto the table. Vikram automatically shouted "WHERE?", and stepped onto his chair from where he leapt onto the table knocking the priest over backwards as Powell himself hopped onto his chair. The priest fell flat on the ground and seeing the table fully occupied with the hefty Zamindar, he pointed a finger towards the south, screamed "there", and ran out from under the thatched roof to scamper half way up the flag pole. Vikram Singh and Powell looked towards where the finger had pointed and saw the snake. The sight caused the Zamindar to hop on the table. He felt that his present perch was not high enough for safety and he needed a higher one. Since there was none available, he had to make do by hopping to elevate himself.

The Englishman felt relieved and foolish. In his fright he had nearly pulled out his service revolver form its holster. He was facing his Jeep now and could see his driver and the other policemen suppress their laugh so he got down, removed his hand from the holster, adjusted his shirt and straightened his cap. Snake or no snake, he was an important officer of the Raj, and would not let down the stiff upper lip of his race or the composure of his Majesties Government of India, in India.

Powell looked up at the Zamindar who was still hopping on the table and the pundit who was halfway up the flag pole.

"Get back on the chair sahib", Vikram shouted in between hops, "Get back on the chair".

"I certainly will not", replied the Englishman. "And you Mr. Singh, will you please stop hopping and step down from the table".

"No sahib", Vikram panted, "the snake".

"But the snake is sixty feet away".

"It can fly sahib", panted Vikram, "It can fly. A cobra has been known to fly a hundred feet and bite its victim".

"Hogwash. Snakes cannot fly".

"Of course they can", continued Vikram through pants,"ask the pundit".

"Mr. Singh, will you stop that nonsense and get down. You don't know how ridiculous you look up there".

Vikram Singh stopped hopping. He was extremely tired. He had never exerted himself so much and his wobbly feet had taken a battering. His heart seemed to pound against his chest and the thin fabric of the dhoti he was wearing was torn in places where his toes had got entangled with cloth. "I won't get down from the table", he panted, "but are you sure that snakes don't fly?".

"Of course they don't. The nearest they can get to flying is to spring out of a couple of coils".

"Shush sahib shush", shushed the pundit from halfway up the flag pole.

"What is it?", whispered Vikram from under the thatched roof.

"We have been visited by the lord snake, the Nagraj". It had been sometime since the priest had seen a cobra and though he was frightened, he wanted to pray to it.

"Aha the Nagraj", then turning to the Englishman Vikram

asked again, “Sahib are you sure that snakes cannot fly?”.

“As sure as the sole under my feet”.

“Then shush sahib, we have been visited by the snake lord”.

“By the what lord?”

“By the snake God sahib, the Nagraj”.

“You mean to say you are going to pray to that reptile”.

Vikram singh now had his hands folded in reverence to the snake. “It is not a reptile sahib. It is a holy snake. Lord Shiva’s snake”.

“Preposterous”, exclaimed the englishman, “unthinkable, UNIMAGINABLE”.

“Sahib”, continued Vikram, “Look at the snake. Doesn’t it look beautiful.”

“Horrible”

“Doesn’t it look majestic”.

“Monstrous”, then on second thoughts Powell exclaimed. “You’re most unpredictable Mr. Singh. On one hand you call that creature beautiful when just a minute ago you were hopping on that table”.

“Shush sahib, shush. Look his lordship is looking at us”.

Powell looked at where the snake sat and a shiver ran down his spine. The reptile looked relaxed in the field. The belly plates shone in the afternoon sun and the scales that covered the snout made it look menacing. A bifid tongue flicked out occasionally and the hood looked expressionless. The officer couldn’t make out whether the reptile was pleased, happy, angry, or just peeved as the glazed eyes watched with a glassy stare at the table top standing Zamindar and the flag pole climber pundit. Powell did not know that the forked tongue was actually measuring the presence of the three people under the thatched roof.

"Hey Nagraj", Vikram prayed in chaste hindi so that the english man could not understand. "Till when will we have to play second fiddle to the white man. What have our ancestor's done to bring your wrath on us in this manner. Why do we have to wag our tails to these dumb creatures".

Powell was amused though he did not understand what was being said. He stepped three steps back to allow more privacy to the praying Zamindar.

"Your holiness, the English fume and fawn over us. They think themselves superior to the Brown man and we have to bow before them to hold onto our property or to acquire more land. Your holiness, the white man is a pest, a leech which sucks the blood out of our bodies. He is strong and mighty with tanks and guns and aeroplanes. Only you can deliver us from them".

"Pray harder Mr. Singh".

"Shush sahib, do not make a noise. I am praying for your welfare. For the welfare of the British empire. I have just prayed for the long and happy life of the king so that the English may prosper and rule India for the next one thousand years".

Powell was taken a back. The most he could say was a"thank you".

Halfway up the flag pole the priest had loosened his grip on the pole and was slowly sliding down. It was a long time since he had seen a cobra and he had no intention of leaving Vikram alone at this golden moment. He wouldn't loose this opportunity to ask something for himself. There wasn't any problem in deciding what to ask, the thought was automatic. He would ask for hard cash.

The Pundits feet soon made contact with the ground and he let go of the pole. Turning around he walked carefully towards the thatched roof while he kept an eye on the snake. Fangs did not like the pundit's movement so he gave out a loud "khaaa". The priest panicked and rushed into the thatched roof and leapt onto the Zamindar's table causing the latter to loose balance and fall off. The terrified Zamindar immediately caught hold of the table's edge and hauled himself up. Straightening himself he screamed obscenities at the pundit.

"Shanti, shanti, shanti," quelled the priest.

"Shut up," then turning towards the snake Vikram folded his hands and continued. "Forgive this miserable priest for the disturbance your holiness. You see he has no brains".

The priest also folded his hands. "Hey Nagraj", he prayed silently, "why have you forgotten me?, why have you forsaken me? Why have you made me a poor Brahmin. Please. I repeat, please make me as rich and landed as this fat Zamindar. Why is this useless meatball prosperous? Is it because he wags his tail before the English? If that is so, then give me two tails to wag. Please Nagraj,snatch this fat slouche's lands and give them to me. Make me the Zamindar and him a poor Brahmin. Then I will slap him, box him, twist his arm and scream obscenities every morning at his face before breakfast".

"Punditjee", the Zamindar interrupted.

The priest opened his eyes and realized that Vikram's torso was half turned towards him. "Yes", he replied.

"What were you praying for?"

"For your health and increase in your wealth".

"Don't lie, I heard you mumbling something".

The priest gulped. He had sub-consciously mumbled his prayer and wondered whether the Zamindar had heard it.

I will not allow you to pray in my premises as long as Nagraj resides on my lands and does not fulfill my wishes," retorted Vikram. "He is my property as long as he resides on my lands".

The priest nodded his head so Vikram continued his prayer. He remembered the Englishman so he stopped and apologetically looked aside ."Excuse- me sahib", he said, "while I pray to the snake lord".

Powell understood that the lord snake was more important to the Zamindar than the British government. The British Government could wait so he nodded his head and Vikram continued his prayer while the priest silently prayed. This time not from a mumbling mouth, but from his heart. He prayed for more money and land than the Zamindar so that he could thrash and abuse him daily before breakfast.

" Hey Nagaraja", Vikram continued, "You came in the right time. My wife Narayani is pregnant. She is going to get a child. Please bless her with a boy this time.She had given birth to two girls previously. Lord, I have had enough of them. You know the problems a girl creates after she gains puberty . I had to sell two hundred acres of land to marry off the other two girls. If this carries on I will become a pauper soon. Please lord give me an heir this time,"

Powell decided that he had seen enough He was bored and had better things to do other than watch two cranks praying to a snake. He got up, looked at Vikram and decided not to disturb the Zamindar. A gust of wind brought the stench from the shacks so cupping his nose, Powell turned and walked towards the jeep. Seeing him approach the driver quickly got in and switched on the ignition and the Jeep's engine coughed to life. The boots engulfing the ankles out of which flowed a pair of brown socks letting out white legs which rose up into baggy half pants, stepped into the Jeep, while the bottom sat itself on the front seat. The driver backed the vehicle, turned it around and headed towards the double lioned gate. The Jeep lurched and purred up the rutted driveway and through the gates from where it turned left and vanished out of sight leaving behind a lonely Scarecrow smiling across the road at the two lions.

Vikram stopped his prayer and looked around. Seeing the jeep missing, he turned to look at the pundit who was silently praying. "Punditjee," he interrupted the priest, "I think I had forbidden you."

"Oh sorry," apologized the priest, "I was only praying for your wealth."

"I knew you were praying for my wealth . I know you always pray for my wealth".

The priest gulped as Vikram's eyes hardened. Seeing that the former was properly scared the Zamindar turned to face the snake again. "Hey Nagraj", he continued, "If you fulfill my wish I promise to leave a bowl of milk where you are now sitting for you to drink every day."

The priest was again silently praying."What an idiot this Zamindar is", he thought, "snakes don't drink milk . He offered the wrong thing. He should have offered a lizard, a frog or a mouse."

Vikram had stopped praying and was again looking side ways at the priest. "Punditjee", he said, "shout out to Rama to bring a bowl of milk."

The priest obeyed and soon a short dark chocolate brown skinned servant trotted out of the haveli's verandah. He was a thin, famine-famished, bald headed, half naked servant of the Zamindar who lived in one of the huts from where the smell of shit emanated. In his right hand he held a bowl of milk. "Yes master," he shouted.

"Come here," yelled the priest.

Rama hurriedly walked upto the thatched roof and wondered why the two were standing on the table. "Yes master", he repeated.

"Rama can you see the snake?," asked Vikram who was still facing the reptile

"Where master,?"

"In front of us,"

Rama looked towards where the Zamindar was looking and saw the cobra .A glance at the snout and breast plates sent a shiver down his spine." Yes master," he replied.

"Take the milk and put it in front of the snake".

Rama did not believe what he had just heard. "What did you say master?," he asked.

"Put the milk in front of the snake."

The priest gulped as the happy face of the servant looked perplexed, then surprised, then amazed, then astonished, and finally terrified. The dark face grew darker, the twitching cheek twitched more and the hands shook causing small ripples to form in the milk he was carrying. "Do you want me to put this bowl before the snake?", he asked.

"Yes".

Rama took in his predicament .He wanted to run away. But couldn't. He was a slave of the Zamindar, a bandhwa mazdoor. His grandfather had borrowed two thousand rupees from the master and in return had pledged that he himself and his successors would work free for the master on a meager pay of two meals a day. Rama his sons and their sons were at the mercy of the Zamindar and his successors.

Rama was a devout Hindu himself. He also prayed to the Nagraj but they were photos of snakes wrapped around lord Shiva's neck. He had never prayed to live poisonous reptiles like the one sitting coiled cozily in the field flicking a forked tongue menacingly at him. Rama knew Vikram well. He knew how eccentric the latter was and realized he had two options. Either to obey the order and get bitten by the snake. This was unthinkable since he loved his unbitten hands and was desperate to keep them unbitten. The second was to disobey and get hung from the giant Baobab tree by his legs and receive a thorough beating from the Zamindar's Pehelwans . Rama had come to terms with his regular hanging sessions from one of the trees thick branches due to which he knew the latter very well. He disliked the huge bottle necked tapering trunk and the thick horizontal branches . Due to hours of hanging upside down he knew that the leaves were digitate, having five leaflets radiating from a central point with a hairy surface.The flowers were large pendent on a long thick stalk with creamy white petals. They would bloom at midnight during June and wither away the next day. During the summers the tree would become leafless and its much divided crown would appear gaunt and grotesque and Rama would have to hang with out any shade. The Zamindar was a bully and was in a habit of getting him strung from the tree at the smallest excuse.

"Rama take the milk to the snake,"ordered Vikram.

"To hell with the Zamindar's orders". thought the servant, "The cheek of him. He and the priest are themselves standing safely on the table. They don't even have the guts to come down and I am supposed to go an feed the snake."

"RAMA"

"I can't master", the servant shouted as he moved forward.

"Be quick".

"Have mercy master", Rama pleaded as he shuffled forward.

A visibly irritated Zamindar pulled out a pistol from the folds of his dhoti. It was a little silver coloured 22 Baby Colt whose magazine was tucked neatly in the butt. With his thumb the Zamindar pushed back the safety catch and pointed the weapon at the servants feet. He wasn't going to miss this opportunity to please his holiness the snake or the chance to change the gender of the child in the womb if it was a girl child.

Fangs was now a silent spectator. He occasionally shot out his bifid tongue to get information of what was happening in front of him. The miserable Rama sometimes focused into his view and sometimes became hazy. The snake was bewildered. Why did the humans always fold their hands whenever they saw him?, and why did they always offer him milk? Didn't they realize that he disliked milk. The snake was still contemplating when it felt a vibration. It came from behind Rama's feet in a spurt of dust as a bullet slammed into the ground a split second after the pistol spat flame. The snake did not hear the crack of the pistol but felt the thud and thought that it was menacing so he turned his hood towards Rama.

The little weapon had spat its venom at Rama's feet. Words weren't needed , the language of the pistol was enough. It meant that the Zamindar meant business.

Rama took three hasty steps forward and realized that the snake was looking at him. The creature looked horrible with the snout and beady eyes pointed at him. How he wished that some one would batter the creature to death. He didn't know that the snake was fangless and was sure that the latter wanted to bite him to death. He unfortunately shuffled four steps forward.

"Go on quick," goaded Vikram, "or the snake may slither away"

Fangs quietly watched as Rama approached. He lowered the angle of his hood to align his beady eyes with the servant who was now crouched and was creeping towards him. The human slowly crept into the snakes view and Fangs now recognized what was in the silver bowl. It was the white liquid he hated. It was milk." Yuck," he thought, "Yuck, yuck, Yuck. I feel like vomiting".

Rama crept on.

The snake studied Rama. "What was the fellow doing?,"he

thought ," He is behaving just like the snake charmer."

The pistol muzzle followed Rama

"Come closer you fool," Fangs thought , "even though I don't have my fangs , I'm not one to run away. I ll give you a taste of my bone teeth".

The pistol followed Rama's slow approach as Vikram's hand slowly pulled the muzzle back and cocked it.

Rama was perspiring as he inched towards the snake.

"Come on nearer you fool," thought the snake, "I'll show you what snakes are made of".

Rama's teeth were now chattering as he moved on.

Fangs tensed his snaky muscles as his gaze concentrated on the hand holding the bowl. He was waiting for the correct moment to strike,when with lighting speed he would hurl his hood forward and with an open mouth would draw his jaws around a portion of the man's hand. If he had had his fangs and venom bags, he would have injected an overdose of the deadly liquid into the hand.

The bowl came closer.

The pistol followed impatiently.

The bowl come closer.

"Now", thought the snake as it let go off a coil and shot its head forward and missing the hand by just two inches splashed into the milk in the bowl, splashing milk on the terrified Rama who dropped the bowl and screaming ran back to the thatched roof." Master, the snake bit me", he yelled , "now I will die."

"Shut up you idiot", growled Vikram, "I saw the snake miss your hand".

Rama looked at his hands and a relieved half smile crossed his face.

Fangs had drawn back his hood and had straightened himself to regain his composure. The lord snake had struck and had missed and now felt like an idiot with drops of milk dribbling down his scaly body. He disliked the human and their milk and decided to slither off. Uncoiling himself he turned his hood to the right and straightened his body to create the S shaped curves when he saw something interesting. It was a yellow frog hopping across his path seventy feet away. To be certain he rapidly shot out his forked tongue and collected molecules that were passed on to his Jacobsons organs. "Now that's what I call good food," he thought. "Delicious bull frog in the belly. What an exotic dish".

Vikram Singh now had a stubborn look of piousness on his face while his pistol hung from his hand. "The snake is looking away from the milk." he commented, "we will have to bring back its attention to the milk."

"Yes master?", Rama half heartedly agreed as the priest nodded his head.

"Rama".

"Yes master?"

"Go and shake the snakes tail and bring its attention back to the milk."

Rama gawked . "But master it will bite me."

"The secret to a long life is to be quick in thinking and quick in action".

"But it will bite me. It nearly did so."

"Shake the snake's tail Rama."

"Shake the snake's tail", Rama thought, "Shake its tail my foot. If I had my way I would shake my tail to this job and leave this damned place."

"Rama."

"May I use a stick master?"

"You can," was the reply, "but bring its attention back to the milk."

Rama picked up a six foot long stick from the ground and crept up to the snake and stretching out his stick holding hand he rudely prodded the tail.The result was a backlash from the reptile. Its head whipped around, and hit the stick hurting its own snout in the process. Rama let go off the stick and scampered off to the haveli."You can kill me master", he shouted as he ran, "but I will not go any where near the snake,"

"Come back Rama", shouted Vikram.

Fangs had decided he had had enough, so he lowered his head and creating his S shaped curves, he slithered off towards the row of shacks and the field beyond, leaving behind a cheatingly praying priest and a stubbornly pious Zamindar who was yelling the choicest Behari abuses to his servant who had just disappeared into the haveli.

A Dead Miss Rat

The disturbed cows mooed their uneasiness at the snake which slithered past them. Fangs could not hear the deep throated calls they were making to each other. But understood by the way they pulled at their tethers that they did not want him around. He himself did not want to stay back. He wanted to be as far away as possible from the humans and the bowl of milk he had dived into. Specially the human with a menacing stick which had prodded his tail. As he was passing a little black Jersey cow which did not have any horns, the tether tying the cow snapped and the animal was free. It lifted its tail in the air and pranced around. Realizing it was free it bucked, and kicked and dashed about raising a cloud of dust as it did a funny jig.

Fangs was startled so he stopped and raised his hood. He

did not want to get trampled under the creatures hooves. The cow pranced around as though it knew no restraint and suddenly stopped looked at the snakes upraised hood, belched and dashed off past the other bovines into the wheat harvested fields beyond.

"Hey stop", yelled a cowherd who had suddenly appeared from behind a shack. He was a thin dark fifteen year old boy and wore nothing except a torn khakhi half pant. He was Rama's younger brother and was in charge of the master's cattle. He hadn't seen the snake and wondering at what had provoked the cow, he ran off after the fast receding bovine.

Fangs watched the cowherd run and after he had disappeared behind the rump of a particularly huge Haryanvi cow, he lowered his hood and closed the rib muscles into the neck. He then continued slithering across the dung pasted hard ground and was soon passing between two thatched houses. Slithering on,he turned a bend around a mud wall where he saw a unique scene. A group of red warrior ants were carrying a green caterpillar which they had just killed. Seeing the snake they let go off their load and scampered off in different directions while some scampered up the mud wall from where they watched the snake slither past. After the reptile had gone they gathered their courage and slowly climbed down and reorganized themselves and were soon lugging and tugging and heave-hoing at the caterpillar to carry it back to their nest which was in the field behind the shack.

Fangs slithered on and entered a clump of dried yellow grass and soon broke out into the open on the other side in time to scare an angular headed, prehensile tailed Chameleon who had just flicked out a long tongue , trapped a mosquito and flicked it back into its mouth. Seeing the snakes, the Chameleon scampered up a mud mound where it turned and nodded its head vehemently at the passing reptile,which soon disappeared in another clump of grass. The Chameleon's large turret like eyes stared at the place where it had last seen the snake and saw a yellow winged locust leap into the air and fly a short distance with the help of its brightly coloured hind wings which produced a clicking sound as it flew. The locust suddenly shut its wings and dropped to the ground where it seated itself on a dried leaf.

Fangs had now increased speed and was approaching the Baobab tree which sometimes had Rama hanging from it upside down. Zipping on he realized that he was being chased from the air. A couple of dragon flies with large eyes and two pairs of richly veined wings were flying above him. Fangs stopped and looked up. Making a few calculations he shot his head up to catch one of them. The dragon flies were quicker and like helicopters elevated themselves to a higher altitude and flew off in different directions only to fly in a curving arc which brought them back to where the snake lay.

Fangs watched the two helicopter like insects and did not realize that he had trespassed over the male dragonflies property.

The latter was just checking on him and his intentions. The two airborne insects were out of reach and Fangs couldn't do any thing about them. Neither could he do anything about the small blue kingfisher which had scared the dragonflies, and was hovering above him. It was a dapper little blue and green bird with deep rust colored underparts, a short stumpy tail and a long straight pointed bill. It had been on it's way to a pond that was two hundred meters behind the Baobab tree,and seeing the snake it had stopped in mid air, and hovering over the reptile was letting out loud and shrill chichee-chichee noises. The king- fisher was soon accompanied by a dozen earthy brown untidy looking Jungle Babbler's whose harsh conversational chatter and squeaking could be heard before the birds had actually arrived. The Babblers were now flying in circles around the kingfisher adding their noise to the chorus.

Fangs was irritated and let out a couple of loud 'khaa's' through his mouth at the birds. This failed to scare them who simply increased the din and attracted a host gray necked house crows who were soon flying in circles around the field caw-cawing their irritation at the snake. Fangs forked tongue shot out as he sensed danger. He knew that the birds would attract larger birds like the brown Pariah kites from which he had just escaped, or the white headed Brahminy hawk which was as dangerous as the Pariah.

Lowering his head, Fangs slithered to the edge of the field across which was a little patch of land on which corn grew.

Crossing the field's boundary he noticed a hole in the ground. Ignoring it he slipped into the cornfield and lay hidden as the din which followed him slowly died down.

Fangs waited and waited and only when he was sure that the birds had flown off did he venture out. Moving slowly in a straight line with the help of the scutes along his underbelly, he slowly scuted along a shallow mud drain which was used to water the cornfield. Reaching the end of the drain he crawled out and moved towards the field's boundary where he had seen the hole which he suspected housed a rat.

It was a rat hole and to Fangs' delight his bifid tongue picked up the molecules of a fat mouse and a litter of mice. Poking his head into the hole he looked in. It was dark and musty and the hole fell a feet into the ground after which it curved slightly to the left ending up in a small cavern. It was actually a dungeon with a nest of sticks and leaves spread out at the bottom. On the bed lay a fat field mouse with a litter of six blind mice who were all squabbling and drinking from the double line of tits that lined her underbelly. Next to this cave was the larder. It was another little cavern stocked with approximately five kilograms of wheat which the Mouse had pilfered from the wheat fields from the ground above.

Fangs realized his luck had turned for the better. He had trapped a field mouse and a whole litter. He would now enter and gobble up the complaining land lady and her delicious children after which he would annex the house and spend the hot summer relaxing in the cool hole till the waters of the monsoon rain finally flooded him out. The mouse had been lying content that she had done her work well. She had burrowed down into the ground and had dug two caves. One she had filled with the paddy she had pilfered which would last her the whole year. The second, she had converted into her bedroom cum living room cum toilet. She had unfortunately missed out on one major detail. She should have made an emergency exit like the humans who lived on the land above. She hadn't so she was now trapped in her own little home. Sensing danger she had got up and was sniffing the air while her litter kicked and flailed their little limbs as they groped in the dark for her invigorating tits.

Miss mouse did not have to sniff hard. The smell was all pervasive and filled her nostrils and almost choked her with fright .She gave an alarmed squeak, and a terrified shriek and backed to the back of her cave where she cowered in fright. She had forgotten about her little ones whom she had just a minute before dreamt would become mighty rats. They would now end up as nutrition for the snake helping it become stronger and bigger and more venomous.

Fangs used his scutes again and entered four inches into the hole. He was careful. It was always wise to be careful so he rapidly shot out his forked tongue to get the information that could be got pertaining the hole. Sensing no danger he pushed himself deeper in as his forked tongue repeatedly shot out of his mouth.

Poor Miss mouse could feel and hear the scrapping noise as the cobra lowered itself into her home. Her legs felt weak as she trembled and the strong scent of the snake caused her to defecate. Her blind litter were still flailing their limbs and groping for her tits. Fortunately for them their senses hadn't developed so they did not realize the danger that was stalking them

Miss Mouse was looking towards the hole in the cave wall which was the mouth of the tunnel down which the snake was coming, when the snout appeared. It was pitch dark and both the hunter and the hunted were relying on their sensory organs. Fangs rapidly shot out his forked tongue while Miss Mouse used the sensory hairs which were on her snout.

"Aha", thought Fangs, "there you are at last".

"Have mercy please," petitioned Miss Mouse," devour my children but spare me ,"

"No mercy maa'm. I'm too hungry for that . It'll be you first then your children"

Miss Mouse panicked and ran into her larder. In pursuit Fangs shot after her and slamming through the bunch of mice his head shot into the second hole. Flicking his forked tongue he made his calculations, shot his head forward and caught Miss Mouse between his gums.

"Help me," squealed the mouse," Please someone help me," she squeaked as she flailed her legs and lashed her little tail.

The squeaks reveberated and seemed to bounce from wall to wall of the cave making her plight scarier still.

"No luv," Fangs hissed through his nose, "there's no one who'll come to your rescue just now."

Miss Mouse continued squeaking and kicking and Fangs had to lift his head and whump her a couple of times on the floor. Miss Mouse went on squeaking and flailing and Fangs realized that whumping her on the floor was useless since it was padded with an eight inch thick layer of paddy grains so he slammed her against the mud wall. Miss Mouse however went on squeaking so the snake violently jerked his head from left to right causing the mouses snout to repeatedly ram against the cave wall . This silenced her though her tail squirmed.

Fangs had had to change his style. Previously he would have simply punctured the body with his fangs injecting a lethal dose of venom into her, thereby killing her. She would have slowly died and all he had to do was to slowly pull her body down an elongated mouth,neck and stomach. He would now have to hold the vermin in his mouth for some time till life finally squeezed out of her. This he did as the little mice who were still alive kicked and groped at his belly scales thinking they would find their mothers nourishing tits there.

Fangs squeezed his jaws tighter and felt a leg twitch. The squeeze caused the mouse to kick out with her free limbs and scrape with the clawed digits on her feet against the paddy grains and the cave wall. The snake however did not loosen his grip and held on and when he felt the vermin was becoming a nuisance he shook his head and slammed the mouses snout repeatedly against the cave wall again. This seemed to paralyze the creature whose flailing and tail squirming stopped so Fangs let go of the body and with his snout he pushed the back of the vermin around so that the face of the mouse faced his mouth which he opened as wide as possible by elongating his mouth muscles. His jaw bones had a row of sharply pointed inwardly curving cones which were his teeth which were attached to his skull only by muscles and ligaments. Due to this each of his teeth could move independently up and down, back and fourth and from side to side. With the help of these teeth Fangs caught hold of the mouses snout and head and walked the vermin slowly back into his gullet. As he sucked, his neck muscles elongated and the inwardly curved bone cones on his jaws moved back and forth alternately slowly dragging Miss Mouse in. It took the snake half an our to finish his meal and when Miss Mouse had finally entered his esophagus he formed a sharp curve in his neck behind her causing her to get pushed downward into his stomach.

"Aaah", thought Fangs as he rested his head on the paddy bed. "That tasted nice".

The little mice still clawed and tickled his belly plates so the snake drew his head out of the larder back into the living room. Turning his neck around his mouth opened and grasped a flailing creature and gulped it in. He then gobbled up the rest of the litter and adjusted himself and drew the entire length of his body into the cave. He realized that he was too large for the hole so he let the latter part of his body flow into the larder until he felt comfortable. Laying his mouth on the bed of twigs, he lazily shot his forked tongue out and decided to have a proper rest. The house now belonged to him and he could occupy it as long as he liked till the monsoon rains flooded him out. He would rest till Miss Mouse and her litter were properly digested and he felt hungry again. Till then he would stay away from the harsh world outside.

Girl Child

It was the eighth of February 1942 and the great war was at its peak. It was the third year and the allied countries were pitted against Nazi Germany and Fascist Italy. Japan had entered the war inviting America to do so by bombing Pearl Harbor. Hitler had gallantly driven his forces through Poland and had overtaken France and was now gloating over his blitzkrieg over London. Hordes of Stukas screamed over the city while swarms of Heinkels dived and unloaded their deadly loads and screamed back into the London skies leaving behind a trail of death and misery to the people living in the heart of the British empire. Where there was victory, people rejoiced and where there was defeat, people cried.

People cried too in a remote village in Bihar. It was the Haveli of Bahadur Vikram Singh. A huge bomb had dropped into the

Zamindar's house. As the dive bombers of the Luftwaffe rose up with their engines screaming into the London skies, a little girl came out of Narayanies' body screaming at the irritated household. The Zamindar's wife had given birth to a girl child.

Vikram Singh had been tense since the morning as his wife's labor pain increased. He was seated bear bodied and cross legged under the thatched roof on the ground while his mustachioed Pehelwan's smacked mustard oil on his body giving him a proper massage. They rubbed his legs, thighs, arms and back while one of them even put some oil in his nostrils for good luck. The little group of villagers who were sitting cross legged in front of him on the ground, were also tense. They were all listening to a radio which stood in the south eastern corner of the shed near the hole in the brick wall. They were listening to the Hindi edition of the B.B. C and were all silent. Only the short, stocky, headman of the village spoke. "This is a very opportune time to get our independence" , he said.

No one answered.

"It seems that Germany is winning the war. I wonder what has happened to Gandhi? Why is he opposing the Germans?"

No one replied.

"The Congress Party should tie up with the Germans, and with their help throw the English out of this country."

No one replied.

"It will be another case of missing the bus."

The headman stopped when he saw Rama run out of the

Haveli's verandah towards the thatched roof. "Glory be to god", the servant shouted, "The Goddess Laxmi has come to reside in the masters house again."

"What", shouted Vikram, "is it a boy?"

"Glory be to God", repeated the servant, "the goddess Laxmi has come to reside in the masters house."

"Speak up you idiot", growled the Zamindar, "what is it?"

"A girl child has been born."

Vikram Singh's right hand shot up and smacked his own forehead in an expression of frustration and partly covered his face as he leaned back against the brick wall. "Look at the idiot", he said, "he is rejoicing over a girl child."

The villagers remained silent.

"Look at that brainless idiot", Vikram growled again as he picked up the radio and threw it at the servant. "He's rejoicing over a girl child."

The radio broke and fell silent.

"Cool down", retorted the village headman as he got up to block Vikram who was attempting to get up to attack the servant.

Vikram slumped back onto the ground. "What have I done to deserve this?", he wailed, "why have the Gods forsaken me? Why don't they bless me with a son."

"You must have missed something somewhere", interrupted the headman who was desperately suppressing a smile, "may be you didn't pray hard enough".

"I prayed very hard Mukhiaji, I promise you I prayed very hard. I prayed during Holi, during Diwali,during Nag Panchami, during Shiva Ratri, during Ram Navami and during Dussehera. I regularly sacrificed two goats to the goddess Durga".

"Then most probably you didn't go on a pilgrimage".

"Yes I did", retorted Vikram, "I went to Deogarh, to Benaras to Mathura, to Ayodhya and even to Vaishno Devi".

"Then what went wrong?", asked the headman.

Vikram Singh fell silent as he thought and wracked his brains. "I don't know", he said.

"You'll have to accept, said the headman in a resigned tone that, "the goddess Laxmi has come to reside in your house again"

"Now listen Mukhiaji", retorted Vikram, "you know very well that it is the third time she has entered my house. I had to sell two hundred acres to marry off the other two. I will have to sell another hundred to marry this one off".

The village headman looked back at the other villagers and realized that they were all suppressing smiles and were desperately putting on stern faces. Vikram realized this as he continued "And you idiots know very well that people don't invite the goddess to enter one's house in the form of a new born daughter. People invite her into homes in the form of currency notes snatched from the useless peasants".

The congregation nodded their heads.

"I know you all are enjoying this moment. If I don't get an

heir I know what you all will do. Like vultures and dogs you will peck and gouge into my property after I die".

"You are abusing us Vikram", the headman retorted.

Vikram fell silent and thought and remembered and suddenly sat bolt upright. "I got it", he said, "I know what went wrong".

"What?", asked the headman.

"It is this miserable Rama's fault".

The villagers turned their heads towards the servant who looked perplexed.

"A couple of months ago I was visited by the Snake God. It was a beautiful creature with a spectacle on its hood and its face seemed to glow. It looked just like the one we see in the photo's wrapped around the lord's neck".

"Then what happened?", asked the headman.

"I was sure that it was a "Nagraj', so I prayed to it. I asked this miserable person to pay it proper respect and present it with a bowl of milk".

"But I gave it the bowl of milk", retorted the exasperated Rama who realized that another session under the old Baobab tree as imminent. "It nearly bit me".

"Shut up", growled Vikram who had got up. "This idiot attracted the snake's wrath," he shouted as he rushed forward and caught the scared servant's hair and shook it wildly.

"Have mercy master", wailed Rama, "have mercy, I am innocent".

"Why should I pay for your mistake", shouted Vikram.

"I made no mistake", wailed Rama.

"You know Mukhiaji", continued Vikram who was now facing the villagers, "the Lord snake was looking away from the milk and I told this idiot to bring his attention back to it. The idiot took a stick and rudely prodded the tail. He should have done it reverently with his hands".

"But I asked your permission to use the stick".

"Shut up", growled Vikram.

"God help me", Rama wailed, "If I touched the tail".

"Shut up", interrupted Vikram, "you will be punished for this." He pushed Rama towards the two Pehelwan's, take him to the tree", he ordered, "he will hang from there till he repents".

"I already repent master".

"You must repent only after your punishment", Vikram retorted as he turned towards the south and started walking through the paddy fields towards the old Baobab tree which could be seen in the distance. The villagers were perplexed and felt that Vikram was unjust. "How did he expect the poor man to touch the snake's tail reverently?", they thought, "the person was sure to get bitten". However nothing could be done to save the servant since he was the private property of the zamindar. They in fact had a couple of slaves themselves and did not want to get involved in useless arguments so they shrugged the matter off and quietly watched Vikram lead the way through the empty paddy fields with his two Pehelwan's in tow who dragged the wretched servant along.

Vikram's wobbly feet led the way as Rama pleaded for mercy. "Master have mercy on me, and God will bless you with a boy child the next time", he said, "Master, I will pray to him personally for the child."

Vikram did not reply but walked on. His feet scared two stag Beetles who had their horn's locked in a fight over a female. They scampered off when the humans approached. Further on a glossy black chestnut winged Crow-Pheasant which had been walking around purposefully in search of food was disturbed. It hopped, then flew out of the way and perched itself on the fields boundary from where it called in a deep resonant "ook" followed by a trail of musical 'coop-coop-coops' which was heard by a green Asian bullfrog further on. It saw the approaching humans and desperately hopped out of the way.

"Give me a stick", ordered Vikram as a grasshopper barely saved itself by jumping out of the way just as Vikram's pointed shoe crunched onto the ground where it had sat a fraction of a second earlier. "These parts have become the home of the snake Lord", the Zamindar said.

The little group walked on and one of the Pehelwans lifted a stone and threw it at a couple of fawn colored Hoopoe birds with black and white zebra markings on their backs. The birds had been walking about on the ground on their squat legs with a somewhat waddling quail like gait as they busily probed into the soil with their bills which were partly open like a pair of forceps. The stone landed between them and the brown crests on their heads flicked open as the birds looked up at the passing humans. Disturbed, they flew off in an undulating undecided sort of way and resettled on the ground further away where they again raised their crests and bobbed their heads as they called out in soft musical 'hoo-poo hoo poo' noises.

The little group were soon standing under the great Baobab tree and were looking up into the foliage for the rope which had been left on one of the branches. It was a giant deciduous tree with a smooth bottle shaped trunk which tapered to the top and sent out thick horizontal branches. Due to long hours of hanging upside down from the tree Rama had come to know it well. He knew the flowers which were like large pendants on long thick stalk with creamy white petals. They bloomed in July during midnight and withered away by the next afternoon. He liked eating the spongy acidic pulp which was packed in the white, velvety, hairy surfaced gourd like fruits which hung from the branches. In fact that was the only bright spot in his hanging sessions.

"Its on that branch", said one of the Pehelwan's.

"Climb up the tree and send it down", ordered Vikram.

The taller Pehelwan jumped up and caught hold of a hanging branch which had broken in the middle. Like a monkey he clambered up and reached the branch which held the rope. On his way he disturbed a small stout Mahratta Woodpecker.

It had a pointed bill and a stiff wedge shaped tail. Its upper plumage was spotted black and white with a brownish yellow fore crown and scarlet crest. It had been scuttling up and down in jerky spurts directly or in spirals halting at intervals to tap on the bark or peer inquisitively into crevices for lurking insects. Seeing the intruding human it uttered a few sharp click, click-clickrrr noises and flew away. Higher up a brown colored fork tailed Brahminy kite which had been sitting in the foliage on the upper branches, got disturbed. It had been gouging on a Rohu fish it had scooped up from the pond further on. Dropping the fish, it spread its broad wings and flapping heavily lifted itself out of danger. Seeing the Brahminy fly a dozen House Crows, a couple of Parrots and a Blue Jay took to their wings disturbing the insect world that resided in the tree.

Two ladybirds colored black and red who were selecting their mates flew away. Black and yellow Assassin Bugs who had been eating on a dead caterpillar scampered off. Green coloured tree Hoppers curled up to resemble thorns to escape detection and Lynx spiders who were sitting motionless on leaves were now leaping nimbly from leaf to leaf to be far away as possible from the human intruder. The insects probably knew that Rama was going to be hanged.

"Here take the rope", shouted the Pehelwan as he threw both the ends of the rope down from both the sides of the branch. The Pehelwan on the ground caught both the ends and made a noose on one end. He turned to Rama who was miserably looking up at the tree. "Master please forgive me", he requested the Zamindar.

"I will forgive you in one condition", stated Vikram. "If you promise to feed the snake with milk the next time it appears".

"But how can I do that master", Rama wailed, "it will bite me".

"It won't if you're quick enough".

"But I'm not quick enough".

"Then hang him from the tree".

The second Pehelwan drew his arms under Rama's thighs, lifted him and threw him on the ground.

"Mercy master mercy", Rama cried.

"Will you feed the snake the next time it shows up".

"It will bite me master".

"Then hang him".

The Pehelwan tied the noose around Rama's ankles while the other Pehelwan clambered down the tree trunk to join him.

"Now pull him up", Vikram ordered.

The two Pehelwans took the other end of the rope and heaved. The rope pulled Rama's feet three feet up. The Pehelwans pulled again and Rama's head left the ground. The Pehelwan's pulled harder and Rama went higher till his overturned face was at level with Vikram's.

"Master you will get a boy child the next time", the servant wailed.

Vikram swung his hand and his pudgy right palm smacked the servants cheek causing the face to turn and the body to swing a bit. The body swung back and Vikram moved back and motioned to a Pehelwan who smacked the servant across the cheek again. Vikram had hurt his palm by the slap he had given the servant so he watched as the body swung back again. "Tell me Rama will you feed the snake when it shows itself",he asked.

"Yes master", wailed Rama.

"And you will touch the tail reverently with your hands?"

"But it will bite me master".

"Give him a few more slaps".

"No, no master", wailed Rama, "I will touch the tail reverently with my hands. I will touch its mouth reverently with my hands if you want me to. But please don't hit me again".

Vikram walked over and caught the swaying servant's hair and looked into the eyes as the body stopped swaying. "And what if you don't?", he asked.

"Then you can hang me from here again and get me stoned with bricks".

"Good", exclaimed Vikram. "Do you realize what your mistake will cost me? I will have to sell a hundred acres to marry that miserable girl who has been born today. If you had respected the snake Lord then I would most probably have been the proud father of a boy child. I would have had an heir if it wasn't for your impudence".

"I won't be impudent in future", begged Rama, "I will be most respectful to the snake and I will touch the tail reverently with my own hands".

"Promise?"

"Promise".

"Good". Then turning towards the two Pehelwans Vikram ordered, "The two of you send him up higher and wait for an hour. Then you can put him down and send him to the Haveli to prepare tea for me".

The Pehelwan's nodded their heads and Vikram turned and walked away after which the two wrestlers pulled at the rope and sent Rama higher up into the foliage. Satisfied that he was high enough, they tied the rope around the trunk and sat down cross legged at the base of the tree to rub tobacco in their palms to later place it in their mouths in between the teeth and the gums.

Up in the tree Rama looked around. He did not feel like an outsider since he knew his surroundings well. He was at home as he watched a green colored Lynx spider settle down and sit motionless on a leaf as its ogre like eyes stared at him. Somewhere else black and yellow Assassin Bugs carefully crept back to where they had left the dead caterpillar. Green coloured tree hoppers that had curled themselves to resemble thorns, uncurled themselves as black and red ladybirds went back to the task of choosing a mate. Half a dozen House Crows flew over and perched themselves a few branches above the dangling human and caw-cawed their irritation at him while the Brahminy kite dived under the tree in search of the half eaten fish it had dropped.

Rama hung and watched the two humans below him dunk tobacco in their mouths. "It is a beautiful world", he thought. The only thing that irritated him was a pair of spotted doves that had flown over and had perched themselves on a branch ten feet away from him. They had white spotted, pinkish brown and gray underparts with white speckled black chessboards on their hind necks. They occasionally bent their heads and called out mournfully in "Kroo-kruk-kruk-kroo", calls.

"What could they be saying?", Rama wondered.

"Kroo-kruk-kroo", said the male dove, "Why does this human always come up here?"

"Don't know", krooed back the female dove,"you know the world better than me".

"Kroo-kruk-kroo", continued the male dove, "this human seems to belong to a different species. It behaves like the spider".

"It doesn't look like the spider", replied the female dove.

"Kroo-kruk-kroo but it does behave like one. It belongs to the species that hangs from a thread".

"But I don't see any other humans hanging like he does".

"Kroo-kruk-kroo", continued the male dove, "The species is very rare. Must have belonged to the Paleolithic age. It's predecessor must have had something to do with spiders. They most probably imbibed the genes from them.

"Kroo-kroo-kroo", wailed the female dove.

"Shoo", shouted an irritated Rama as he waved his hands at the doves. "Go away from here".

"What's he saying?", krooed the male dove.

"Don't know", replied the female dove, "but he doesn't seem to look friendly".

"Shoo", yelled Rama as he waved his hands, "get out of here. Your wailing is getting on my nerves".

The doves felt that the human belonged to a dangerous species and disgusted they krooed a,"to hell with you", and flew off leaving the hanging human to himself and to the mercy of the caw-cawing irritated crows.

Aha My Fangs

During summer the crows gouged on the luscious yellow pulp of the ripened mango fruits just after the flame coloured flowers had formed a gorgeous canopy on the upper portion of the trees. Trees like the Baobab lost their leaves during the hot weather when their crown appeared gaunt and grotesque. July saw the Ashoka tree producing egg shaped fruits which when ripe was eaten by bats during the nights and the seeds were scattered over the ground the next morning. The Australian Phyllode Acacia bloomed bright yellow flowers during the monsoons and the repeated showers made the fruit of the Neem tree stink. The Pampas grass waved its plumes in Autumn while the Jamun tree shed its leaves in Winter. In Spring the Hyacinth weeds in the water opened spiky flowers of fresh mauve while the 'Horse Radish' tree bore loose clusters of creamy white honey scented flowers which appeared along with the leaves.

Winter had seen Fangs cooped in a Rat hole he had annexed and spring saw him making excursions outside his rat hole to get some food. He was enjoying his freedom and was delighted with the arrival of a fresh pair of Fangs. By the end of spring they had grown to their full length and Fangs was now a snake with confidence with a pair of milky white teeth folded neatly in his mouth, backed by a bagful of deadly creamy white venom.

The snake cruised through the grass and was soon passing under the Baobab tree where he stopped and looked up. He was immediately met with a chorus of squawks from a group of crows who flew off and circled the tree. They were accompanied by half a dozen agitated Common Babblers who added their musical "which-which which-ri-ri" whistle to the chorus. This in turn attracted a Blue Jay, a couple of Red whiskered Bulbuls and some glossy black, and bright yellow coloured common Ioras. Together the birds made a terrible din causing the insect world living in the tree to scurry to safety.

The din could not be heard by the snake whose forked tongue and sensory glands told him that it wasn't safe to hang around. Lowering his head he slithered on creating his S shaped curves till he entered a wheat field. Through experience Fangs knew that it wasn't wise to stay out in the open for too long.

Once in the wheat field the snake felt relaxed since he was hidden amongst the tall wheat stalks so he cruised along with his snout carving a path through the haze of stout yellow green stems. Fangs was hungry as he came to the end of the field where he used his scutes to slither over the fields boundary after which he entered a clump of grass which swayed in the breeze. Fangs slithered on with his forked tongue rapidly shooting out of his mouth. His snout burst out into open ground where he disturbed a swarm of yellow winged locusts who jumped into the air and flew on brightly colored hind wings which produced a chorus of clicking noises. The snake realized that he was on the banks of a little pond so he turned right and continued his journey over the damp loamy soil. He startled three white faced, stub tailed white breasted Water Hens. They scampered out cf the snakes path and from a safe distance on top of some bushes they called out in raucous grunts, croaks and chuckles. Further on a leggy Bronze winged Jacana spread its wings and flew off calling in a shrill wheezing noise. In the water the water stick insects which hung from the surface film by their respiratory siphons used their raptorical legs to go to a safer place while the water boatman swam to the middle of the pond.

Fangs slithered on though he did not like the musty smell of the humus that made up the banks of the pond. Reaching the western edge he turned south and slithered over sticky clayey soil and was soon slipping over a dead tree trunk where he disturbed a myriad of bugs and insects who all scampered off to safety. He snapped at a 'Day roosting moth' which thought that its wing pattern which resembled the mottled lichen covered wood, had properly camouflaged itself. The startled creature took to flight and headed north towards the Baobab tree.

Fangs crossed the dead tree and increased his speed. He was hungry. Flicking out his tongue he realized that a huge tree was some distance ahead so he headed towards it. He moved fast, sometimes over gravel, sometimes over clayey soil, sometimes through humus and shrubs and thick grass till he was under the tree. It was a huge Banyan tree with rope like structures called prop roots hanging from the branches. These ropes entered the ground and sent out roots which caused them to thicken and became pillars which supported the thick long branches of the tree themselves.

Flicking his forked tongue Fangs realized that there was plenty of food above so he decided to climb one of the prop roots. Curling up around the closest one he tightened his muscles around the root and with the help of his scutes he slowly crawled up with his body moving around in circles. Slowly and steadily he climbed up and reached a thick branch and pulled himself up to lie on it. Lifting his head he scuted into a thin leafy branch and taking proper hold of it he scuted on with the twigs and leaves acting as supports through which he meandered and climbed up to another branch. Turning to the right he used his ventral scutes in groups with some pushing back against the branch while others slid forward causing him to travel in a straight line over the wood. His Jacobson's organs told him that there was a nest straight ahead amongst a bushel of leaves, so flicking out his forked tongue he scuted on when he felt some movement above him. A host of crows were sitting on a branch four feet above and were caw-cawing their anger at him. They knew that he was headed for their nest which had four eggs cradled neatly at the base.

The crows were joined by Brown Babblers, Red Munias and black headed Buntings who screeched and cawed a variety of noises at the snake. The more adventurous of the crows especially the female whose nest the snake was headed for, dived at the reptile only to pull away when they were still at a safe distance.

Fangs wasn't perturbed by the commotion. What he wanted was to gobble down a couple of eggs which he suspected would be in the nest. Pushing through the leaves, his snout broke out of the foliage and he was delighted to see the nest. It was actually an untidy platform of sticks with a central depression lined with coir, fiber, tow, and other bits and pieces pilfered from the human world. Cradled in it were four pale, blue green speckled, and brown streaked eggs.

"Yummy", thought Fangs as he drew his body up and barked out a loud "Khaa" at the desperate female crow who had dived too close. The snake let out half a dozen more 'Khaas' at the crows that were sitting on the branch above him. By now a swarm of the angered birds were encircling the tree calling out loudly for more of their fellow creatures to assemble.

Fangs flicked out his forked tongue and pushed his head forward. He slowly approached an egg and opening his mouth as wide as possible he took a corner into it. His elasticized neck muscles readily expanded with the teeth cones on the upper and lower jaws moving back and forth which slowly walked the egg into the gullet. To push the egg further in Fangs made a bend in his neck behind the egg and sent it further down into his stomach. He then straightened his head and by mistake hit an egg which rolled to the edge of the nest. There was a flurry of wings above him so the snake hastily drew his body back, shot his head up and snapped at the intruders'. A couple of crows swerved and flew off to the safety of the upper branches squawking their despair to their friends as two eggs fell off the nest and got smashed on the ground below.

"Oops, must be careful", thought Fangs as he regurgitated the egg shell which had split in his stomach. "Might as well finish this one and leave this place", he thought as he turned his attention to the remaining egg.

Opening his mouth wide open the snake engulfed the second egg and using his cone like bone teeth he walked it into his gullet as the elastic skin behind the mouth expanded and contracted to let the egg in. The shell again cracked which the snake again regurgitated and turned his head around to go back the way he had come. Using his scutes he traveled down the length of his own body and was soon scuting down the branch with a host of crows caw-cawing above him. He reached the thin leafy branch up which he had climbed and crawled down it. Weaving in and out of leaves and twigs he reached the lower branch where he again scuted to the point where he had climbed onto the branch. The prop root he had climbed up was directly below him so he allowed his head to travel down but had to hastily pull it back as a couple of crows dived too close for comfort. Shooting his head up and snapping at them Fangs went back to the task of climbing down. His head went a foot down the prop root after which the body started moving in circles around the fibrous wood as it took a firm grip on the latter.

Fangs was soon on the ground and looking upward he realized that the crows were still after him so he hastily slithered away towards the pond from where he had come. Traversing the edge of the water over the black humus the snake entered a clump of grass which led him to the paddy field. Traveling through the field, he soon broke out of the paddy stalks and realized that he had lost the crows. They were still cawing at the clump of grass he had entered so he slithered on and passing below the Baobab tree he disturbed a pair of pink necked Chameleons who scampered up the trunk. Further on a couple of grasshoppers leapt to out of his way and a pair of brown colored moths hovered above and followed the snake from a safe distance.

Fangs was soon back at his rat hole home. Peering down into the hole he allowed his head to travel six inches into it.

His forked tongue did not receive any suspicious molecules so he entered deeper into the hole and was soon lying in the cave which had once been owned by a field rat.

The next day unknown to Fangs a group of children were preparing themselves for the days work. They were of the 'Mussahar' community which was a branch of the Harijan caste which in turn was the lowest in the ranks of the Hindu caste hierarchy. They were a landless community and earned a living as agricultural laborers in the fields of different landlords that owned the land in the area. The children lived with their parents in single roomed mud houses with thatched roofs and no latrines. They all defecated outside in the fields.

The village itself was situated on the outskirts of Vikram Singh's property and constituted of a cluster of mud houses with thatched roofs around a bare plot of land in which a giant Pakur tree stood erect and proud lending its shade to one of the most miserable specimens of humanity.

The Mussahar's themselves were short, dark and stocky compared to their tall Aryan masters. They had been suppressed from ancient pre-Christian times and were forced to work for a couple of meager meals a day. Due to hunger they were forced to eat rats and snails and other unsavory delicacies which these children were going to hunt today. The village elders would go to the Zamindar's fields to work while the little ones would hunt for vermin or little river crabs which would give the family the much needed nourishment.

The children were all naked and stood in an untidy group before an old man. Their hair was matted and most of their noses ran while some of them were pot bellied. The old man had white hair, was bare backed and bent double with age. A stick in his right hand seemed to help his old feet to hold him up.

"Remember", the old man said, "when ever you prod a hole always use a stick first. Make sure it goes down deep enough. If a rat lives in it, it will scamper out and you may catch it. And remember that a rat hole sometimes contains a cache of paddy. Always remember to dig it out".

Some of the children scratched their matted hair as they carefully listened to the old man. They were looking forward to unearthing these caches. They knew that field mice were big thieves and stored paddy in their dungeons. Caches up to a quintal had sometimes been unearthed and the landlords had made it a rule that the person who unearthed the grain could take it as long as he killed the vermin. This resulted in three months of undisturbed rice eating for the family if they were lucky.

"And if your stick touches something hard you can expect it to be a crab or a snail", continued the old man, "so take a couple of spades along and dig into the hole till you finally catch the creature. Remember snails meat is good for tuberculosis and we have a couple of people suffering from the disease. The snails meat will help them to recuperate".

The children nodded their heads.

"And remember", warned the old man", there are chances that a snake may be hidden in the hole so never probe with your hands. Always use your sticks. Do you understand? Never probe with your hands".

The children nodded their heads.

"Good, then repeat the last part of what I said".

"Never probe with our hands", the children repeated in a chorus, "and always use a stick to poke into the ground".

"Good, and god bless you".

The children wished the old man a 'thank you' and scampered off behind the tallest boy. There was something peculiar about the Mussahar children. Due to malnourishment they didn't look their age. The eldest boy looked like a ten year old while the rest seemed to average between five and ten years. They all looked five years younger than what their actual age was.

The children ran on behind the tall boy. Some skipped, some hopped, and some did a weird dance while they happily followed their leader. They liked rats and crab meat and were looking forward to catching plenty of them.

"Come on", shouted the tall boy. "I am your leader now and every one must do as I say".

The children nodded their heads.

"Remember", the tall boy continued, "no one must put his hand into a hole. We will use a stick".

The children nodded and chatted and sang Mussahar songs as they ran after the tall boy. They knew that if they did not catch these creatures, they would have to eat coarse chappaties with salt, flavored by a single green chilly, and they shuddered at the thought. Who in this world did not want to eat a full meal?

The children were soon running past the Banyan tree with the hanging prop roots which Fangs had just climbed down. They dashed into the little pond as the younger ones squealed and splashed around in delight. They were soon out on the other side and were running towards the Baobab tree with a rope hanging from it. They knew what the rope was meant for as they ran past it into the fields beyond.

"There's a hole", shouted one of the boys.

"And another".

"Look there's another".

"Well try this one first", stated the tall boy who sat down on his knees and taking a stick he slowly let it enter the hole. Pushing the stick in deeper and deeper he waited for some noise of protest from below. None came and his stick touched the mud floor. He pulled it out and shook his head. "There's nothing in there", he said.

"Then lets try that one", said a boy.

The tall boy shuffled on his knees to another hole and let his stick down into it and heard a squeak. The children got exited as he rudely jabbed into the hole and squealed as a rat twice the size of a cricket ball scampered out.

"Catch it", squealed a girl as she dived and missed. The rat scampered towards an empty plot of land vegetated with short hard grass. The children ran after it and the leading ones dived at the vermin just as it turned to the left. They missed and fell flat on the grass while some of those running behind toppled over them.

"There it is", shouted a boy as he scampered after it with piece of cloth. The other children followed while the fallen ones disentangled themselves.

The rat scampered on turning left then right and was soon surrounded by the children. It went on running desperately and finally stopped when a boy holding a piece of cloth dived on it and trapped it in the cloth. A cheer rang out from the children and the tall boy walked over to the cloth and slipping his hand in, he caught hold of the vermin and pulled it out. Grinning from ear to ear he showed the captive to his friends and waved to a boy who was holding a small sack. The boy ran over and the rat was unceremoniously dumped into it.

"Let's try another hole", the tall boy announced as he walked over and sat down next to a hole. Lowering the stick in, he was at once rewarded and a vermin as large as the previous one scampered out causing the children to rush at it. This time the chase was short as the boy with the cloth made an accurate dive and the cloth landed properly on the rat. The brown creature was soon in the sack with the other one.

"There's something hard here", shouted a boy who had picked up a stick and was prodding it into a hole. Quite a few of the children now had sticks in their hands and were prodding into several holes. "Lets dig this one out", said the boy.

A boy with a spade ran over and hacked into the soil. He dug a foot into the ground and saw the crab which scampered up the mud wall in an attempt to run away. A blow from the spade caused it to flail and roll back into the pit from where it was picked up and put into the gunny sack to accompany the two rats.

Unknown to the group of children a little pot bellied naked eight year old girl who had been running amongst them got over excited and impatient. She couldn't find a stick long enough to prod into the holes so she decided to use her hands. She was a little child after all and children did have the tendency to break rules so seeing a hole, she sat down on her knees next to it and lowered her right hand in. Pushing down, she bent over as her elbow entered the hole.She opened and closed her palms to catch something and screamed as she felt a sting which seemed to pierce her palm and shoot up her hand, past her shoulder, up her neck and to her head. With one jerk she pulled her hand out and went on screaming.

Fangs had struck. The little girl had put her hand into his rat hole and he had watched it come down as the palm opened and closed. He had rapidly shot out his forked tongue and had pushed his head into the tunnel down which the hand was coming. Without warning he had lunged up and bitten the back of the hand when the palm was closed. It was the first time he had used his newly acquired Fangs and he pulled back with satisfaction to survey what he had done. The hand however disappeared back up the hole.

The other children stopped what they were doing and looked at the girl who was now clutching her right hand and was screaming wretchedly. They understood something was badly wrong and ran up to her.

"Stop screaming", ordered the tall boy. "What happened?"

The little girl went on screaming.

"What happened?"

"Something bit me".

"Where?"

The girl still screaming lifted up her hand and the boy grabbed it and looked at the puncture marks. He grew suspicious.

"What bit you?", he asked.

"In that hole".

"You put your hand in that hole?"

The screaming girl nodded her head.

"You idiot, you could have been bitten by a snake". Then turning around he shouted, "bring a spade over and dig into this hole. Let's see what bit her".

The boy with the spade ran over and the children drew back to allow him to swing it at the hole. The spade hacked into the mud and scooped some out and had dug six inches when they heard a loud "Khaa". It was Fang's warning to them.

The spade digger stopped and looked down and stepped back. He recognized the sound. Too many Mussahar's had died of snake bite and there was no Mussahar who did not recognize this sound.

The boy swung his spade down which was received by another loud "Khaa". They then saw it. Fangs lifted his head out of the hole and opened his hood as he spat two more menacing "Khaa's" at the spade holding boy. This caused the children to scamper off in different directions.

The tall boy however ran after the little girl shouting "she's been bitten by the cobra, by the Nagraj, lets take her to the village and try to save her".

The children encircled the little girl and ran with her towards the village. Unfortunately for them an elder Mussahar wasn't around or he would have simply taken an axe or the spade which was available and would have hacked off the hand from the wrist. The child would have fainted but herbs and some unique Mussahar medicines would have been pressed over the amputated limb and soon the wound would have healed with the girl still alive.

Unfortunately the opposite happened. The girl's running caused her blood circulation to increase and her heart to beat faster. She first felt something cold travel up her hand and to the other parts of her body. The cold feeling soon turned into a burning sensation till she collapsed a few feet away from the Baobab tree. The desperate children got together and lifted her on their shoulders and took her back to the village.

Back in the hole Fangs decided that enough was enough. He had been disturbed and his hole was half dug out so using his scutes he climbed out and slithered towards the distant row of shacks which bordered the Zamindar's supposed to be beautiful garden plot. Zig zagging through tufts of grass, over little mounds and in and out of little troughs in the ground he reached an eight foot long dead log that was lying on the ground. The dead wood teemed with minute living organisms which disappeared as he approached.

Reaching the wood, Fangs decided to rest under it since he wasn't in a hurry to find another resting place. Spring had arrived which in Bihar was actually the start of the hot season. It didn't make a difference now where he relaxed. He needed the hole during the winters to hibernate from the cold. It was difficult to move around during the cold season because of the dew which transformed the grass into blades which seemed to cut into his belly plates. The dew hurt him, but now for eight months he was free to go where he willed with no restrictions from mother nature.

Drawing himself alongside the branch and partially covered by the curved wood, Fangs lay still to relax. Soon the only sign of life from him was the occasional flick of his forked tongue.

Fangs couldn't have been luckier. He was destined to live

longer and eat more rats and frogs and lizards and maybe bite more humans. His decision to leave the rat hole was a wise one because the girl had died by the time the group of children reached the village. A few people scampered off to call the villagers and the girl's parents from the nearby fields while others ran to get the OJHA or the witch doctor to bring the girl back to life. The witch doctor came and made the villagers carry the child's body and laid her under the Pakur tree. He lit some incense sticks and taking his broom, he had sat cross legged next to her abdomen and blew incense smoke over her blue tinted body. He blew the smoke, rang a little bell and muttered some prayers, but to no avail. The girl didn't get up, so he continued ringing the bell and blowing smoke over the dead body as he muttered more prayers. Nothing happened so the villagers decided to get a better OJHA from the next Mussahar village. A short stocky bare bodied fellow was brought over and he too tried to get back the little girls life. He too blew incense smoke over the body and rang a bell over it. He too muttered prayers and when nothing happened, blamed his failure on the previous OJHA.

The girl died and the Mussahars decided to dispose her off. They tied her dead body to a couple of banana stumps and let her float away down the holy Ganges to where ever the river took her. It was a common belief that the cool waters of the Ganges and the cooling effects of the banana stumps might combine to suck out the poison causing the dead person to come to life.

As the little body floated away sandwiched between the green stumps, the father and uncle of the girl were overcome by grief and swore. “Let’s kill the snake”, whispered the father.

The girl’s uncle looked at his brother and nodded his head, “yes let’s kill it”, he said.

“Let’s kill the demon”, roared the girl’s father as he watched his little girls body grow smaller as it floated away. “Let’s kill the Rakshasa”.

The girls uncle who was short and dark complexioned like his brother turned to the rest of the Mussahars. “Everyone collect spears and axes and spades and lets kill that snake and make it float on this river”, he yelled.

The little group of short dark complexioned, half naked humans went to their huts and returned with a weapon each and soon the children were leading them towards the Baobab tree and the rat hole where Fangs had lived a couple of hours earlier.

Lying relaxed under the dead wood Fangs saw the little group approach. He saw some of the children point to his rat hole, and how like maniacs they dug into it. Finding nothing they dug up another hole and another and another and Fangs realized that it wasn’t wise to stay back since digging up the holes the little group was slowly approaching the dead branch under which he was lying.

Turning around Fangs looked up, flicked his forked tongue

and quietly slipped out from under the dead branch. The humans were too busy digging up the various holes in the ground so no one noticed him slither towards the distant row of shacks which was the boundary of Vikram Singh's supposed to be beautiful garden plot.

Slithering through shrub and grass, Fangs felt a wee bit scared since he was now in the open and could be easily seen. He knew what the result would be if he was seen. The people would throw sticks and stones and he knew how painful these missiles could be so he increased speed and tried his best to keep himself hidden in the greenery while he moved on.

Back where the Mussahars were digging, the latter got tired and spat at the ground and cursed it for having swallowed up the snake. They couldn't figure out where the reptile could have gone and looked around in exasperation at the nearby fields and the fields beyond. "It was impossible to search for the snake in all those fields", they thought as they sat down cross legged on the ground to rub some tobacco in their palm's and dunked the stuff into their mouths. They had finally given up.

Fangs had reached the edge of the field which led to the row of shacks. Peering over the boundary, he used his forked tongue to make sure that everything was clear. His sensory organs told him that there was a cluster of Magnolia trees to his right so he turned and slithered towards the cluster of bushes.

The Magnolia is actually a hardy shrub or a small tree with

spreading branches, and from above it is very hard to make out what is below it. So this was a perfect hiding place for Fangs who arrived and slithered into the protective green canopy of leaves and lapped his body around the short trunk deciding to have a rest till night came when he would be safe.

Fangs lay there and through the leaves watched the sun travel from mid-day to evening to sunset and finally till darkness shrouded the earth. He had watched the different low flying birds fly overhead, the grasshoppers and dragonflies as they ushered in the evening. He was now watching a multitude of fireflies which were switching on and off the phosphorous glow that was on the tip of their abdomens in synchronized flashes as they flew. This exasperated Fangs as he watched the little glowing things dance in the darkness occasionally leaping higher when a cricket called out to a mate or when they heard the distant cry of a Cicada. Fangs could not hear these noises so when the host of lights shot up, he thought that it was a part of the dance.

The snake soon got tired of watching the fireflies and lazily uncurled himself. It was spring and the climate had changed from bitter cold to warm so he felt relaxed as he slipped out from under the Magnolia tree and headed towards the row of shacks which he sometimes frequented. The humans attracted mosquitoes and flies which in turn attracted lizards and frogs and mice which in turn attracted him. He relished these creatures and knew he would find them near human habitation.

That's why he was soon passing in between two mud walls when he scared two rows of ants who were about to wage war. Seeing the snake pass in between them, they desperately scampered up their respective walls. The ones which weren't fast enough were thrown or hurt under the reptiles belly plates as it scraped over the ground on its way past the shacks.

Fangs soon reached the other side and was in the open again. In front of him was the row of bovines tethered to their troughs. Ahead and slightly to his left was the thatched roof with the low wall traveling around three parts of it. Some men were sitting under the thatched roof with their legs akimbo while others sat cross legged as they chatted under the yellow light of a lantern. Further to the left was the flag pole and the dung heap. To the extreme left was the Haveli's verandah.

And there was a rat. It scampered past just twenty feet ahead of the snake so Fangs let go of his curls and gave a chase. He zipped through the stubby grass as the rat squeaked and picked up speed. Creating his curls in well timed precision Fangs increased speed and zipped after the rat. The vermin ran on and changing its direction it headed for the Haveli's verandah. Fangs was in hot pursuit and was catching up.

"Rama" shouted Vikram from under the thatched roof. "Close the Haveli's doors and tell the mistress not to wait for me. Tell her to retire if she wants to. I will be up till late tonight".

Rama was sitting dozing in the dark verandah. The Haveli did not have electricity and the master did not believe in using more than two lanterns at a time. One was for the mistress and the other was for himself. The rest of the Haveli and compound had to spend the nights in eerie darkness. That's why Rama did not see the rat and snake racing towards him.

"Yes master", Rama replied as he yawned and got up. Walking towards the door in the south eastern corner of the verandah he took hold of the double door and shut the right one first.

In the darkness the rat hit Rama's ankle and was thrown squeaking over the lower door frame to the other side. "These rats", thought Rama as he proceeded to close the other door. "These rats are always creating trouble in the dark. I wish there was a snake around".

Rama did not know that while the other door was closing, Fangs had narrowly missed his leg and was zipping over the lower door a frame in hot pursuit of the rat. He was three quarters across the doorframe with only eight inches of tail left on Rama's side when the servant slammed the door shut. This jerked the snake to a halt who whipped around and hit the door splatting venom on the wood. Desperate with pain as it was squeezed between the door and the frame it let out three vicious "Khaa's" and attacked the door causing his Fangs to hit wood, spattering venom on it again.

Rama heard the commotion and pressed harder. He heard the loud 'Khaa's and was confused and thought that the rats were a nuisance. "To think of it", he thought, "they are even scolding me. May be one of them has been caught between the wood. Might as well release it. Then maybe the commotion will stop".

Rama felt sorry for what he thought was stuck rat and opened the door for a second. Fangs felt relieved and in the dark did not know where to go. His Jacobson's organs told him that human feet were just inches away but he had broken his backbone just eight inches up his tail and any movement made it hurt. Moreover he had hurt his fangs against the door. He was confused and was still contemplating on whether to cross back across the door frame or to continue when Rama decided he had given the rat enough time to escape and slammed the doors shut and latched the bolt.

Fangs immediately screamed out half a dozen deadly "Khaas" which echoed in the Haveli's corridors and reverberated down the verandah and through the door all the way to the thatched roof causing Vikram Singh and the others to sit up straight. "That sounds like a snake", said Vikram.

"Like a cobra's mad hiss", commented a villager.

"Yes its a snake", said Vikram as he got up. "It is the Nagraj. Some of you come with sticks".

Vikram took the lantern off its hook and walked toward's the Haveli's verandah while the villagers picked up their sticks and followed him.

"What's happening Rama?", Vikram shouted at the servant's silhouette.

"Master the rats are scolding me".

Fangs squirmed madly on both sides of the door. He had hit his teeth and hurt them several times on the wood but the unbearable pain kept him on. The tip of the squirming tail hit Rama's feet several times and the confused servant thought that there were quite a few rats down their and in the darkness they were all attacking him with their tails. It was not until the snakes tail wrapped around his leg did he realize what was actually down there. To his horror he realized that a snake was wrapped around his right leg.

"Master", he cried, "help, it has bitten me".

"What has bitten you?", asked Vikram who had arrived and was holding up the lantern.

"My leg master, my leg, a rope is around it".

Vikram let down the lantern and saw a coil around the leg. Rama also saw the coil and his suspicion was confirmed as he screamed and sprang. The coil was wrenched open and Rama was a free man to stand and watch the squirming tail with the rest from a safe distance after he had properly checked his feet for puncture marks.

"It is a cobra's tail", whispered the short stocky village head man.

"Open the door", ordered Vikram.

Rama bent over, slid open the latch, pushed the double doors open and jumped back. Fangs was lying with his head on the ground. Seeing the door open he felt relief as his squeezed portion was released. He opened his hood and was startled to see the bunch of humans all peering down at him in the pale light of the lantern. He barked at them and saw them jump back but inch forward again, so he barked a second "Khaa" causing them to jump back once more. The Zamindar of course had jumped onto the elder Pehelwan's back for elevation and was riding piggy back on him. He felt safe there because the Pehelwan's back was broad, strong and reassuring.

"Some one put this lantern on a long stick and put the lantern near the snake", whispered Vikram from behind the Pehelwan's back, "It looks majestic, I want to have a proper look at it".

Fangs turned his hood as he surveyed each and every face. It was like the horrible old days with the snake charmer when the humans seemed to be perennially peering down at him. He thought that this group also, after having satisfied their curiosity, would fish out a pair of hands in prayer to him so he flicked out his forked tongue for more information.

"Look he is flicking his tongue at us", commented Vikram.

"It looks dangerous".

"Why isn't the snake moving away?", asked the village headman, "It seems to be hurt. I think Rama squeezed its tail in between the doors and broke it. That's why it was making all that ruckus".

"It is the snake lord nevertheless", Vikram whispered from behind the Pehelwan's back.

"Yes, and Rama broke his back", commented a villager.

Vikram turned his head towards Rama, "Did you break its back?", he asked.

"No master".

"Of course you did", replied Vikram, "you squeezed it between the two doors".

"But it was a mistake master".

"How would you feel if I squeezed your finger between the doors and said it was a mistake".

"Please don't do that master".

Vikram turned to the snake and folded his hands around the Pehelwan's face in a prayer to the reptile. "Oh Snake Lord", he said, "forgive this miserable servant for he knows not what he does".

"There it was", Fangs thought. "He has fished his hands out in prayer. Must try and get out of here".

The snake flexed his muscles and realized he could move his body. Only the part of the tail which had been squashed in the door hurt so Fangs drew up his body in a straight line. He knew that he couldn't use the last six inches in creating his S shaped curves so he decided to use his scutes to move forward. Moving them up and down alternately, he traveled in a straight line and crawled over the lower door frame. Moving his scutes he travelled across the verandah while an exasperated Zamindar tried to stop him. "Wait your holiness", Vikram pleaded from behind the Pehelwan's back. "Please wait, I have got some milk to offer you".

Rama was dreading this and knew that it was coming. He had promised the Zamindar that he would feed the snake with milk if it showed itself again. And if necessary, he would touch the tail reverently with his hands. The snake however continued scuting. It wanted to get out of the human menace as soon as possible.

"Rama get some milk", Vikram ordered, "and be quick with it".

Rama disappeared into the Haveli and hid in one of the dark rooms as Fangs continued his slow journey across the verandah.

"Rama bring the milk quick", Vikram shouted, "the Nagraj is reaching the edge of the verandah".

"I'm searching for the milk", shouted back the servant, "I can't see in the dark".

"Then take the mistresses' lantern", shouted back Vikram.

"Okay master".

Fangs had now reached the mouth of the verandah and was slithering down the double steps to the grass below.

"Bring the milk quick Rama".

"I'm boiling it", Rama shouted back.

"You idiot bring it cold or the snake will disappear".

"Okay master".

Vikram now understood that Rama was playing truant so he jumped off the tired Pehelwan's back and rushed past the villagers into the hall way and into the kitchen. It was pitch dark. "Rama where are you?", he shouted.

There was no reply.

"Rama, where's the milk?"

There was no reply so an exasperated Vikram Singh ran back to the verandah. "Where's the snake?", he asked.

"It disappeared into the grass", answered the headman pointing a finger towards the silhouette of the row of shacks in the distance. "It went that way".

Vikram Singh was furious. He had missed a second chance to please the lord snake because of Rama. "Rama", he screamed, "you will hang from the tree the first thing in the morning and this time no one will save you".

The Daughter's Marriage

It was 1946 and Vikram Singh's daughter was four years old. She had been named Shanti in a special naming ceremony which was conducted by the hook beak nosed Brahmin priest who always had pride of place next to him. The Zamindar had conveniently absented himself. He didn't care what they named her. They could call her a cat, a mouse, or a leopard for all he cared.

The priest had however named the girl Shanti since he felt the name suited the occasion. "Shanti" because the world needed it, 'Shanti' because blitzkrieged London had cried out for it. 'Shanti' because the prophet Gandhi asked for it. Vikram thought it was the most stupid name that had been chosen. He deeply felt that Shanti would elude him, and the girl would cause problems for him in the future.

Narayani had fallen ill a couple of years after Shanti's birth and now looked like a ghost of her previous self. She had been beautiful once with a roundish face, thin lips, large eyes, fair skin and a slim body. She was thin now and her cheek bones protruded out of her face. Black shades surrounded her eyes which were embedded deep in their sockets. The village quack had advised her total rest so that she would get well soon. The English doctors of the government hospital in the district town of Monghyr had diagnosed cancer in her uterus. They advised her to get her uterus taken out if she wanted to live and Vikram went into a daze. "If they took out her uterus then how would she be able to bear him a boy child", he reasoned. The doctor's however persisted that she should undergo the operation if he wanted to see her alive for some time.

Vikram had nearly replied, "then let her die", but kept his mouth shut and like a proper husband accompanied her to the hospital and sat on the lawn outside all through the operation. A nurse had come out after the operation and informed him that the operation had been successful. Later, the chaprasi showed him the miserable lump of flesh that had been the womb. Vikram Singh now understood that his miserable wife's miserable abdomen would bear him no more children. She was a Falcon now. A Baaz.

Narayani knew that she could die soon. She knew that the removed uterus hadn't finally cured her and that cancer could still be lurking in her insides. She knew that her husband's craze for a boy child would lead him to re-marry after her death. She did not like the idea of her little Shanti being in the hands of an unknown woman who would be her stepmother. She distrusted step mothers and decided to marry off her little child safely into a rich Zamindar family before she herself died.

Narayani pestered Vikram who readily succumbed. He knew that his wife was ill and the doctors hadn't guaranteed how long she would live. They had told him that they had done their best and the rest was in the hands of God so Vikram had looked up at the skies with a pleading look in his eyes. "Please take her away", he had mentally prayed, "her medicines are eating up all my money". Seeing his pleading eyes looking up at the sky, the doctor thought the Zamindar was asking for the Almighty's mercy so that his wife would be delivered from the sickness. The doctor felt sorry for him.

Vikram Singh did have a deep desire to marry again. That's why he hoped that Narayani would leave for her heavenly abode, and it would be nice if little Shanti was also out of the way. Then there would be a clean house, a new wife and a fresh new life to live all over again with a stronger attempt at a boy child.

The match maker was called the next day. He was a fat Brahmin Priest who had three vermilion lines running across his forehead and was richly dressed in a silk kurta and dhoti. He doubled as a Priest and a sort of a broker. He knew of most of the marriageable girls and boys of the area and catered to all castes except for the poor Sudra's and the Harijans. At a request from Vikram he fished out a list of addresses and a sheaf photos of tiny tots to strapping twenty five year old young men. Shanti was five and a half years old so a cute looking seven year old boy was chosen from the photographs. The Bio-data of the child was perfect. He was the son of Zamindar Shree Balbir Singh of Rampur. The photo was sent to Narayani who was lying on her bed. Seeing the eyes smiling out of the picture, she put the paper against her breasts and closed her eyes in silent prayer after which she murmured. "I want this boy at all costs. No matter what the dowry is. I want this boy wedded to my daughter".

The next day Vikram Singh got himself dressed up as smartly as possible, as Zamindarly as possible and as nawably as possible. He wore white churidar Pajamas under a silken kurta made out of the finest silk of Bhagalpur. Over the kurta he wore a pink colored, gold brocaded, golden bordered coat which flowed down to his knees and was called a Sherwani. It smelt of a rose flavored perfume called attar. On his head he wore a little gold brocaded pink Lucknowi cap and his feet had stepped into a pair of gold brocaded pink shoes whose tips were turned upwards in a half circle.

"Rama", shouted the Zamindar, "bring me my walking stick".

"Yes master", shouted back the servant who had been brushing the already shining stick with a piece of cloth. It was an intricately carved expensive piece of wood which was well polished and had a curved handle which was made of ivory. It wasn't that Vikram Singh was lame or he couldn't walk. It was just a fashion of those days. A Zamindar had to have an expensive stick in one hand while the other twirled a moustache on either side of a bulbous nose.

Rama ran over and politely handed the stick to Vikram who walked over to the two framed paintings that hung on the verandah's northern wall. One was a portrait of his father the late Zamindar who was wearing breaches under a red hunting coat and whose right hand's fore finger was placed on a globe which sat on a round table while the other hand twirled a moustache to the left of a bulbous nose. Vikram did a namastay and asked for his blessings and moved over to the second portrait which belonged to his grandfather. The elderly gentleman's features were similar to Vikram's father's except that the hair was white. The lordly fellow wore a kurta over a Pajama and had a sword hanging from his hips while his right hand was placed on an oblong globe which rested on an oblong table. The other hand of course was twirling a moustache on the left side of another bulbous nose.

Vikram Singh lowered his head for a second time and asked the painting for its blessings. Confident that he had received them he turned around and shouted to Rama.

"Yes master?", the servant replied, "I'm just behind you".

"Good. Then go and tell the driver to take out the car and you and the Priest go and look for a snake. A cobra. I would like to pray to it before I start my journey".

"But master", replied Rama, "where do I search for a cobra?".

"On the ground you idiot, or in a rat hole or on a branch of a tree,or under a bush".

The servant nodded his head and scampered off to the thatched roof under which the thin hook beak nosed Brahmin Priest sat dressed in his best. He wore a well ironed white kurta over a well ironed dhoti and his hair and beard were properly combed. He had his chillum safely hidden in his kurta pocket and had high hopes for the day. It was a rule among the Zamindars that if a deal was clinched and a marriage was fixed, the two parties would offer gold coins to the Brahmin Priest's accompanying them.

"Punditji", shouted Rama, "you wait here while I tell the driver to start the car. The two of us will then go in search of a snake".

"A snake?", shouted back the Priest.

"Yes Punditji. The master wants to pray to the snake for good luck before he goes to Rampur".

Punditji shook his head while Rama ran over to the Garage next to which the driver lived in a little low ceilinged corrugated roofed room. "Driver sahib", he shouted. "The master wants you to wash the car and park it in front of the verandah".

The driver was a thin dark man with a medium sized moustache and a piercing look in his eyes which were embedded in deep sockets in a longish face. He was lying on his cot and grunted when he heard Rama speak. “When does he want the car?”, he asked.

“In half an hour”, Rama blurted as he ran back towards the thatched roof under which the Brahmin Priest sat. Accompanied by the latter the servant set off towards the row of shacks from where the smell of shit emanated. Passing the shacks the two picked their way through cakes of shit as they headed towards the distant Baobab tree. On the way Rama took a stick and prodded a couple of rat holes. He was unlucky and jumped in fright when an irritated rat scampered out and ran to safety.

“How are we to search for a cobra?”, the Brahmin wondered loudly, “this Zamindar is completely mad”.

“Shush, Panditji, warned Rama, “even the air and trees in this area have ears. The Zamindar seems to know everything that goes on around here. Even the birds seem to behave like his spies”.

“I know”, mumbled the Priest as he walked on.

“And if you say something sacrilegious against him, he somehow comes to know about it and hangs you from that big tree over there”.

“He dare not hang a Brahmin”, retorted the Priest.

“And why not?”

“Because we are the chosen ones of God. The Brahmin has a special place in society and is respected and revered by all castes and no one can touch him or hurt a hair on his head.

Whoever tries will burn his fingers, his arms will melt and he will be cursed in hell. And the Zamindar knows that".

"Yes", thought Rama, "you are truly the chosen one. You don't have to work and pretend to pray and smoke hashish while the rest of society toils and works and provides you with free food and lodging every day".

The two soon reached the Baobab tree and looked up into its thick branches. The tree was dressed in a new dress of bright green leaves. There were large flowers which were present on long thick stalks with creamy white petals which had bloomed last night and were now in the process of withering away. But there was no snake so Rama and the Priest walked on and studied the banks of the pond. There was no snake, only a few river crabs that scampered back into the water. On the opposite bank there was a dead tree trunk on which a red necked chameleon sat and nodded its head at the humans. In the pond itself, stepping gingerly on the water surface, on the lotus leaves were a group of Purple Moor hens. They had long bear red legs with bald red foreheads and a white patch under their stumpy tails which was conspicuous when it was flicked up at each step. Some sauntered over floating weeds while a couple of males went through a ludicrous courtship display by holding water weeds to their bills and bowing to their mates to the accompaniment of loud cackles and hoots and harsh notes which emanated from the other birds.

"Noisy birds", muttered Rama as he picked up a stone and

threw it at the hens. The stone splashed in the water in the middle of the group causing some of them to run for cover while the others took to flight. They flapped their wings and awkwardly lifted themselves up in a labored and feeble flight with their long and ungainly red legs dangling from behind.

Rama and the pundit traversed the pond and walked to the other side and were soon standing under the Banyan tree. They looked up into the foliage and saw a few disturbed crows, some common yellow beaked Mynah's, and a scarlet chested, Myhna. Rama studied the prop roots which hung from the tree's branches and entered the ground as roots. Choosing a particularly thick root the servant climbed to the lowest branch and looked around while the scared crows and Mynah's took to flight. They flew around the tree caw-cawing and chattering and making sharp irritated calls at the human who persisted on climbing onto a higher branch to get a better look into the foliage. Satisfied that there was no snake to be seen Rama climbed down and accompanied with the Pundit, he walked towards the little Mussahar village where the little girl had died.

Rama stopped under a Neem tree and looked up. It was a medium sized tree with a straight trunk, evergreen and elegant in form. The leaves were compound and green and crowded at the ends of the branches. There were a couple of common Mynah's and a Blue Jay perched on the upper branches, but there was no snake.

"You idiot", teased the Pundit, "why are you looking up into the Neem tree. Snakes don't climb Neem trees. They don't like the smell of the leaves".

Rama looked at the Pundit and smiled. "How do you know that snakes don't climb up Neem trees?"

"Because I am a Brahmin", retorted the Priest, "and Brahmins have all knowledge".

Rama nodded his head and walked on. Seeing a couple of rat holes he took a stick and prodded deeply into them. There was no reply so the duo walked on till they reached a couple of Crepe flower trees. They were deciduous with a rounded crown, short boles and smooth branches with light gray barks. The leaves were bright green on the upper reaches of the tree and paler green on the lower branches and were veined heavily on the underparts. The duo looked up and saw the usual crows, a couple of sparrows, a green colored small Bee-eater, and a smoky black, white rumped, House swift which had a short square tail. But there was no snake so Rama slumped down onto the ground. "Now what do we do Panditji?", he asked. "do we look up into every tree in this world?"

"The Zamindar is mad", the Priest commented, "come on lets go back to the Haveli".

"But what will we tell the master?"

"That we saw no snake, you silly".

"But he will hang me from the tree".

"And if you're late he will still hang you from the tree".

"Oh god, why doesn't this earth swallow me up".

"You better get up and start heading back or the Zamindar will swallow you up".

Rama reluctantly got up and walked behind the Brahmin. They left the Crepe trees and the Neem trees behind and were soon passing under the Banyan tree. They traversed the pond and were soon walking under the Baobab tree and Rama looked up at the rope which he suspected would soon have him hanging from it. The Priest carried on and the servant reluctantly followed and they soon crossed the line of shacks and saw the black 1930 model battered Buick parked in from of the verandah with Vikram Singh standing in front of it. The two Pehelwans were standing behind the Zamindar and were wearing yellow colored dhoties under a white kurta and had yellow turbans wrapped around their heads. The driver was dressed in similar attire.

"What happened?", Vikram asked.

"We didn't see any snake", replied the Priest. Rama was standing two feet behind him.

"Then you didn't search hard enough".

"Yes we did Judgemaan". Being a Brahmin the Priest did not call the Zamindar master. The latter was his client and it was his job to recite prayers for the former for a fee. Since the Zamindar was his client, he called him his Judgemaan".

"You didn't search hard enough", Vikram repeated.

"Yes we did Judgemaan", the Priest swore. "We looked into

rat holes and sometimes dug them up. And this miserable Rama climbed up every tree we saw to see if there was a snake on the branches. He even climbed up a Neem tree".

"I didn't", retorted Rama, "I only climbed up the Banyan tree".

"See you're telling lies", Vikram grumbled, "you're the worst Priest I've ever put mine eyes on".

"Now are you going to believe me Judgemaan, or will you believe this miserable servant?"

"I don't believe you", retorted Vikram, "you're the biggest Brahmin liar I ever saw".

"Shanti, Shanti, Shanti", quelled the Priest, "shame, shame, shame, you shouldn't be saying such things to a Brahmin".

"Now shut up and get into the car", ordered Vikram as he himself opened the rear door on the drivers side and climbed in.

The bearded Priest climbed in from the other door and seated himself beside the Zamindar. Being his spiritual advisor he always got the priviledged place next to the Zamindar.

The two turbaned Pehelwans got into the front seat next to the driver, as one of them proudly held Vikrams double barrel shot gun. The turbaned driver took out a handle from the dickey and pushed it into the hole in the bumper connecting the T end of the handle in the slot of the crank pulley. Yanking the handle in a full circle the six cylindered engine coughed to life. Most of the six cylindered vehicles those days weren't self started since the vehicles were mostly bought in the second hand car markets of Calcutta and the spare parts weren't available locally. The only cities which had shops dealing in spare parts were Patna and Muzaffarpur which were generally a couple of hundred kilometers away. So the vehicles were push started or yanked to life with the help of a strong iron handle while the driver doubled as an engineer and was always at his wits end to somehow keep the vehicle going. The old Buick didn't have a silencer which had rusted and had fallen off a long time ago. It had since been discarded and was now lying among the dung heaps busily returning to dust. The result was a deafening ear splitting loud pra-ta-ta-taa when the engine roared to life.

Vikram Singh expectantly doubled his right leg over the left one as the driver put the handle in the dickey and climbed in behind the wheel. He let go off the clutch and the old Buick roared up the supposed to be gravelled driveway and for an instant it seemed that it was headed straight for the Scarecrow that stood in the field opposite the cement lions. The pot that was supposed to be the Scarecrows head seemed to be perennially smiling in a gesture of welcome with outstretched hands at the two lions that guarded Vikram's gate. The Buick turned after passing the lions and traveled along a rutted dirt track over which the heavy car bucked and bounced on its coil springs. It soon reached the highway which was actually a fifteen feet broad stretch of a pot holed layer of tarmac which traveled from the capital city of Patna to the district town of Monghyr. The turbaned driver turned left towards Patna and covered twenty kilometers in two hours before the Buick reached the village of Rampur where it left the tarmaced road and entered a dirt track which led to Zamindar Balbir Singhs double lioned gate. Village urchins screamed and shouted and chased the slow moving vehicle while the elder peasants looked enviously at Vikram Singh proudly sitting in the back seat of his pra-ta-taaing big car. He had one leg over the other while he leant back against musty, plush made in America upholstery, dressed in his pink gold brocaded Sherwani and white Churidar with his right hand holding an expensive polished ivory topped walking stick.

The black Buick had roared along luckily with none of the usual breakdowns which was very rare for a Zamindar's car in those days. It would have spoilt Vikram's style and composure. The vehicle pra-ta-taa'd into Zamindar Balbir Singh's double lioned gate, down the supposed to be graveled driveway, past a row of shacks which smelt of shit, past the row of irritated bovines and the dung heap in the corner. It roared into Balbir's portico and stopped in front of an old white six cylindered Ford which was parked proudly in the portico.

Vikram did not move to get out of his vehicle. He just sat back and twirled his moustache as he waited for his driver to open the door. All the while the fat round faced Balbir, who was sitting with his family on the verandah of the house, looked on and at a signal from him his obese double chinned wife pulled her ghunghat low over her head and taking her seven year old son's hand she shuffled into the houses interior to later peep from a window.

Balbir looked on as the fat saffron clad Priest who always had pride of place next to him looked at the skinny Priest who had pride of place next to Vikram. The driver got out of the Buick and walked back to Vikrams door and opened it. He then walked over to the front of the car and opened the bonnet and covering his right hand with a cloth he yanked out the radiator cap releasing a huge spume of steam from the gurgling boiling radiator.

Vikram Singh got out of the car as the skinny Brahmin got out from the other side. Together they climbed the six stairs to the verandah where Vikram in his nawably attire was face to face with Balbir Singh who was in his dhoti and vest. The two namastayed each other with folded hands after which Vikram twirled his moustache as he looked Balbir in the eye. Balbir stared back and twirled his moustache. The two were searching each others faces and were trying to remember where they had last met. Yes they had met before and knew each other well.

Twirling their moustaches the faces suddenly lit up in recognition and their mouths emanated loud 'Aahs" causing both the pot bellied paunches to twitch up in an effort to press the stomach and squeeze the air out of the lungs to create the 'aah'. With outstretched arms they gave each other a huge hug as their paunches clashed and squeezed as they held each other tight. Yes they had met before and knew each other well. They had met in the brothels of Gaya where the two frequented. Especially in the apartment of the twin sistered nautch girls whom they had fallen in love with. That's why they called each other brother in law.

"Vikram Singh my friend", Balbir spoke first as he hugged the Zamindar of Ramnagar. "How come you are in my house? What a pleasant surprise! And forgive me for not recognizing you".

"I made the same mistake dear brother in law", Vikram replied as he guffawed at the joke as Balbir also roared in laughter. "Are you going to offer your brother in law a place to sit or do I start my business standing".

"Of course sit down, sit down my dear brother in law", Balbir replied as he himself broke out guffawing. "Would you like some tea or some rosogulla's first".

Vikram Singh grew serious. "I have come here on some important work", he said, "only after my problem is solved can I eat in your house".

Balbir also grew serious and curiosity overtook him as he stared back into Vikram's eyes. "Yes what is it?", he asked.

Vikram motioned to the skinny hook beak nosed Brahmin who had pride of place next to him. The latter got up and with folded hands and requested Balbir. "My client here is the father of a four year old pretty looking girl. We heard from a respected

Brahmin that you are the father of a good looking seven year old boy".

Balbir nodded his head as he got the gist of Vikram's work.

"My client", continued the thin Brahmin, "would like to marry off his daughter to your son and with folded hands we pray for your acceptance. We are ready to turn the world over upside down if it is necessary to get our daughter wedded to your son".

Balbir looked into Vikram's nervous eyes then at the skinny Brahmin who had his hands folded in prayer. He looked down at the ground and thought for a while. "Won't you have some sweets first", he offered.

"Sweats are eaten when there is happiness", replied the thin hook beak nosed Brahmin, "sweats are tasteless when there is tension".

"But I'd like some time to think", replied Balbir.

"It is well known in these areas that the royal Balbir makes quick decisions", lied the Priest.

Balbir looked down at the ground then again at Vikram who was trying to hide his nervousness by twirling his moustache. Balbir then turned his back to Vikram and nudged the fat Brahmin Priest who had pride of place next to him. The Brahmin looked at Balbir who winked and made a gesture to reply. Getting up, the fat Brahmin pleaded with folded hands. "My client here is overjoyed to receive the great Vikram Singh as a guest. He is overjoyed more at the cause of the great

Zamindar's coming. He would be delighted to change the unreal relationship he had with the Zamindar sahib in the brothels of Gaya to a real one. There is unfortunately a small hitch. His son is only seven years old and my client thinks he is too young to marry".

Vikram Singhs' heart sank as he watched Balbir twirl his moustache. To show that he was unaffected by the fat Brahmin's words he continued twirling his while his thin Brahmin gulped and continued. "Brother Brahmin, who are we to make or break marriages? These things are written in heaven in the holy books. The holy clerks of the lord almighty maintain books where marriages are registered when the infant is born itself. Who are you or me to go against what is written in those books".

"How do you know what is written in those books", asked the fat Brahmin who had his hands folded towards the thin Brahmin.

"It is written in the girl's horoscope. A respected Brahmin gave me a copy of the boys horoscope and I realized the stars and the planets were perfectly matched. The boy and girl were made for each other and it will be a crime on our part to break up such a holy arrangement".

The fat Brahmin looked down at Balbir who hid his hands from Vikram's view and raised two fingers. His lips moved to form the word Jeep and the Brahmin understood and folded his hands in prayer again. "My client here is overjoyed at your coming here", he said while Balbir continued twirling his moustache. "he is overjoyed that you want to change an unreal relationship to a real one. He was formerly against the marriage of his underage son and wanted the boy to grow up attending school and college".

"He can attend school and college even after marriage", interrupted Vikrams thin Brahmin, "My client here will send his son in law to the best schools and colleges in this country".

"Please let me finish what I have to say", interrupted the fat Brahmin. "My client here as I have said is overjoyed to see the Zamindar of Ramnagar in his house. He cannot bear to see his royal self go away from his house empty handed. More so without eating a single sweet. Therefore he is happy to give his son in marriage to your client's daughter if that will allow you to eat in his house".

Vikram Singh's eyes brightened with relief and he and Balbir got up and hugged each other. In the process Vikram winked at his skinny Priest while Balbir lifted two fingers from behind Vikrams' back which both the Brahmins saw and understood. The two Zamindars disengaged themselves and went back to their respective seats while the two Brahmins remained standing with their hands folded towards each other.

"Are you happy with my client's decision?", asked the fat Brahmin.

The thin Brahmin nodded his head.

"Then lets get down to business", continued the fat Brahmin, "As you know nothing is cheap now a days with the British rulers unable to control inflation".

Vikram's thin Brahmin nodded his head. He had prepared himself for the bomb that was coming and had his answers on the tip of his tongue. He was a cut throat haggler himself and was just waiting for the questions.

"You see my client is a kind person", continued the fat Priest", and he is not at all interested in money. Money is dirt for him and he is in a habit of distributing it amongst the poor. He is a great giver and regularly goes on pilgrimages and showers money on beggars and temple Priests".

Vikram Singh's thin Priest nodded his head adding "our clients have the same characteristics. My client is also not interested in money. Money is dirt for him which he presents to us poor Brahmins".

"My client", continued the fat Priest, "has one problem. Fate caused him to marry a very very greedy woman. She is exactly opposite to what my client is. Her life revolves around money only for which my client is a very unhappy man. Being a respectful person he believes in woman's liberty and he personally feels that the mother has more right to the child than the father".

Vikram's thin Priest nodded his head in approval. "yes of course it is very wise thinking on the part of your client", he interrupted, "after all it is the woman who nurses the child for nine months in the womb".

"True", continued the fat Priest, "the mistress of this house returned four offers of marriage because the parties that came offered only twenty thousand rupees and a second hand Jeep".

The thin Priest looked down at Vikram. He didn't know what a Jeep was. "What is a jeep Judgemaan?", he asked.

"It is the vehicle on which the English officer comes to meet me", replied Vikram Singh.

The thin Priest looked perplexed. "Are they for sale?", he asked.

The fat Priest looked down at Balbir for an answer. He also didn't know what a Jeep was. Balbir nodded his head. "I have heard that the British Indian army and the police have started auctioning the older vehicles", he said, "They are available in the second hand car markets of Calcutta".

The fat Priest looked at the thin Priest for an answer who in turn looked at Vikram who slightly shook his head.

"Don't you think the mistress is demanding a little too much?", asked the thin Priest.

"I told you before that my client was very unhappy with the demand. But what can he do. His wife has more right to the child than him and she is rigid".

"But her demand is outrageous", stated Vikram's Priest, "she is demanding money that is the dowry for a full grown male. For twenty thousand rupees you can get a powerful ICS officer working for the British government of India".

"What to do, but the lady persists. After all the boy is better placed than an ICS officer. He is the sole heir to Balbir Singh's

Zamindari".

"What guarantee do you have that the boy will remain the sole heir to your clients property. Your client is young, his wife is young and the boy is only seven years old. Your client has many years before him and can produce many more heirs. What guarantee is there that he won't produce ten more children. What guarantee is there that he won't produce twenty more children. Tell me what guarantee is there that his wife is not pregnant at the moment".

The fat Priest was foxed. He was cornered. "My client will give you his word", he stammered.

Balbir Singh gulped. The haggling had taken a funny turn so he looked at Vikram who was proudly looking at his hook beak nosed Priest and was wandering at the latent energy stored in the latter's brains.

"Can you give a guarantee that the lady is infertile?", the thin Brahmin continued.

"Look lets stop discussing my client's private life", the fat Priest answered. "All we know is that my clients son is worth twenty thousand rupees and a second hand Jeep. And that's final".

"What is the price of a jeep?"

"Around three thousand rupees", interrupted Balbir.

"My God, twenty three thousand rupees for a seven year old boy".

"He is worth it".

"He isn't worth it".

"He is".

"He isn't".

"You are abusing us", stated the fat Brahmin.

"We would like to see the boy", demanded the thin Brahmin.

The fat Priest got up and went to the door which led to the women's section of the Haveli. "Ganesh", he shouted "bring Mahesh with you. Some people want to see him".

The Priest went back to stand in place in front of Vikram's Brahmin. A couple of minutes later a little boy dressed in a red shirt and yellow half pants was led by a thin half naked dark servant who left the boy standing in between the two Brahmins and disappeared back into the ladies quarters.

"Look at him properly", suggested the fat Brahmin, "and you can decide for yourself".

The thin Priest looked approvingly at the boy, then looked at Vikram who gave a slight nod with his head.

"My client approves of the child", the thin Priest continued, "that's why we are here. The respected Brahmin told us that he was healthy and good looking".

"Then what is you're decision?"

"He isn't worth what you are demanding".

"Then what is he worth? You haven't given an offer yet".

"Fifteen thousand rupees and no Jeep".

"Preposterous".

"Most reasonable".

"Impossible. My client's wife will never accept".

"She will have to".

"She won't".

"Then I think we will leave". The thin Priest looked at Vikram and made a gesture to get up as the fat Priest looked at Balbir for further orders. Seeing Vikram getting up Balbir hastily showed the fat Priest ten fingers and added seven more and formed the word Jeep on his lips.

"Wait brother Brahmin it seems you have become angry", stated the fat Priest, "Ask your client to sit down".

Vikram Singh sat back and twirled his moustache.

"Now what is it?", asked the thin Priest.

"Why are you going without finishing your work?"

"You are demanding too much".

"Okay we will be kind with you. You see my client doesn't want your client to leave this house empty handed. Deep down in his heart he has the desire to marry his son to your clients daughter and is prepared to go against his greedy wife's will".

"State the amount".

"You see my client has five thousand acres of land and his Ford car cannot travel over the fields. His son will soon grow up and will have to oversee the property. For that he will need a Jeep. So a Jeep is a must".

"The money".

"My client's wife will take nothing less than nineteen thousand rupees".

"Impossible".

"Not a rupee less".

"We will pay fifteen thousand and not a rupee more".

"And what about the Jeep".

The thin Priest looked at Vikram who nodded his head.

"We will present the boy a Jeep", the thin Priest announced, "but we won't pay more than fifteen thousand rupees".

The fat Priest looked at Balbir who winked back.

"My client is eveready to adjust. He is a kindly man and is ready to bear the wrath of his greedy wife. He will take nothing less than eighteen thousand five hundred rupees".

"You are still demanding too much".

"Eighteen thousand and not a rupee less".

"Look at the boy", said the thin Priest, "He is young and has his whole life before him. He may grow up to be a good man but what guarantee is there that he won't grow up to be a drunkard, a womanizer and a rascal. What guarantee is there that he isn't infertile at the moment. He may make life a living hell for my client's daughter".

"Look now don't abuse the boy".

"I'm speaking facts".

"Eighteen thousand and not a rupee less".

"Fifteen thousand five hundred and not a rupee more".

"Not accepted".

"Sixteen thousand and not a rupee more".

"May I intervene?", requested Balbir as he stood up. "You

two Brahmins are heading for a stale mate". Then looking at Vikram he asked, "Will you accept my decision?".

Vikram was gawking open mouthed at his Priest. He didn't know that the latter could haggle so effectively. "I will accept only if it is reasonable", he replied.

"Okay. One Priest is holding onto eighteen thousand like a stuck record", continued Balbir, "and the other is behaving like another stuck record. How much is he repeating?"

"Sixteen thousand", Vikram interceded.

"Both the Priests cannot have their way so let's decide on a middle figure. It won't be eighteen, neither will it be sixteen. The middle number is seventeen and that is fixed. I will not take a rupee less".

"You're swindling me", replied Vikram.

"It's up to you to decide. Take it or leave it. I don't care now if you leave my house without eating any sweets".

"Accepted".

"Good show my brother good show", Balbir bellowed as he got up. "Get up my brother and let us hug each other".

The Zamindars guffawed as their paunches clashed and pressed into each other as the two bear hugged.

The thin and fat Priests guffawed and bear hugged. The thin Priest was literally lifted off his feet.

Balbir's Pehelwans had arrived so they guffawed and bear hugged Vikram's guffawing turbaned Pehelwans.

Balbir's driver had arrived so the drivers also guffawed and bear hugged.

The black Buick and white Ford wanted to guffaw and bear hug but couldn't since they were just machines. They had to make do with the black Buick winking at the white Ford. The right eye fell off. The right sealed beam of the vehicles headlight had come loose on the rattling journey to Balbir's house. The sound waves from the loud guffaws had given the felling blow.

It was decided to go to the village temple and pay obeisance to the village deity. Balbir got into his smart churidars, Bhagalpur silk kurta and gold brocaded pink Sherwani. He perched a gold brocaded pink Lucknowi cap on his head and stepped into a pair of gold brocaded pink shoes. His fat wife handed him an expensive polished ivory topped walking stick which he held in his right hand. He was now looking as nawably and Zamindarly as Vikram Singh.

Both the Zamindars got into the back seats of their respective cars with one leg over the other and the Brahmins piled in to take their pride of place next to their clients as the Pehelwans climbed in next to the drivers seat. The two turbaned drivers took out the handles from the dickeys, did the preliminaries and yanked at the handles. To Vikram's delight the Buicks' engine was the first to roar into life while the Ford's engine coughed a couple of times and the driver had to keep yanking at the handle before the old engine finally coughed to life. It let out an ear splitting loud pra-ta-taa which was equal in intensity to the roar of Vikram's Buick. The Ford had also lost its silencer which was rotting in the dung heaps nearby.

The vehicles roared down the supposed to be gravelled drive way and passed the irritated bovines. They roared past the shit smelling shacks and out of the double lioned gates to turn left and travel down the dusty mud track leading to the temple. The springs squeaked and squelched as the vehicles bumped and bounced over the uneven road and came to a stop in front of the temple. The turbaned drivers first opened the doors of their respective masters and then the bonnets of their respective vehicles and unscrewed the radiator caps to let out steam from the boiling gurgling radiators. This delighted village urchins who shouted and screamed and had surrounded the vehicles.

The Zamindars paid obeisance to the deities. The temple's Priest and the Priests accompanying the Zamindars argued and decided on the date of the marriage. It was fixed for the fourth of May. The happy Zamindars got back into their cars and drove back to Balbir's house where a date was fixed for the payment of the money and the delivery of the four wheel drive 'British Indian army' auctioned Willy's Jeep. Balbir had told Vikram as a joke that the marriage proceedings could be stalled if the vehicle and money failed to come on the accepted dates. Vikram was in a good mood and happily accepted the veiled threat.

It was a happy Vikram who left a happy Balbir after stuffing himself with Rosogullas and Rasmalais. With a full stomach he entered the Buick while the hook beak nosed bearded

Brahmin who was two gold coins richer, piled in next to him. Vikram had presented the fat Brahmin with two gold coins while Balbir had presented his skinny Brahmin with the coins. The turbaned driver who had been baksheeshed did the preliminaries after the baksheeshed Pehelwans had climbed in. The Buick was soon roaring out of Balbir's double lioned gate with its happy load. It turned right and soon left the dirt track to roar down the thin strip of tarmac that was the highway along which the Buick lost another eye. The left sealed beam fell off, this time causing the vehicle to pra-ta-taa into the dark night without any lights all the way back to Vikram's house.

Vikram gave the news to Narayani. There was a hitch. He didn't have the money for the dowry and the jeep. This wasn't a surprise as the Zamindars had squandered their money on the twin sister nautch girls in a brothel in Gaya. If they had cash then their vehicles would have had self starters and silencers and would not pra-ta-taa all over the place heralding the arrival of their masters. The only way to overcome this problem was by extorting money from his peasants and selling some land.

Time flew as Vikram arranged the money and made a trip to Calcutta to buy the Jeep. The vehicle and money were delivered on the date decided and the first of May soon arrived. There was only three days left for the marriage.

The bovines were irritated as they bravely faced blast after blast of Pra-ta-taas with each one breaking the sound barrier as they heralded the arrival of another Zamindar relative. The cars entered the double lioned gate to drive down the driveway to finally stop in front of Vikram Singh's verandah.

The servants realized that it was now perfectly safe to defecate further on in the fields since the snakes that would have bitten their bottoms most probably had slithered off. Their sensory organs wouldn't be able to bear the vibrations emanating from the pra-ta-taaing six cylindcred petrol engines.

It was a happy over-crowded household now full of aunts and uncles and nephews and nieces with servants scurrying around desperately trying to cope with the extremely increased work load. Cooks had been brought from the district town of Monghyr. They were accompanied with huge utensils to cook the food in.

The servants got up early in the morning to supply the guests with lotas of water to defecate in the fields from where the snakes had slithered off. It had been decided to leave the two latrines of the Haveli for the women folk. The servants then provided the guests with Neem sticks to chew and scrub their teeth with. The sticks also doubled as tongue cleaners wiping out the saliva from the tongue surface. The guests then sat cross legged on the five foot broad pavement encircling the well as their servants massaged mustard oil, and later soap over them, to be finally dunked under buckets of water which washed away the dirt from their bodies.

Breakfast was excellent, half English, half Hindustani. There were eggs, butter, chappaties washed down with a glass of milk or cups of tea.

Lunch was delicious. Piping hot red chillied mutton curry and rice with the duo burning down the gullets of the hugely paunched Zamindars, causing them to let out obnoxious air all through the afternoon and into the evening until they defecated in the fields.

Evenings were pleasant with exotic sweets concocted by the local Halwai who didn't mind the swarms of fleas, blue bottles and hornets swarming over his concoctions. Of course people could help themselves to these delicacies only if the hot mutton curry had left some place in the stomach.

Dinner was an equally hot affair competing with lunch. The star attractions were red chillied fish or red chillied chicken curry with butter smeared chappaties washed down with brandy or Rum, heating the insides and making the Zamindars feel excited.

The great day came. Caparisoned elephants which had been brought by some relatives were accompanied by Vikram's elephant and were made to stand in a line in front of the double lioned gate with their rumps facing the smiling Scarecrow as they waited for the caparisoned elephants that would lead young Mahesh's Baraat. The woman had donned their gold brocaded heavy Benarasi sarees with their necks ringed in heavy jewellery glittering and competing with each other. The half naked servants were now liveried and wore red half jackets over white trousers and scampered around the bustling crowd doing something or the other.

The excitement grew. The Baraat was coming. The lights from the Petromax lamps could be seen from the roofs and the blaring band and pra-ta-taas could be heard from the ground. Amidst squeals of irritated elephants and the barking of excited dogs and blaring music from a brass band, the over lit Baraat come into view. As it came closer, the host of old cars behind the open convertible six cylindered Dodge in which little Mahesh sat, made a beautiful sight. The vehicles looked majestic as the engines roared under the bonnets which had red and yellow paper flowers on green sticks stuck in grooves in the old faultily dented bodywork. The paint on the cars glistened as their masters sat in the back seats in expensive churidars and attar smelling Sherwanis, with one leg over the other, and a hand holding a polished ivory topped walking stick while the other twirled a moustache. The chillum smoking Priests had pride of place beside their erstwhile clients.

Of course the local people envied the back seated Babus in their big cars which were of varied hues and shapes and sizes. Half of the vehicles had West Bengal number plates since they had been bought in the second hand car markets of Calcutta. Sitting here in Ramnagar one could see the variety that had been discarded by the rich businessmen of Calcutta. There were Fords, Buicks, Studebakers, Fiats, Dodges, Plymouths, Desotos, hooded Jeeps, open Jeeps still with the faded British Indian army colors, Mercedes Benzs, Daimlers, Bugattis, Cherolets, some hooded, some hard topped. All had paper flowers stuck to the bonnets and the corners of the windscreens. These vehicles had bulbous front mudguards, mountainous bonnets, divided windscreens, well curved rear mudguards over which flowed a round bottomed dickey.

Of course the local people envied the back seated Babus in their big cars even if some of the majestic machines had stalled. The slow moving Baraat played havoc with the engines and clutch facings of the vehicles peppering the regalia with perspiring drivers who madly yanked at the handles to bring the overheated stalled engines back to life.

So it was that the chaotically majestic Baraat of Zamindar Balbir Singh's seven year old son limped to the front of the verandah of Vikram Singh's generator lit Haveli. The Dodge convertible with the little bridegroom, and whose over heated radiator was spewing out steam, drew up in front the verandah.

The elephant keepers of the caparisoned elephants were baksheeshed, the band that played the blaring music was baksheeshed, the people carrying the Petromax lamps were baksheeshed, and the temple Priest who accompanied the bridegroom was richer by five gold coins which he stashed in his saffron dhoti after which he helped the womenfolk with the rituals. A photographer was brought to photograph the groom and the flashlight illuminated everything around for a split second causing the elephants little eyes to wince and close shut.

With the music of Shehnais in the background the Zamindars were taken to a brightly lit Shamiana where they would be entertained by nautch girls brought from Muzaffarpur and Gaya. They were as usual accompanied by their spiritual advisors, the chillum smoking Priests.

Shanti was dressed for the occasion in a little red sari, with little ornaments decorating her hands neck and forehead as she accepted exclamations that she looked very cute. She was told that she would soon be married like her father and mother. Today she was the center of attraction with everyone lovingly pulling her cheek, patting her as she enjoyed the attention she was receiving.

The male doll from Rampur sat pink faced from the attention he was also receiving. He was in the sitting room waiting for the Priests call. The child was fair, wore a little gold colored, gold brocaded Sherwani over a pair of little silken churidars. Around his waist was a red cloth belt from which hung a little sword.

The Priest soon called the boy over to the square thatch roofed mandap and made him sit next to the girl who was looking wide eyed at her husband to be. Since the boy and girl weren't supposed to look at each other till the rituals ended, Narayani pulled the ghunghat low over Shanti's face. The Priest started the rites and chanted verses in Sanskrit. The children could not understand what was being said. To them it was simply 'Blah, blah, blah' and the rest of the crowd chorused in with a 'swaha' following which they had to throw what ever the Priest had put in their hands into a fire that was burning in front of them.

While the Priest carried on with the rituals there was excitement in the Shamiana. People were getting ready to be entertained. The Shamiana itself was thirty feet broad and forty feet long and was held up by bamboo poles with the ground below draped in white linen. The North eastern corner was draped in a blue velvet carpet with velvet masnads which were huge sausage shaped pillows. This corner was reserved for the Zamindars while the north western corner was reserved for their chillum smoking Priests who had their chillums safely in their kurta pockets and were eying the nautch girls. The south side of the Shamiana was occupied by the village folk of Ramnagar and Balbir's Pehelwans who now doubled as crowd controllers. They threw out any person who got too exited and became unruly.

The nautch girls sat in the middle of the Shamiana with the musicians in an empty square patch which was approximately twenty feet broad and twenty feet long. There were two people with harmoniums and two people with a set of tablas each and they watched the crowd which was eying the girls. Everyone was sitting cross legged except the Zamindars who were leaning on the masnads and were stuffing wads of green paan leaves into red mouths with rotten teeth. Amongst them were two thin fair looking teenaged Zamindars who were Vikram's elder son in laws, the miserable boys for whom he had sold two hundred acres of land.

As the nautch girls prepared themselves to dance, the Priest continued with his boring rituals which caused the two children to fall asleep. In their dreams they heard him say, "Blah blah, blah and everyone chorused in saying 'swaha'.

Back in the Shamiana it was a free for all. The Zamindars were relaxed on masnads and drank a cheap tiger brand beer. The nautch girls danced as the musicians made noises while the crowd and the Brahmin Priests eyed and ogled at the girls. Some one pinched a bottom while another hopped out of the crowd and kissed a girl while they goaded them on. They were paid for this, so one of them winked at a fellow while another girl pointed a bottom at one and shot out a pelvic thrust at another as they sang lurid songs in hoarse voices to the sounds emanating from the musicians with the musical instruments.

The Zamindars were soon sozzled and excited. They stopped twirling their moustaches and were concentrating on the girls. The little cuties would be called over to sit in front of them or on their laps and render a hoarse voiced lurid song while the latter ran his fingers over her body in full view of everyone and drunkenly kissed her to the "yaays", of his fellow Zamindars. Happy with the cheer, and the nice feel of the body the Zamindar would pull out some money from his kurta pocket and stuff it into the blouse of the pleased girl, to another round of cheers. This was the signal for the remaining girls who fanned out amongst the erstwhile rulers. They knew that a competition was building up. A competition where the Zamindars would try to out do each other in stuffing money into the bodies of these girls thereby proving that they were richer. The competing Zamindars would fan out currency notes, as you do with cards, show it to everyone, then stuff it into the blouse. Another Zamindar would try to outdo him and fan out more currency notes and stuff it into the girls clothes. This continued through out the night till the wee hours of the morning till the Zamindars and girls got tired and retired to their respective rooms.

Back in the Haveli, in the mandap, the 'blah, blah, blah', and everyone said 'swaha', had ended. The children were woken and taken into the bridal chamber and seated on a flower covered bridal bed which was covered with a red bed sheet after which the elders left and closed the doors on the two children.

Shanti suddenly found herself alone with the seven year old Mahesh. Her lips parted, smile vanished, cheeks went up, eyes watered and mouth opened to let out a cry. She didn't like the boy and wanted to be with her mother. Getting off the bed, she went crying to pound at the door with her little fists.

Mahesh had a better idea. He took out a fist full of marbles from his Sherwani and got down from the bed to sit on his haunches on the ground. He put the left hand thumb to the ground and with the right hand he connected the marble to the middle finger of the left hand and pulled the finger back to let it go. The middle finger shot forward and caused the marble to shoot across the room and stop on the other side. Another marble was taken out and aimed at the first marble. Mahesh's aim was perfect and the second marble hit the first one. Mahesh then took out a third marble, and as he let his finger go, he noticed from the corner of his eye something red run past him to the other side of the room. It was Shanti. She had stopped crying and had decided to join in the marble game, deciding that Mahesh was likable after all. Taking the marble she shot it at the one in front of Mahesh. The marble hit and reflected off the piece of glass ball to fly into the air and hit Mahesh on the nose. Mahesh sat back rubbing his nose as Shanti laughed. The boy smiled and the two carried on playing, thoroughly enjoying their first night of marital bliss.

The Female Cobra

The little girl who had been bitten by Fangs had died before she reached the village. She had been made to lie on the ground under the Peepal tree while some people ran and fetched a second OJHA. The first one had been proved useless. The second Ojha ran a broom over her body and blew incense smoke over her to no avail. He muttered prayer after prayer and finally accepted defeat but did not blame himself and his inability to drive out the venom. He blamed it on the snake saying that it wasn't an ordinary reptile that bit the child, but a disciple of Satan himself who had come in the form of a snake. So according to popular belief the girl wasn't burnt on a funeral pyre but was tied between two six foot long banana stumps and taken in a procession to the banks of the Ganges. After the witch doctor had said a little prayer the banana stumps and body were taken into the river and pushed into the currents to slowly float away while the villagers looked on. It was believed that venom heated the body and caused the victim to die and the cool waters of the Ganges with the help of the cool banana stumps would cool down the body and in the process maybe suck out the venom. There were stories of people who had died and had been left to float tied to banana stumps. They regained consciousness a couple of kilometers downstream, and clinging to the stumps had paddled back to the shore.

The girl however did not come back from the river and entered the score board of the villages snake bite victims. It was believed that the soul of a girl who was less than ten years old and who had died of snake bite, did not die but her soul lived on and roamed the village searching for some one in distress whom she could help. The little girl was made into a deity and every full moon night the villagers gathered under the Peepal tree which was in the middle of the village square, and sang praises to her.

So it was today as the people sat in a little circle under the tree singing praises to the girl's soul so that she would bring prosperity to the village and its inhabitants. Cymbals clashed and tablas made noises and the singers screamed out the words they sang. This was the reason why the little square was void of other living things. Bugs, beetles, spiders and other beings had all scampered off because of the ruckus the humans were making.

Except for a big yellow Bullfrog.

It was a foolish amphibian. Just like the humans, other living creatures too had their dumb ones and this bull frog was dumb. It had hopped out of the water, out of a little pond that was adjacent to the village and had hopped across a fallow field attracting the attention of a cobra. The snake wasn't Fangs though it was of the same length and colour. It was a female who was wandering around the area in search of food and the Bull frog looked delicious so she used her scutes to quietly follow the dumb creature who did not care to look back. Or it couldn't look back. It had no constricted neck. The nostrils and eyes were on top of the skull which allowed the creature to sit submerged in water with its eyes above the water. The eyes were large and weren't fitted in the skull to enable it to see what was happening behind it since they were inclined slightly forward. To check its behind the frog had to hop to its left or to its right and this bull frog was too lazy to do that. It just hopped on and on with the female cobra stealthily following it. When the amphibian hopped, the cobra moved forward and when it stopped, the former lay very still.

The frog was a beautiful creature and it was unfortunate that snakes relished it. Its body was slender and elongated with a long head and a tapering snout and extremely long hind legs which was ideal for jumping and swimming. The belly looked like a Zamindar's paunch with loose belly skin which could be pressed tightly against any surface, and the sticky webbing between the fingers and toes was also used in a similar manner. The amphibian did have ears in the form of large and conspicuous eardrums behind the eyes which sent sound vibrations to a middle ear cavity which in turn transferred the vibrations from the ear drum to an inner ear. In spite of this the bullfrog did not manage to hear any movement behind it. Instead it used its larynx to let out a couple of croaks before it went on hopping with the snake stealthily stalking it.

The frog did not fear humans or where the humans inhabited. It was in a habit of regularly visiting the village because of the flies and mosquitoes the humans attracted. The amphibian relished these and would greedily shoot out a long tongue which would catch a fly on its sticky surface and flick it back into its mouth. It knew that the humans would not harm it since it was of no use to them. The frog was regarded as a dirty creature and no one ate it. The only danger the humans posed was in the form of naughty children who carelessly squashed some to death. Infact a dead squashed frog was regarded dirtier and no one wanted any around.

The snake however feared the humans and had started feeling uneasy. Its flicking tongue and Jacobson's organs told it that it was in forbidden territory so she was extra cautious. The eyes kept a rigid look out over the area it could scan at the same time concentrating on the frog which seemed to hop deeper into danger. The two were stopping and moving down a little path between two rows of mud walled thatched houses and the snake got jittery fearing that the frog might escape amongst the humans. So opening her mouth wide she increased her speed and stealthily drew closer as the frog hopped, stopped and hopped on.

Still using her scutes the snake closed in and was four inches behind the amphibian and was about to pounce on the creature when a door opened ten feet ahead and a human stepped out. In a flash the snake zipped back soundlessly and turned right into an alley and stopped. Her head moved around and she drew her body along the mud wall of the thatched house. Peeping around the corner she saw the frog had also turned and was hopping back towards where she lay. The human's mouth moved as it muttered something and spat at the frog after which it turned and walked towards the village square where the singing was going on.

The frog sensed that the human had walked away so it stopped, hopped around and hopped on along its original coarse. The snake had been unlucky because the frog had stopped just three feet away from it. A couple of more hops would have brought it within the snake's striking range. This minor aberration did not lower the reptile's spirit who was used to these minor hiccups in her hunting forays. She decided to have a second go and again used her scutes to travel around the bend of the mud wall. She was soon stealthily scuting behind the frog with a gaping mouth and alert eyes which were watching everything around including the frog.

The open mouth drew closer and closer and was just three inches behind the frog and was about to shoot forward when another thatched door opened and a naked child jumped out. In a jiffy the snake turned and zipped back to the place where it had hidden earlier. Drawing its body along the mud wall it looked around the corner down the path from which it had come. The child was running down the path and the frog had turned to its left and had disappeared behind the opposite mud wall of the thatched house behind which the female snake was hiding.

The frog had turned and had entered an alley parallel to the one the snake lying in. If it carried on hopping it would travel to the end of the alley and enter the field behind the house. This was where the snake would intercept it so turning around she used her S shaped curves to slither down the alley till she reached a field. She turned right and using her scutes she traveled along the rear wall of the thatched house till she reached the end where she drew her body up behind two bricks which were piled over each other. Peeping between the lower brick and the mud wall she waited and was pleased to see the frog hop into her view. She did not move and let it hop on after which she opened her mouth wide and slowly slithered over the brick. Crossing it she moved stealthily towards the frog and stopped when she was just six inches behind her prey with her mouth still wide open. The dumb amphibian seemed to at last sense danger so it stopped, gave a croak and hopped to its right in time to see the gaping mouth shoot forward and engulf its belly. It felt the pain as the Fangs pierced it and injected venom into it as the jaws closed in on each other with the frog trapped firmly in them. It tried to kick out and hop, but in vain. The left hind leg only kicked. The right was folded between the snakes lower jaw and its belly.

The female cobra was exultant. She had caught her prey and would now swallow it down, but to first squeeze the life out of it she pressed the jaws harder. Being earless she could not hear the sorry croaks of the frog. When the kicking finally stopped she let go off the dead body and turned it with her snout so that its bottom faced her. Opening her mouth wide she took the bottom in, and her sharply pointed inwardly curving cone like teeth moved back and forth alternately and slowly pulled half of the croaking frog into the gaping mouth. The cone like teeth continued moving and the frog continued its slow journey in. Its snout was the last to enter the mouth while its body stretched the snakes skin which was flexible enough to let a large body stretch it on the way down without tearing it. The cobra then formed a sharp curve in its neck behind the frog and pushed it down into her stomach.

The female snake had had its full and could relax for the next seven or eight days. It decided to relax behind the mud wall and wait for the frog to settle down after which she would venture into the field that was in front of her. The fading light told her that it was evening and it would soon become dark so she lay where she was and watched as twilight drew over the land.

A little brown door mouse scampered across the field that faced the female snake. She scampered up the fields boundary and had no inkling that she was running straight into danger. How could she, since the wind was blowing from behind her. Reaching the top of the boundary she saw the snake lying along the base of the wall. Squeaking, she scampered off to her right.

A little later a group of black ants marched in single file down the way the female snake had come. The leader saw the tail and not recognizing it marched on just three inches parallel to the snake. Marching half way down the body the supreme commander noticed some movement so he stopped and asked his second in command, "Did you see that?"

"Yes", replied the subordinate.

The commander looked down the way they had come and up the way they were supposed to go. "This doesn't look like a hill or mud, it looks like skin".

"Yes", replied the second in command.

"What do you think it could be?"

"It's a snake".

"A snake? My God such a huge snake. What caste does it belong to".

"A cobra".

"A cobra?, my God a cobra". The commander was shivering all over "should we fight it?"

"Yes we should".

"Then you lead the battle. That's my order".

"And what will you do sir?"

"I will courageously watch from here and gallantly goad you on".

"On second thoughts sir. I think it will be wise to do the disappearing act".

"Ants don't back out of battle. It is clearly written in the rule books".

"It's also clearly written that if the enemy is too large and strong, the commander should save his army and do a dignified retreat".

The commander was now angry. "I will not stand insubordination", he shouted, "I will not stand a junior speaking back to me before or during or after a battle. You will be court martialled for this".

"I apologize sir".

"Into the battle with you".

The female cobra got tired of lying in a straight line so she shifted a few muscles and created two slight curves down her body.

"I think the enemy is about to attack", shouted the supreme commander, "prepare for battle".

There was no answer so he turned around to scold his second in command. There wasn't any second in command and the commander was faced by a jittery third in command. "Where's your officer?", he asked.

"There", the third in command answered pointing his bald head towards the mud embankment up which the second in command was desperately climbing.

"Come back here", bellowed the Supreme Commander, "come back you gutless, lily livered nincompoop".

"Not in my life sir", replied the terrified ant, "I am going to apply for a decommissioning. I'll opt for general labour or may become a cook".

"I'll get you hanged- oh sorry- eaten for this", then turning to his third in command the supreme commander ordered. "I have promoted you so you are now the second in command, so prepare for battle".

"I will sir, but there is a minor problem".

"What is it?"

"The army is about to state a mutiny".

The supreme commander looked down the line of his mighty army and saw only grumpy faces. They were the faces of would be deserters", so he fell back in line. "What should a commander do in such a situation?", he asked.

"A dignified retreat".

"How can a retreat be dignified?"

"It's written in the rule books sir. If you engage the enemy and retreat, then it means you have lost the battle and have run away from war. It is a disgrace. But if you see the enemy is too strong for you and you retreat without engaging it. It is regarded as a tactical retreat".

"And a tactical retreat is dignified?"

"Yes sir".

The supreme commander took a second look down his ranks and realized that the grumpy faces had grown grumpier still. "Okay then it's a tactical retreat for us. Legions, about turn", he bellowed.

The line of ants turned around but the order to march did not come. The supreme commander and his second in command were marching down the ranks. After all it was he who had to lead his army from the front. He couldn't be seen trailing from the back. The line of ants were soon marching down the path they had come.

It had become dark by the time the ants had gone and the female snake decided it was time to search for a safer place to relax in. Creating her S shaped curves, she climbed up the fields boundary and slithered to the other side. She was soon gracefully slithering across the field which she left behind and was cruising through shrubs and grass. Seeing a little dot of light fly over, her she stopped to look up. It was a little fire fly.

Lowering her head she continued her journey and did not hear something scamper into the dark to her right. She kept going but stopped again when her flicking tongue picked up the molecules of a dog. She lifted her head and uttered a vicious "Khaa" at the startled canine who got up, barked at the snake, whined and slunk away.

Seeing the silhouette move on, the snake carried on her zig-zagging path as she repeatedly flicked out her forked tongue. It was her only guide in the dark. She soon reached a piece of land which was hard and smooth and seemed to have been flattened by something or the other. She felt comfortable on it so she decided to curl up and rest. Doing so she noticed her surroundings and saw a myriad of synchronized flashes around her. They were fireflies and the sky seemed to be full of them. Looking up the snake did not realize that she was lying on the little path the humans used to walk from the Baobab tree via the pond to the little Mussahar village.

The female cobra lay relaxed as she enjoyed the feeling of a full stomach. She couldn't hear the lonely cry of a cicada nor the mating call of a cricket or the lonely howl of a jackal. She did see the silhouette of a jackal slink past her after which clouds covered the moon. It became pitch dark and the snake quietly watched the flashes of the fireflies flying around her. She didn't know that three humans were walking down the path and were headed straight for her.

The humans were agricultural labourers who had migrated to the southern coal fields of Bihar. They worked alternately in the fields back home or in the mines far away on the Chota Nagpur plateau. The men had just ended their stint at the coal mines and were returning to their homes which was in a couple of villages south of the Mussahar village where the female snake had just eaten a frog. The three knew the area well and somehow managed to keep on the track even in the dark. They were all thin and were of medium height and wore only half dhotis from their hips to their thighs and carried their belongings in a bundle tied to their backs. None of them wore anything above their dhotis and were all bare backed.

It was the first person who stepped on the snake. He felt something soft below his feet and then a searing pain as though two needles had punctured the flesh an inch above the right legs ankle. He let out a yell which was followed by two loud "Khaas", from below and the bitten man realized what had happened. Panicked, he hopped a couple of times and ran a little distance shouting.

The female cobra was furious on being stepped on and had hastily uncurled herself when the second man in an attempt to spring out of the path, stepped on her tail. The pain was excruciating so she whipped around and bit the ankle and gave out a couple of more "Khaas". This caused the man to scream and kick out with his leg as the snake withdrew just as the clouds uncovered the moon. The enraged snake saw the silhouette of the third person in the moonlight who had frozen with fright. He did not know what to do in the dark. The snake could be anywhere and it was too late when he saw the dark form on the ground lunge for his feet. He couldn't jump and felt the fangs pierce his skin just above his heel.

Satisfied that her venom was spent, the female cobra slithered off to her right while the third person limped up to the other two.

"Did it bite you also?", asked the first man.

"Yes".

"Have you got matches".

"Yes".

"Then light one you idiot".

The third person was sitting on the ground and was rubbing the place where he had been bitten.

"Quick light a match".

The third man dug into his bundle and pulled out a match box and lit a stick. In the dim light the other two sat down on the ground and surveyed their own feet. The two bluish puncture marks were easily discernible in all three feet. The bluish tint was less on the third person's ankle.

"Quick, take out some cloth", ordered the first man as he pulled out a dhoti from his bundle and tore off a thin long piece and tied it tightly around his own calf. The other two also desperately tore out pieces of cloth and tied them around their calves.

"We are very close to the Mussahar village", spoke the first man, "let's go there. An Ojha will drive the venom out".

The three got up and limped towards the village. They were careful not to put pressure on their bitten feet and sometimes winced when the affected ankle sent up a throbbing pain.

The three soon reached the village and limped to the village square where a fire was burning and some singing was taking place. They slumped down onto the ground near the singers. The singing stopped and the villagers turned around to look at the new comers. They recognized the three as belonging to the next village and were suspicious when they saw the bandaged feet. Too many people had died of snake bite in the area and the people knew the symptoms of someone who had been bitten. The bandaged limb and scared eyes of the person told the story.

"We have been bitten by a Naag", pleaded one of the three, "Please help us. Please get on Ojha".

No one asked questions. They all knew that it was an emergency as five people rushed off into the dark. A witch doctor lived in a hut in a nearby field and the latter soon arrived holding a lantern and was accompanied by the five people who carried the paraphernalia to drive out the venom. They were simple. An old broom with long bristles, an incense cup, incense sticks, sandalwood chips and a photograph of a bearded dead person. The witch doctor himself was short, dark, bare backed and wore a black lungi around his waist which flowed down to his ankles. His head was capped with curly hair and two round brass rings hung from his ear lobes.

The photograph was made to stand on the ground near the fire and the three people who had been bitten were made to lie down in a row next to each other. The incense sticks were lit and two of them were poked into the ground before the dead bearded man's photograph. Sandalwood chips were filled in the incense cup and lit, and the witch doctor blew the smoke one by one over the three people. He took the broom and muttered some prayers and swept it over the three bodies from the head to the feet. He did this five times over each body after which he reverted to the incense cup and blew incense smoke over the three scared humans again. Satisfied that he had blown enough smoke he put down the incense cup and picked up the broom. Continuing to mutter his prayers, he swept it down the bodies a second time after which he put the broom down and leant on the ground before the bearded corpses photo. He folded his hands in prayer and muttered something. Then he turned around and in a loud voice asked the villagers to open the bandages.

Three people walked out of the silent crowd that had gathered around the witch doctor and the people lying on the ground. They bent down and opened the bandages as the witch doctor raised his hands with a flourish and screamed something into the skies. The people lying on the ground felt something cold travel up their snake bitten feet as the bandages were opened. The cold feeling reached the calf and travelled to the knees after which it engulfed the thighs and spread slowly to their torsos. The cold sensation grew warm and hot causing the three to swoon.

"How are you feeling", asked the witch doctor.

"My body is burning", spoke the first person in a nasal voice.

"Don't you feel any relief".

"I'm feeling giddy. I think I'll faint".

"And how do you feel?", the witch doctor asked the second person.

"My body is burning", was reply as the fellow tried to sit up but fell back on the ground.

The three traveller's were soon lifeless with a bluish tint covering the first two bodies.

"They are dead", said a villager.

"Yes", muttered the witch doctor. "They weren't bitten by a snake. They were bitten by the Shaitan that had bitten the little girl".

The villagers nodded their heads as the witch doctor told them to beware of the Shaitan's evil. "Beware o villagers", he shouted, "this area is plagued by a messenger of death. There is no medicine that can cure his sting and no holy powers that can wash away his curse. So beware and look after yourselves".

The witch doctor had a little chat with the villagers and left for his thatched hut in the nearby field with a villager leading the way with a lantern. Some people took long sticks called lathis and rushed off to the nearby villages to inform the family members of the people that had died. Soon people were rushing back to the Mussahar village where a miracle had taken place. One of the dead people had come back to life and his relatives were overjoyed to see him alive while other people cried over the other two corpses.

One of the villagers standing near the dazed person

remembered something. "Isn't this the spot where the little girl had been lying?", he asked.

"Which little girl?", asked another villager.

"The little one that died of snake bite".

"You mean Jagdish's daughter".

The villager nodded his head.

"She didn't die of snake bite. The Shaitan killed her. That's what the Ojha said".

"But look at the spot where this man is sitting?"

"Hmmmmmmm".

"Isn't it the same spot?"

"Yes it is the same spot", the man said. " It seems the girl's spirit drew out the poison and brought the man back to life".

The villager saw a stool nearby and walked upto it and climbed up to stand on it. "Friends", he shouted. "A miracle has taken place".

The villagers turned towards him.

"Do you remember the little girl who died a few months ago?"

The villagers looked up at him.

"The little girl who was killed by the Shaitan?"

The villagers nodded their heads.

"She has shown herself today".

"How?" asked a bare bodied onlooker.

"The man who has come back from the dead is sitting on the same spot that she lay on before we took her to the Ganges".

The villagers looked at the dazed man who was sitting surrounded by his relatives. They remembered. That was the exact spot where the little girl had lain before she had been tied to the banana stumps.

"Do you recognize the spot?", the man on the stool asked.

"Yes", shouted a villager, "It is the spot where the dead Chunni was made to lie".

"And she drew out the poison from this persons leg", shouted another villager.

"Let's ask the Zamindar for help and build a temple as a memorial to the girl on this spot", a person shouted, "from now on if a snake or the Shaitan attacks any one, he will be brought here and made to lie on this spot. No evil spirit can hurt us now because Chunni's spirit is our protector. Now everyone shout with me. Chunni Beti Amar Rahe".

"Amar Rahe, Amar Rahe", the dumb people shouted back.

The Englishman's Advice

Fangs was cruising over the hard dry ground behind the row of troughs that bordered Vikram's compound. The bovines tied to the troughs had not seen the snake and were relaxed as they chewed their food. The thatched roof under which the Zamindar usually sat was further away with a couple of villagers sitting cross legged on the ground discussing something or the other.

Fangs looked up and was irritated to see a pair of dragonflies flying overhead so he shot his head up and snapped at one; only to see it elevate itself like a helicopter. They were a couple of busy bodies and it seemed as though they did not have anything else to do. Realizing the futility of his attack Fangs lowered his head and continued on his zig zagging path and passed three feet by a group of black and yellow Assassin bugs that were feeding on a dead caterpillar. Further on two yellow backed Rhinoceros Beetles were engaged in a wrestling match. The bigger of the two grabbed the rival in its spiny hairy grip and with its horn, which extended from it's head and thorax, slammed the rival down on its back. From the corner of its eye it saw the snake approach.

"Hey a snake is coming", said the victorious Beetle.

"It's better to die than live with defeat", replied the fallen Beetle.

"Then you can die, I'm getting out of here". The Beetle scampered off to its right. The fallen Beetle saw the snake approach and became desperate. It hadn't meant what it had just said. It was lying on its back and was flailing its thin stick like limbs to somehow roll back on its feet. It was too late, the snake was nearly on him. "Aagh", he screamed, "I don't want to end up as a snake's food".

The Beetle was lucky as Fangs wasn't interested in it. He was interested in a rat hole further on, so he by-passed the terrified insect and one of its curves overturned the creature. The desperate beetle opened the hard casing which was its front pair of wings and released the rear wings which fluttered madly and lifted it into the air. The airborne Beetle flew away to the left towards a group of short Magnolia trees.

Fangs soon reached the rat hole and shooting out his forked tongue he repeatedly touched the ground with it. He picked up the molecules of a rat but they were old so he carefully entered the hole. His bifid tongue regularly shot out to give him the information he wanted as he slowly scuted into the tunnel. He soon reached the cob-webbed cave in which the rat had lived. It seemed that the unfortunate creature had ended up as someone else's food and the premise was uninhabited. Fangs continued his scuting and entered another tunnel that was in the opposite side of the little cave. He did not know that the tunnel led to the little brick wall which surrounded the thatched roof under which Vikram sat. So flicking his forked tongue Fangs scuted up the dark musty tunnel and stopped. He could see light further on and a dark dangerous silhouette before it. It was a black scorpion with large menacing pincer like pedpalps and a narrow tail arched over the body on whose tip was a poison gland opening into a sting. The Arachnid was walking backwards on its six legs and seemed to tell the snake to watch out or it would attack.

Fangs slowly scuted forward and realized that he was nearing the opening of the tunnel and the scorpion would soon be out in the open. The Arachnid walked out of the hole and was seen by a villager.

"Scorpion", the man shouted as he promptly pulled out a slipper from under his feet and flung it at the creature. The slipper hit the scorpion who was thrown against the brick wall and found itself lying on its back. It promptly flailed its legs and using its tail it rolled over. Furious at being attacked, it once again arched its tail over its body and with its sting ready, rushed towards the humans.

One of the villagers swung a stick at the attacking creature and missed. The stick landed two inches in front of the running scorpion who simply scampered up on it. The terrified villager lifted the stick and saw the scorpion rush for his hand. He desperately let go of the stick which fell as the other villager pulled out another slipper and threw it at the offending creature. The slipper hit the overturned scorpion on its soft underbelly and threw it against the wall. This shot stunned the Arachnid who lay still on its back as the villager picked up the stick and slammed it into the abdomen. The second villager joined in with another stick and together they clubbed the creature to death.

Fangs had reached the opening of the hole and saw the whole episode. He hadn't been seen so turning his head and neck around he scuted down the length of his own body and was soon scuting through the tunnel along which he had come. Reaching the opening where he had entered the hole, he gracefully flowed out and was soon sliding over the grass. He passed a hundred feet behind the bovines and the thatched roof in which the two humans were studying the dead scorpion. Slithering on he passed behind the garage and the 'Hathikhana' with the lone elephant in it and soon reached the boundary wall where he turned left and traveled parallel to the wall till he reached the double lioned gate from where he turned left again. Slithering below the perennially growling lions, Fangs reached the other side of the road where he slipped gracefully into the wheat field. Cruising through the wheat stalks he reached the bamboo stick which was the Scarecrow's skeletal structure. Pushing his head eight inches up he slowly crawled up the bamboo moving in circles as his long body engulfed the latter in his tight curls.

The Scarecrow smelt bad. It was wearing a filthy old tattered black kurta into which the snake entered as it climbed up the bamboo. The reptile soon reached the cross which was the Scarecrow's hands and crawling up the neck it's head came out of the kurta collar with the forked tongue repeatedly shooting out. Pushing up higher Fangs soon found himself sitting curled up on the 'bird droppings' lacerated mud pot that was the smiling head of the Scarecrow. Feeling a cool breeze, the snake lifted its head up to spread its long thin neck ribs and tighten its loose skin into a beautiful hood after which it surveyed the area around it. It was now the master of the Scarecrow and lord of the paddy field that seemed to bow below it in the wind.

The snake was short sighted and as it turned its hood around it did not see the cloud of dust in the distance. It was the little police jeep which was bouncing down the rutted path towards the double lioned gate. Sitting under the cloth hood of the vehicle in the front seat was James Powell who looked smart in his police uniform. Next to him behind the steering wheel sat Maan Singh who cruised the lurching vehicle down the rutted track. Behind the Englishman sat two Indian policemen who held, 303 rifles in their hands.

Sitting relaxed and surveying the road in front of the wind shield, Powell contemplated on his meeting with the Zamindar. Today he hadn't come to get information of a Bengali or any other Indian who had killed an English officer but had come with a bigger request. He wanted a list of the names of all the active sympathizers of the Congress party who lived in the various villages in the area. The party had become a nuisance and had stepped up its campaign against the English. He had been ordered to clamp down on these people and arrest them if it was possible.

Powell was jolted and thrown six inches up as the Jeep skipped over an obstacle the diver hadn't seen. "Oop's", he exclaimed as he touched seat with a thud, "we'll get blisters on our bottoms if you continue driving like this".

The two policemen sitting at the back of the vehicle had been tossed up and landed heavily on their bottoms causing one of them to lose his cap which left his head and fell on the floor of the vehicle. It was because of the English officers presence that they did not openly abuse the Nepalese driver. They satisfied themselves by muttering under their breaths.

"Drive carefully", advised the Englishman.

"Sorry sahib", replied the Nepalese driver, "I did not see that mound".

Powell settled down to relax as he looked forward through

the wind shield and realized that the double lioned gates and the Scare-crow were much closer. He looked forward to reaching the Zamindar's thatched roof and to relaxing on his wooden chair. He had been travelling in the jeep for the last four hours, and most of the journey was over mud tracks along which the wooden wheels of bullock carts had cut deep ruts. The jeep had sometimes behaved like a bucking bronco and it would be pleasant to sit on a still chair on firm ground.

The jeep lurched on and approached a one and a half foot broad drain that had been cut across the road to allow water from a nearby pond to flow to the fields on the other side of the road. The drain was eight inches deep and Powell thought the vehicle would slow down as the latter approached it. The jeep however did not check its speed. "Driver, watch out", Powell shouted at the last moment.

It was too late. The front wheels hit the bottom of the drain and its opposite wall and bounced up sending the wheel shooting into the air one and a half feet above the road. The vehicle seemed to pounce out of the drain first with the grill and bonnet facing up with the rear following suite. In the air the jeep hastily changed stance with the grill and bonnet headed downwards with the rear wheels still up. The front wheels hit the road with a jarring thud followed by the back wheels which did the same. As expected the officer and driver were thrown a foot above their seats and landed with their hip girdles taking most of the shock and passing the rest up their spinal cords.

"Goodness gracious", exclaimed Powell, "what's wrong with you?"

The policemen in the back had been tossed up and one of them landed on the floor board. "This driver will kill us", the policeman muttered as the driver slammed on the brakes.

"What's the matter with you Maan Singh?", asked Powell as he adjusted his cap on his head which had fallen off, "you can do better than that. That's not the way to drive. What's wrong with you?"

"Sorry sahib".

"Now buck up and concentrate on the road."

"Sahib look at the man standing in the middle of the field".

"That's not a man silly. It's a Scarecrow".

The Nepalese driver looked at the Scarecrow and recognized it and felt foolish. "Sahib I am a good driver", he said, "but please look at that man's head".

"It's not a man silly, its a Scarecrow", repeated Powell.

"I know its a Scarecrow sahib, but look at what is on its head".

Powell looked at the head and saw the snake sitting coiled on the mud pot. "Jumping Jesophats", he exclaimed, "what a creature". He motioned to the driver to carry on as he gazed at it. The reptile was facing the cement lions as the Jeep slowly approached the gate where it stopped. A shiver ran down Powell's spine as he stepped out of the vehicle onto terra-firma and stood there watching the snake. The reptile was now watching him and his men who had all got off the vehicle. Powell realized that he had mixed feelings for the creature. "It looks monstrous", he whispered.

"Yes sahib", whispered back the driver.

It was one thing to see a snake on the ground and another to see it coiled on a Scarecrow's head with its hood majestically surveying the area around it. "Majestic isn't it", muttered the Englishman.

"Yes sahib".

"No wonder the Indoo's pray to it".

"Yes sahib".

Inside Vikram's compound the two people who were sitting under the thatched roof saw the jeep stop in front of the gate and the English officer step out. They shouted out to Rama who came running out of the Haveli. "What is it?", the servant asked.

"The English sahib is standing at the gate".

Rama turned and saw Powell and the policemen gazing out towards the field on the other side of the road. He found it weird and trotted upto the people. Reaching the vehicle he saw Powell turn towards him so he stopped and folding his hands he bent down low in a very cautious, very reverent namastay.

"Where's Mr. Singh", asked Powell.

Rama did not understand English so he hemmed and hawed.

"Maan Singh", ordered Powell turning to his driver, "ask

him where Mr. Singh is?"

The driver asked the servant in Hindi where the Zamindar was and was told that the latter had gone to the nearby Mussahar village to supervise the building of a temple on the spot where the child's spirit had brought the snake bite victim back to life.

"Go and tell your master that the English sahib has come", said the driver.

Rama scampered off as Powell and his men continued watching the snake. "This area seems to be infested with these creatures", he muttered to himself.

"Yes sahib?", asked the Nepalese driver, "did you say something?"

"No its nothing Maan Singh".

The snake flicked out its forked tongue. The humans and the jeep were hardly discernible to it. It was the bifid tongue that picked up the molecules as the hood continued enjoying the soft breeze and surveyed the area around it.

Soon eight pallbearers came huffing and puffing down the road. They were carrying a long pole from the middle of which hung a little cot called a Doli. There were four pall bearers in front of the cot and four pall bearers behind the cot and sitting on the cot suspended in mid air was Vikram Singh who was goading the dark half naked men to move faster. Behind him a group of men followed led by the short stocky village headman and the hook beak nosed Priest. Seeing the jeep and the policemen, the villagers slowly slunk away and the bearded Priest found himself alone following the Doli. His chillum was safely tucked away in the folds of his dhoti on his right hip.

The people carrying the Doli were of the Kahaar caste, and it was their sole job to carry these suspended cots around for a fee. The eight "Kahaar's", stopped behind the jeep, put the Doli down and Vikram Singh got up and stepped out of the cot. "Namastay sahib", he wished as he folded his hands and bent down low, "It is my pleasure to receive you near my humble abode".

"Hello Mr. Singh", the Englishman replied, "isn't it a nice day today. I hear you're constructing a new temple".

"It is true sahib", replied Vikram, "It is a nice day and I am constructing a temple sahib. After all there should be a proper place to pray to the – to the – to God, to ask him to save the king, sahib".

"Now you're at it again Mr. Singh", interrupted Powell, "you're overdoing the loyalty bit".

Vikram Singh looked startled. "What has happened sahib?", he asked, "are you against the king?"

"Not on my life", replied Powell, "its just that you make me uncomfortable when you overdo the loyalty bit".

Vikram Singh shrugged. "I will never understand the English", he said while the bearded Priest smiled and nodded his head as though he understood what was being said.

Vikram suddenly looked concerned and looked deep into

the English man's eyes. "Is something wrong sahib?", he asked, "are you angry with me?"

"Certainly not, and what makes you think that I am?"

"Your Jeep hasn't entered my compound? Why is it standing outside my gate?, and why are you standing outside my gate, sahib?"

Powell smiled at the minor misunderstanding. "Oh, it's nothing to worry about", he said, "I was just watching that snake lord of yours".

"What snake Lord sahib?"

"That cobra of yours, that reptile you were praying to".

"Is it here?"

"Yes over there", Powell pointed to the Scarecrow.

Seeing the snake sitting coiled with it's open hood Vikram's body hair stood up with fright. "Aaagh", he screamed, "its the Nagraj", and hopped onto the jeeps bumper from where he stepped on the mudguard and climbed onto the bonnet. He wasn't alone because the bearded Priest had climbed on from the other side while the pall bearers scampered into the compound gates.

"Aaagh it's the Nagraj", Vikram shouted again as he hopped on the bonnet to get more elevation. He still felt he wasn't high enough from the ground and hearing his shouts the bearded Priest also started hopping.

Powell was taken by surprise. He first looked at the hopping Zamindar and the hopping Priest and then their hopping feet.

He saw the smart olive green bonnet of his jeep slowly cave in so he became desperate. "Get down Mr. Singh", he yelled, "get down from the jeep".

Vikram Singh and the Priest went on hopping as though they hadn't heard. "It is the snake lord", Vikram panted, "it is the snake lord".

"You're destroying my jeep", Powell shouted again, "Mr. Singh please get down".

Unhindered by the appeals Vikram and the Priest went on hopping on the properly caved in bonnet which had found its support on the engine below. It now took the load of the two people hopping on it.

Aghast, Powell turned to his equally exasperated driver. "Maan Singh", he yelled, "pull that idiot Sadhu down", and turning to the two astonished policemen he ordered, "the two of you get that Zamindar off the vehicle".

The Nepalese driver caught hold of the Priests saffron dhoti and pulled hard. The old cloth ripped off, and the driver found the dhoti in his hands as he lost balance and fell back on the ground. The terrified Priest who was naked now with only a thin piece of cloth around his waist, grabbed an end of Vikram's flowing dhoti and draping it around himself went on hopping. The two policemen had to climb onto the Jeeps mudguard and push the Zamindar and the Priest off to vacate the properly crumpled bonnet.

Vikram Singh realized he was falling so he caught the hand

of one of the policemen and pulled him along as he fell onto the mudguard from where he slipped to the ground with the policeman above him. The latter hurriedly pulled himself together while the fat Zamindar sat up against the wheel and moaned as he held his back with his right hand. "My back is broken", he said, "the English police broke my back in return for all I did for them".

"You dumb oaf", shouted Powell, "look what you did to my jeep".

Vikram looked up and realized the officer was furious so he pulled himself together and got up to look at the cause of the anger. He saw the crumpled bonnet and the Priest on the other side hastily wrapping on the dhoti which he had retrieved from the driver. Seeing the dented bonnet Vikram felt squeamish as he turned around and apologized to Powell. "Sorry sahib", he said.

"Idiot", yelled the Englishman, "you'll jolly well have to pay for this".

"Sorry sahib".

"Nincompoop".

"I'm sorry sahib".

"Imbecile".

"I'm very very sorry Sahib".

"Scatter brained idiot".

"What work do you have sahib?"

This brought Powell to his senses and lowered his adrenaline.

He looked at Vikram and shrugged. "You will have to pay for this", he said, "it'll cost you a pretty penny".

"I will pay double the amount sahib", Vikram offered, "but please smile. You see it was the visitation of the snake lord". Vikram remembered the snake and looked at the Scare-crow. The snake wasn't there. It had disappeared. "How about entering my compound", he continued, "we could talk over a cup of tea".

Powell agreed and walked behind the slightly limping Vikram. Entering the gate he turned and looked at the driver. "Maan Singh", he ordered, "take a hammer and try to straighten the bonnet".

"Yes sahib".

The little group walked down the supposed to be gravelled driveway and passing below the Union Jack, Powell was forced to put his hands to his nose. "This place stinks", he commented.

"What smell sahib?, I cannot smell anything".

"Cow dung Mr. Singh, and cow urine".

A wisp of wind brought the odour of shit from the shacks.

"My god this place smells awful".

"That smell sahib. It is those miserable people who live in those shacks. Very unhygienic they are. They defecate in the fields near their shacks and I tell them to go and do the job further away. What to do sahib, they are scared of the snakes, like the Nagraj we just saw. They are scared it will bite them on their bare bottoms while they are sitting doing the needful".

"Excuses Mr. Singh, only excuses".

"I'm telling you the truth sahib. Ask this miserable Rama".

Powell seated himself on a chair under the thatched roof as the bearded Priest seated himself on the bench. Vikram sent Rama to make some tea as he himself took his seat.

"Can't you get that hole covered?", asked Powell.

"Which hole?"

"That one in the corner of the wall".

"Oh that one!", exclaimed Vikram. "It is unoccupied sahib. Previously a rat lived in it. Then a scorpion. It was killed today so the house is empty. Ha-Ha-Ha". Vikram laughed at his own joke.

"Something else could occupy it. It could be deadlier than a scorpion".

"What work do you have sahib?"

"Oh yes. I forgot. My Government would like you to give us the names of all the active Congress party workers of this area".

"Oh that. Very simple. There is Ram Singh son of Gajanand Singh of village Barahiya. Baktar Singh son of Ganesh Singh of Barahiya, Jagadish Singh son of Krishna Singh of village Murlighar, Ramashray son of Devaki of Rahatpur".

"Wait I don't want it verbally just now. Take your time and study the area and give me a list in writing".

Vikram nodded his head. "Will that be enough payment for your damaged jeep?", he asked.

Powell looked at Vikram and broke out laughing. "That was

a dumb thing to do", he said, "This is the second time I've seen you praying to a snake".

"The snake lord, sahib".

"A snake nevertheless".

"You should speak reverently about the lord".

"Mr. Singh, you seem to forget that I am a Christian. And a devout one mind you. The sun never sets on the British empire and there are many pagan religions thriving under it. We Christians regard a snake as a snake and a cow as a cow".

"But cow is our 'Maata' sahib. Mother cow".

"A cow nevertheless. A dumb looking creature".

Vikram Singh fell silent as he lowered his head. He was offended but being used to only fawning before Powell he did not have the courage to speak back. The English man recognized the offended face. "I don't mean any offense to your religion", he said, "but you Indoo's do have a lot of contradictions".

Vikram looked up.

"You just said that those people living in those shacks are scared of getting bitten on their bottoms?"

Vikram nodded his head.

"Then if it bites you on the bottom. Why pray to it?"

Vikram opened his mouth to speak.

"Supposing a snake bites a person, tell me what happens?"

"The Ojha will drive out the poison".

"The who will drive out the poison?"

"The Ojha".

"You mean the witch doctor. Don't fool your self Mr. Singh. These things don't happen".

"He has supernatural powers Sahib. He can command spirits".

"Hogwash".

"He can bring a dead person back to life Sahib".

"Old folks tales".

"It happened last night sahib. Three people were bitten by a Naag and they died".

"By a cobra?"

"Yes sahib, a cobra. They were made to lie on the village square and one of them was lying on the spot where a seven year old girl had earlier died of snake bite. Her spirit roams around the area saving people from snakes. The person was lying where her dead body had lain, came back to life while the other two died. How did that happen?"

"Did your witch doctor bring him back to life?"

"No sahib. It was the girls spirit".

"And you believe it?"

"What else is there to believe. Tell me sahib. How did that man come back to life?"

"It's simple. A snake has a certain amount of venom in its venom bags. I think you know that?"

Vikram nodded his head.

All snake bites aren't fatal. I assume you don't know that?"

Vikram shook his head.

"Many people faint or get a heart attack due to fright when they are bitten by a snake".

"But how did the person yesterday come back to life?"

"Simple. The cobra bit three people. The first bite was fatal. The second could have been fatal and the third wasn't fatal. The cobra's venom was spent in the first two bites and in the third there was only enough to send the person into a coma".

Vikram Singh was thoughtful. "You speak with meaning sahib", he said, "your words have weight. The person who came back to life was the third man to be bitten".

"I don't think you know of a tribe that lives in the deserts of Rajasthan. I was posted in Bikaner before I came here. These people trap snakes and keep them for a cheap form of intoxication. The very cobra you pray to are caught by the neck and brought to the mouth. Due to the pressure on the neck the mouth of the snake remains wide open with the fangs sticking out. The villagers prick themselves taking in just the amount of venom they need to intoxicate themselves. And they are Indoo's too".

The bearded Priest nodded his head as though he understood.

"Weird", commented Vikram, "What about the Ojha sahib? I know of some people who have been bitten and died and were brought back to life".

"There's a simple explanation to that too. All snake bites aren't fatal".

"What is fatal sahib".

"All snake bites don't kill. Venom has different qualities. Some can kill a person while others can only paralyze while others send the person into a coma. It also depends on the bite. The snake may have managed to inject a full dose or it may not have. The venom injected may have been only enough to intoxicate the person or send him into a coma to recover later. These people are brought to the witch doctor who I hear, sweeps a broom over the body. Just see the foolishness of it. How can a broom drive out venom? If the bite was fatal and the person dies, the witch doctor blames something or the other. If the bite wasn't fatal and the victim comes out of a coma, it is attributed to the witch doctor's powers".

The bearded Priest nodded his head again as though he understood what was being said. Vikram Singh was serious and in deep thought and did not notice the police Jeep enter his gate and trundle down the supposed to be gravelled drive way to finally stop in front of the thatched roof. Maan Singh had straightened the bonnet as best as he could though it still looked crumpled.

"Your words have meaning sahib", Vikram spoke slowly, "they have weight. But the snake lord. My father and his father and his fore fathers prayed to it".

"I think I've sermonized enough", spoke Powell as he got up

to leave. Vikram Singh and the Priest got up and followed him out of the thatched roof to the Jeep as he seated himself in the front seat.

"When do I expect the list?", Powell asked.

"Within a week. But Sahib your tea is being prepared".

"Thank you, but I think I'd better hurry. I have to meet a couple of more people".

Maan Singh started the vehicle and the two policemen climbed into the back. The jeep reversed and turned around.

"Sahib", Vikram half shouted.

"Yes".

"There are rumors that the English may leave India. Is it true?"

"Over Churchill's dead body Mr. Singh. You can be sure that the sun will never set on the British empire".

The Zamindar and the Priest folded their hands and bowed in deep respect to the English officer as Maan Singh meshed the gears. The vehicle lurched forward and trundled up Vikram's drive way. Passing through the gates the vehicle turned left and disappeared leaving a lonely smiling Scarecrow looking at Vikram Singh from across the gates. A Vikram Singh who was in deep thought. The Englishman's sermon had affected him.

"What did the English sahib say", asked the Priest, "he spoke for a very long time".

Vikram looked at the Priest and thought. He then forced

out a word. "Hogwash", he said. "The Englishman spoke hogwash".

The learned Priest nodded his head as though he understood what had been said.

Young Love

The cold winter shrouded the land sending many of the animal world into hibernation. The Jasmine tree grew silvery white flowers in which gave out a sweet scent during the nights, while the short deciduous temple tree shed its broad lanceolate leaves, preparing itself to bloom highly fragrant waxy white flowers when the weather brightened. The scarlet Cordia bloomed bell shaped brilliant orange red flowers in large open clusters at the ends of branches, while compound leaves appeared on the Barma tree. Paddy stalks ripened and the fields were covered in yellow gold bringing happiness to the people. Come spring and the Jacaranda was flushed with blue mauve tubular flowers. Birds shivered in the cold and felt miserable. They welcomed the morning sun and shook off the misery before taking to flight. The black yellowish green billed Koel became silent and stopped calling. Not hearing its musical Kuoo-Kuoo the humans thought it had migrated. Migratory birds showed themselves in ponds, lakes and rivers and the common crow continued being a pest. It was an unfailing commensal of man and almost an element of his social system with an intelligence and audacity, coupled with an uncanny instinct for scenting and avoiding danger, it triumphantly carried on a life of sin and wrong doing. Nothing was unpalatable to the crow in the matter of food. A dead rat, kitchen refuse, fish pilfered from the protesting fish-monger's basket, meat pilfered from the protesting butchers shop or the egg or toast or chappaty from a humans breakfast table, snatched from almost under his nose.

The female cobra spent the entire winter in a rabbit hole she had annexed. She lay there and watched little creatures who had lost their sense of smell, enter her lair and scamper off in fright. She did have a good meal once when an injured rat who had hurt its nose and sensory hairs had unknowingly entered the dark hole only to be captured, killed and gobbled down into the tubelike body of the snake. Come spring and the female cobra felt it was time to search for food so she uncoiled herself and using her scutes slid out of the hole. She was lucky and did not have to go far. Near the pond she saw a young toad and not minding the warty body she stalked it and captured it and ate it whole with her cone like bone teeth walking it into her oesophagus.

It was a beautiful sunny day and the snake decided to bask

in the warm rays. She slithered to the eastern bank of the pond that lay between the Baobab and the Banyan tree, to the rotting tree trunk that lay on the banks. Slithering over to it she surveyed it and slowly scuted to the top where she lay her entire length on the trunk. Basking in the heat she attracted the anger of a couple of white faced, white breasted, stub-tailed Water hens. They were skulking through the undergrowth when they noticed the snake lying on the log and caterwauled, starting with raucous grunts, croaks and chuckles. They soon tired down and reduced their noises to monotonous Kook-kook-kook sounds which sounded like the 'pooking' of a floor mill's single cylinder diesel engine. Soon a brilliant golden yellow black headed Oriole flew over and flew in circles. Its melodious flute like 'peelow' call was added to the Water Hens caterwauling and attracted a pair of speckled and barred, black and white plumaged Pied Kingfisher's. The birds had typical stout dagger-shaped Kingfisher bills and flew around and sometimes stopped dead in their flight directly above the snake with faces to the wind and bodies tilted upright as if standing on their tails. They hung in mid air poised over the reptile as they rapidly beat their wings.

Hearing this commotion an orange necked Chameleon who had been relaxing under the log on the other side walked out to investigate. Seeing nothing he looked up at the log and still seeing nothing, he climbed up to see for himself, and was horrified to see the snake's tail. With one jump he was back on the ground and scurrying into the undergrowth.

"What happened to the Chameleon?" thought a chocolate brown stag beetle as it walked over to the trunk. "The fellow ran as though a dragon was up there". Opening the hard casing which was its front wing it released its rear wings and flew up to see for itself "Aagh", it screamed before it flew away. "It's the big snake, it's worse than a dragon".

The female cobra lay unperturbed by the disturbance around her and the termites marching up and down the log and feeding on it. She was feeling lazy and sluggish and knew the time had come to shed her old skin for a new one. Basking in the sunlight a hormonal action had been triggered and the semi transparent epidermal layer had loosened around the mouth. This was the time when she was most vulnerable, when she couldn't move easily. She became very lazy and she knew it was dangerous so she somehow slid down the log and lay along it. Finding a stone near the dead wood she rubbed the loose skin against it so that it was pushed back over her head. The old skin was held back by the dead wood and the stone, and the cobra taking her time slowly crawled out of it leaving it behind as a complete inside out replica of herself, showing every scale and also a trace of the colour pattern. The reptile had experienced a year of plenty and had eaten her fill of lizards, rats, mice, and frogs, which was the cause of her oviduct having mature eggs. This in turn had released a chemical signal when her skin had started to molt signaling that she was ready. The female cobra was ready to receive a mate.

Fangs had also shed his skin and was feeling younger and stronger and more virile. He was cruising on the other side of the pond when his bifid tongue picked up the scent. "Hey that's the smell of a female", he thought as he raised his head and opened his hood to survey the area around him. the scent had sent him into a frenzy but he saw nothing and only attracted the attention of the Water Hens who again caterwauled. Fangs however couldn't hear them so he closed his hood and lowered his head and slithered into the pond. Keeping his eyes and snout out of the water he continued making S shaped curves and swam through the water till he reached the other side where he slithered out and slithered to the rotten tree trunk. Yes the smell was strong here. It seemed like the female had moved off an hour ago so he lowered his head and slid into the adjacent undergrowth. He followed the smell and slithered through the grass and passing under a bush he frightened a flock of Red Munias. The crimson billed, crimson rumped sparrow like birds were sitting in globular grass nests in low bushes when one of them saw the snake. It at once took to flight and its disturbed call caused the others to fly also. Further on a couple of fawn coloured Hoopoe birds saw the snake approach. The crests on their heads flicked open and the birds flew off in an undulating undecided sort of way and re-settled on the ground a hundred feet to the left.

Fangs carried on. He was excited as he increased speed and

nearly knocked over a curled Millipede. The brown coloured, black striped creature had seen the snake approach and had curled up secreting a foul smelling poison to deter the reptile. Romeo was however not interested in it and zipped past as he slithered on in his search for Juliet. He did not know where he was going but just followed the molecules his bifid tongue picked up from the ground.

The molecules grew stronger and soon Fangs broke out of grass and passed under a short two feet high Magnolia tree. Cruising on he broke out of grass again and slithered to a stop in the open. There she was sitting with her hood open and coiled up beautifully. "Wow what a gal", he thought, "what a gal".

The female Cobra looked at the new comer with her lovely beady eyes. "Hey she's looking at me", thought Fangs as his tongue flicks increased and became more rapid. She was also rapidly flicking out her tongue.

"My god she's gorgeous", thought Fangs as he lifted his head and opened his hood. "Hey who is that?"

Fangs forked tongue picked up the molecules of another snake which was to the female's right. The other tongue flicking suitor had also picked up the females' signal and had searched her out. He was sitting coiled a hundred feet away and was about to approach her when Fangs arrived.

"Shoo off", the other snake hissed. He didn't like the idea of a rival.

Fangs looked at his rival then at the female snake. "By God she looked beautiful", he thought. He had to get her by any means so he barked a loud 'Khaa' at the other snake. The rival barked back and the two snakes advanced towards each other. Both had transformed themselves from tongue flicking Romeos to tongue flicking young Lockinvars. Approaching each other and when they were just one feet apart the two stopped and coiled up and lifting their heads opened their hoods and snarled at each other. Fangs was eight inches longer than his rival so he could afford to act tough. He raised his hood higher than the rival. The rival raised his head higher than Fangs so Fangs raised his head higher again. The rival followed suite and raised his only to receive a loud 'Khaa' from Fangs who again raised his hood. The two snakes now formed a conspicuous figure standing up erect fifteen inches high and glaring at each other.

Fangs was now furious so he lunged forward and caught hold of the rival's face in his jaws and rammed it to the ground. The other snake was smaller in size and weight and after its head was swung around a couple of times, it gave up. Fangs let go and drew back to strike again and was exultant when he saw the rival beat a hasty retreat. The latter realized that he was no match for the longer and heavier snake and it was better to search for another female who wouldn't have a tough suitor to rival him.

Exultant, Fangs looked around for the female who wasn't there, so he flicked his forked tongue and picked up her molecules. The female snake had thought the duel would turn nasty so she had slithered off knowing that the winner would come searching for her. As expected Fangs transformed himself from a gallant Lochinvar to the desperate Romeo and picking up the molecules he slithered into the grass and was soon travelling as fast as he could. He was desperate to reach the female before any other suitor did.

The female had slithered off to a quiet place knowing full well that the stronger snake would follow her. She had travelled a couple of hundred meters and decided to relax and wait in the shade of a Jamun tree. It was an evergreen tree with a dark stem and shining green foliage with a dense crown. The bark was smooth, light and dark gray in color and the snake was curled up at the base of the thick trunk. Sitting there she saw Fangs approach and felt the excitement grow within her. "Hello there", she seemed to say.

Approaching the female, Fangs' tongue flicked rapidly. He slithered up to her and drew his body alongside hers. "You look gorgeous", he said.

"You're the smartest snake I've ever set mine eyes on", she replied, "you're so strong, you literally threw that other fellow around".

Fangs body was now stuck to hers so he moved his head forward to bring his chin on the nape of her neck. His rapid tongue flicks continued as he rubbed his chin on the nape and overlapped his body with hers. "You feel nice and strong", she seemed to say, "you are my Hercules, my Tarzan, my King Kong".

"You are lovely", Fangs seemed to reply, "better than any other female I ever set my eyes on".

Fangs was now vibrating the entire rear of his body against hers as his chin continued rubbing her nape. He still hadn't got the signal from her that she had fully accepted him. His tail was trying to get under hers but she wasn't lifting it. That was the signal. If she lifted her tail, that meant that she had accepted him fully.

Fangs went on lovingly rubbing her nape and rapidly flicking out his forked tongue. He was taking his time till she was ready. She on her part enjoyed the vibration she was receiving from his body and the feel of his chin rubbing the nape of her neck causing her to also rapidly flick out her tongue. She liked the feel of Fangs' body and finally decided to accept him so she lifted her tail. Fangs hurriedly passed his below hers and inserted one of his two hemipenes into her cloaca and the two tongue flicking lovers were one with Fangs chin still on the nape of the females neck.

The snakes remained overlapped and had forgotten the world around them. The birds in the upper branches of the Jamun tree did not understand what was happening. All they knew was that two snakes meant double trouble so they croaked, and squawked, and chirped and chattered at the lovers. The lizards recognized the embrace and the tails overlapping each other, so they simply scampered away or did what ever they were doing. Up on one of the branches of the Jamun tree a gruesome love act was unfolding. A Praying Mantis was lovingly chewing up her suitor.

It was the bearded hook beak nosed Priest who arrived on the scene undetected by the lovers. He had come to defecate and seeing the snakes he had stopped dead on his tracks. There was a mug of water in his hand in which ripples had formed. The Priest was shivering with excitement. "My God", he thought, "the snakes are mating".

The Brahmin slowly slumped down on his knees, put his Lota down on the ground and folded his hands in silent prayer. He bent down low and kissed the ground. It was a very popular and strong belief that the ground beneath mating snakes contained hidden treasure and the bigger the snakes, the more the treasure. The mating cobras meant a lot of treasure and it seemed that his prayers to the snake lord had at last born fruit. The Lords themselves had shown him the sight of the treasure.

The Pundit's happy face suddenly looked glum. There was a hitch in digging for the treasure. The plot of land on which the snakes were mating on, and the surrounding area belonged to Vikram Singh. Another problem was that he himself was perennially broke and stayed stuck to the Zamindar like a leech for his daily food. He didn't even have the money to get the ground quietly dug up if he wanted to quietly steal the treasure. There was only one way out. Give the good news to the

Zamindar and hope for a fat baksheesh, so he turned around and walked back towards the Zamindar's Haveli.

Four people were soon walking towards the Jamun tree. They were very exited especially the fat person who was huffing and puffing with the exertion of the walk. He was the Zamindar who was led by the bearded Priest who now had an extra happy look on his face. Reaching the Jamun tree the four slowed down and the Priest showed Vikram the spot. The snakes were still there with their bodies still overlapped with the male's chin on the nape of the females neck.

Three of the humans immediately fell on their knees and kissed the ground while the fourth hopped on to stand on the back of one of them. Vikram had taken advantage of the kneeling elder Pehelwan who was lovingly kissing the ground and had stepped onto his back.

"What are you doing master?", the Pehelwan asked.

"Shush, stay silent", Vikram ordered in a whisper as he folded his hands and said a silent prayer.

"But my back will break master".

"Stay still or I'll break you".

"But master".

"Shut up or the snakes will be disturbed".

"Am I telling a lie Judgemaan?", asked the Priest in a whisper.

Vikram Singh nodded his head. He hadn't believed in the Priest and hoped that the latter wasn't lying. He desperately wanted to become more rich and had heard many stories of the fabulous treasures the snakes were supposed to guard. Moreover he wanted to prove the Englishman wrong. Powell's sermon the day he and the Priest had smashed the Jeep's bonnet, had played havoc with his mind. The English officer's words had had weight, and the latter had spoken with meaning giving careful and practical explanations for whatever he had said about snakes. Vikram had nearly believed in what Powell had said. What stopped him was the years of belief that snakes were Gods. His father and grandfather had prayed to them. Their fathers and grandfathers and great grandfathers had prayed to them and it was tough breaking away from a mould that had been built up and hardened through the centuries.

"What should we do?", asked the standing Pehelwan.

"Let them finish and move away", whispered Vikram Singh, "till then no one make a noise".

The four waited two hours for the snakes to disentangle while the Pehelwan on whose back Vikram stood groaned under the Zamindar's weight. The reptiles however remained embraced so Vikram got impatient and ordered the free Pehelwan to go back to the Haveli and fetch Rama and his brother and a couple of axes and spades. "And tell the driver to get a rope and bring the tractor along", he ordered.

The Pehelwan trotted off and was soon sitting on the huge rear mudguard of the blue Fordson Major tractor with Rama and his younger brother sitting on the opposite side. Between them the turbaned driver guided the vehicle through the uneven fields, over mounds and field partitions and stopped when the vehicle reached the plot of land where Vikram was sitting piggy back on the elder Pehelwan's back. He had allowed the wrestler to get up and had climbed onto the back where he felt safe. The snakes were still entangled with each other so Vikram lost his patience. It seemed as though the Pehelwan whom he was riding on, was going to collapse.

"Rama", shouted Vikram, "all of you get together and shoo off the snakes".

Rama, and his thin brother jumped off the tractor's mudguard and walked towards Vikram. The brothers were accompanied by the tractor driver who had left the engine running, and the free Pehelwan.

"Get rid of the snakes", ordered Vikram who was still sitting piggy back on the groaning Pehelwan's back.

The four men clapped, and shooed, and jumped and pranced but the snakes remained entangled so they simply picked up stones and threw them at the reptiles. This brought the desired result and the two snakes disentangled themselves and hurriedly slid away towards the north where they disappeared into the grass. Only then did Vikram step down from the groaning Pehelwan's back who stretched himself and did a couple of push ups.

"Cut down the tree", Vikram ordered.

Rama and his brother took an axe each and positioned themselves on both sides of the trunk. They hacked into the wood and soon had the tree falling to its right. The birds had all flown off earlier when the first axe had struck and were safe. It was the female Praying Mantis that was killed. She had been lovingly chewing up her suitor when the tree fell. She was thrown off balance and died squashed in between two branches. Thus ended the two love stories that took place on and below the Jamun tree.

A rope was tied to a branch of the tree and the other end to the tail end of the tractor which pulled the tree away from the spot that was to be dug up. Rama and his brother took spades and dug into the ground around the tree. They used the spades and axes in turns to cut and dig out the tree's roots after which they dug with the spades in the hope of excavating a room.

Vikram Singh watched from a distance with the Priest sitting silently beside him. Every moment he expected to hear the exited words "Master bricks", which would mean that the diggers had reached an underground room. The words never came and the diggers dug through the afternoon and the evening and soon there was a huge pit fifteen feet long and fifteen feet broad and ten feet deep with no sign of the treasure yet.

Rama got tired digging and his brother got tired digging so the Pehelwan's took over. Soon they were also tired so they gave the spades back to Rama and his brother who soon got tired again. This went on till evening when a visibly off mood Vikram ordered them to stop. He walked over and inspected the pit. "There's nothing in there", he said, "its getting dark so lets go back".

The Pehelwans climbed out of the pit and helped Rama push the tractor. The driver let go off the clutch and the Fordson's diesel engine roared to life. Vikram climbed onto the right side rear mudguard while the Priest climbed onto the left and soon the two were bobbing on the vehicle as it travelled across the uneven fields as the Pehelwans and the servants half walked and half ran behind it.

The tractor sputtered on and Vikram was deep in thought. The mould in him had cracked. The mold that had hardened due to centuries of conditioning – that snakes were a God – had received it's first challenge and Vikram wondered. "Was the Englishman right?", he thought as the tractor bounced on. "If he was right, then were all his ancestors wrong? Did they pray to the wrong God? That meant that they would all be in hell now. How could they all be in hell? They weren't fools. They were learned people so how could they be wrong? They must have been right. The snake was a god, only the stories of the treasures it guarded was untrue.

Vikram was unhappy with his answer. He realized that he was consoling himself and the more he thought, the more muddled he was getting, so he blocked his mind and looked ahead as the tractor noisily chugged on.

Arrest Me

The month of May is the worst season in Bihar when life becomes miserable as the land reels under the heat. The temperature touches forty eight degrees centigrade and burns all who they dare to venture out. Most of rural Bihar walked bare foot and the hot earth caused blisters to appear on the feet. The hot dry easterly wind called the loo blew over the land evaporating water from ponds and lakes and the bodies of living beings. To avoid dehydration, people doubled their water intake which again came out when they perspired. The sun looked extra bright and eyes winced when people left the interiors of their homes. Stray dogs went mad and dead animals decomposed extra fast. Nobody escaped the heat and dust and the sky was void of birds who were most probably snoozing on a branch of a shady tree. The world was silent as everyone was indoors and every living being had retired into the cool of a shade. The heat seemed to shroud the earth like a canopy and it seemed that the world would explode. Bald people were extra cautious and did not venture out without a turban on their heads and birds dived into water if it was available, as fishes gasped and died in drying ponds. The only saving grace was that most of the trees had already shed their leaves and were draped in a brand new gown of sparkling green. Like the kindly Fig tree whose broad evergreen low crowned thick canopy helped to cool the land below and around it. Leathery and opposite, the leaves of the Jamun tree added to the greenery while the Mango tree bore delicious fruits. The big Baobab in Vikram Singh's compound was however leafless and its much divided crown appeared gaunt and grotesque with the rope still hanging from one of the branches.

The climate however did not suit the mood of the people who were happy, exited and expectant. It wasn't an ordinary month but the May of 1947. The British had announced that India would get her independence by August and the date had been fixed for the fifteenth of that month. All the good work done by die hard imperialists had gone down the drain. The Congress party had announced that it would grant general amnesty and all jail doors would be thrown open on that day.

Attlee's decision to grant independence was disliked by people like Powell; people who had worked hard to make sure that the sun would never set on the empire. Indian officers and policemen were a demoralized lot and weren't sure of their future though the Congress party had announced that they would be retained. Their problem were the freedom fighters whom they had harassed and hounded, firmly believing that the British would never leave. These harassed people would now be the rulers and the government employees wondered if they would take their revenge. Illiterate villagers in far flung areas were already in the habit of trooping into police stations they had once feared and proudly announcing to the policemen that after Independence they would be taking orders from them and not the English. Being illiterate they had misunderstood the slogan "rule by the people", and thought that they would become through some weird system, the rulers themselves. Some of course did wonder how each and everyone of the public could become a ruler. This directly affected governance and the controls grew soggy. The English officers valiantly worked on as they prepared their offices for the final hand over of power. In normal times they would have left their districts and mofussils for the cooler hill resorts of Darjeeling and Mussoorie. They stayed back this year and braved the loo they had feared so much and perspired under slow moving electric fans in their Collectoriate's, Commissionaries, Police stations and Courtrooms.

James Powell was also a very busy man but today he wasn't perspiring under an electric fan in a stuffy office but in the front seat of his police jeep which was roughing it along the dirt road which led to Vikram Singhs double lioned gate. As usual there were two policemen sitting in the back and the Nepalese driver who was guiding the vehicle along the rutted road. Powell wasn't visiting the Zamindar for news of the rascals who waged war with the king emperor", or the Bengalis who couldn't hide amongst Behari's because of linguistic differences. Neither did he want a list of the Congress party activists of the area. He personally thought it was his moral duty to call up or meet the people who had helped him carry out his work. He had given Vikram Singh a couple of summons but the Zamindar had failed to turn up. He had wanted to give the pot bellied land lord directions on how to bring down the Union Jack on the fourteenth of August with respect. Powell was adamant that the proud flag which had been brought in by the East India Company, flutter till the last day, till the last hour, till the last minute of the Raj, be brought down with respect and not pulled down by screaming over zealous natives even though he believed that the Zamindar's property was the filthiest piece of British territory over which the Union Jack proudly flew.

The Jeep bucked and bounced on its leaf springs over the uneven road. It did not look as smart as it once was. The cloth hood covering the passenger section of the vehicle was torn with a huge hole in the rear above the two policemen. Some one had thrown a lighted torch at the vehicle and the hood had caught fire. Maan Singh had stopped and taken buckets of water from a roadside well and put out the fire leaving a gaping hole above the rear seat. He had requested Powell to get the hood replaced but the latter had been too busy to get jeep hoods replaced. He had decided to leave that to the new government.

Powell was perspiring profusely as the jeep approached the gates. Salty sweat appeared on his forehead and trickled down to his eyes burning them. Maan Singh was also having problems keeping the liquid from entering his eyes and both of them did not notice the bright new dress the Scarecrow was wearing. Maan Singh turned the vehicle to his right and was soon trundling down the supposed to be gravelled driveway with the Scarecrow smiling in the back. It was proud of its beautiful new dress.

Vikram Singh was sitting with the village headman and a few villagers cross legged under the thatched roof when the jeep approached and stopped fifty feet away. The Zamindar was dressed scantily in his underpants since he was being massaged by the two Pehelwans with mustard oil. His dhoti and kurta and pistol were lying on a nearby chair. Getting up he hastily wrapped the dhoti around himself and stashed the little weapon into a fold in the cloth on his right hip after which he hastily pulled the kurta on and walked upto the Jeep with folded hands. "Namastay sahib", he said and turned around and made a sign to the villagers to leave. They all got up and walked to the Haveli's verandah and sat down on the floor in a little group with their faces turned towards the jeep and the Zamindar.

A shiny Jack boot stepped out of the Jeep followed by another. From the boots flowed out brown socks, shooting out a pair of pink perspiring legs into huge flappy Khaki half pants which was wet in the back. The half pants with a brown buckled, belt and holster was pressed over a Khaki shirt with front pockets on the chest and which was also drenched on the back. A pink perspiring face irritated by the summers heat was perched on a pink neck that flowed into the shirt collar. This example of British Indian policedom was topped with a police cap and a sweat slippery baton held in the right hand.

"Hello Mr. Singh", Powell wished, "and how are you?"

"I am all right sahib".

"And how's your second wife?"

"She is alright", replied Vikram, "my first wife died so I had to marry again".

"What did she die of?"

"Cancer sahib".

"I'm sorry".

"It is alright sahib, my second wife gave birth to a son".

"That's good news, and when was that?"

"Two months ago sahib".

The two walked towards the thatched roof and passed under the drooping flag where Powell did his customary hands to the nose salute as he walked on. Reaching the thatched roof the two entered and seated themselves near the hook beak nosed

Priest who had his chillum hidden safely under his bottom. It was too hot for Powell to feel anything amiss. After the customary complaint of the heat and the stench and the customary excuses peppered with sahibs and sirs with Vikram blaming the peasants for not defecating further away, Powell came to the topic of snakes. "Do you still pray to them", he asked.

Vikram nodded his head.

"My goodness you people are stubborn".

"Its not stubborn sahib. I believed in everything you said. What you told me made sense. But my fathers and their fore fathers prayed to the snake. It is very hard to break away from things that you learned from childhood. And to make matters worse this miserable Pundit won't allow me to break away from this belief".

"Do you feel that it is impractical?"

"What's impractical".

"Praying to the snake".

"No sahib. I should be praying to their photos and not the real ones. That's what this pundit says".

The bearded Priest smiled and nodded his head as though he understood what Vikram had said.

"Well it's upto you to decide".

Powell noticed something wrong with Vikram's speech. "You seem to be ill at ease Mr. Singh?", he asked, "what's the matter?"

"Sahib you said that the sun would never set over the English empire".

"That was a minor miscalculation on my part. It's queer how times can change. Just imagine. The people back home demanded this country's independence from Attlee".

Vikram shook his head. "Then you will be leaving?", he asked.

"Yes. I think so".

"Discarding people like us like old clothes".

"Come on old chap. It's not as bad as you think. Pull yourself together. After all, good things do have to end some day".

Vikram nodded his head and looked towards the verandah and realized the villagers were looking at him so he sat up straight and crossed one leg over the other. Till then Powell hadn't noticed anything wrong with the Flag but later thought he had noticed a glimpse of guilt on Vikram's face. "As the facts stand", he continued, "and whether we like it or not, we are going. I will miss the place. You know old chap, sort of got used to it. Thanks for the help and what you did for us. If you won't any help, something I can do for you before I hand over power, it's yours for the asking. Come over to Monghyr old fellow. They are throwing a farewell party for us there. About the flag.....".

Powell stopped short as he noticed the flag. It wasn't the Union Jack. It was a tri-color. The reality slowly soaked into him as he slowly turned his pink face towards an openly guilty Vikram Singh. "Where's the Union Jack?", he asked in a whisper.

Turning pink Vikram pointed to the Scarecrow that was smiling just out side his double lioned gate. The Scarecrow was wearing the Union Jack and smiling back.

"You rascal".

"What pascal sahib".

"You double crossing rascal".

"Don't abuse me sahib".

The bearded Priest nodded at Powell and smiled as though he understood and approved of the abuse.

"So you've become a turncoat?"

"What turncoat sahib? Don't abuse me. You told me that the English would never leave India and I helped you white people against my brown people. So it's not my fault. You told me that India would get independence over Churchill's dead body. Now you have left me to be torn and eaten by my own people. You English changed your card sahib so I changed mine".

"But you shouldn't have draped that scarecrow with that flag".

Vikram fell silent and from the corner of his eyes he saw the villagers looking at him.

"Mr. Singh will you tell that Sadhu of yours to pull down that flag".

The bearded Priest nodded his head, proud of being mentioned by the Englishman".

“I won’t allow any one to do that sahib”, retorted the Zamindar.

“You have the cheek”.

“Stop don’t abuse me sahib. I’m just asking for your help. Arrest me and I will also become a freedom fighter and fight the elections and become a member of Parliament”.

“Mr. Singh, will you tell that Sadhu of yours to pull down that flag”.

“The villagers are looking at us sahib”, whispered Vikram.

“I don’t care a damn what your villagers think”, Powell said as he got up and shouted to the driver. “Maan Singh go get the flag from the Scare-crow and you”, he shouted to a policeman, “climb up that pole and bring down that goddamn flag”.

“Sahib I won’t allow that”.

“Mr. Singh, I could arrest you for that”.

“That’s what I want sahib. I want you to arrest me”.

James Powell was caught off guard. He knew he should have arrested Vikram Singh. He would have arrested him earlier but knew it was useless. Prisoners would be freed from jails all over India on the fifteenth of August. He had started disliking the Zamindar whom he felt had discarded him and his government and left them on the lurch. Discarded like old clothes for new ones. The only way to punish him now was not to play his game. He wouldn’t arrest the pot bellied Zamindar.

James Powell moved to leave.

"Aren't you going to arrest me sahib?"

Powell did not answer. He simply turned around and glared as Maan Singh came running back to the Jeep with the retrieved Union Jack and the policeman climbed down the pole with the tri-color.

"Then I will give you another excuse to arrest me".

The mustard oil smelling Zamindar walked upto the Englishman till he was only two feet away from the latter. He glanced towards the verandah and saw the villagers watching him, so he straightened himself and swung his pudgy right hand across Powell's face splatting the English man's cheek's, causing the face to swing to its right and the hat to fly off and plop on the ground further away. Vikram was taken aback. Powell was completely bold and his head shone in the heat.

The English officer's reflex was automatic. Recovering he swung his baton across Vikram's face throwing the Zamindar toppling over the aghast Priest. In two strides he crossed over the terrified pundit and pulled his revolver out of its holster. Seeing the weapon the pundit shrieked and folded his hands and begged for mercy. "Sarkar ye Zamindar Paagal ho gaya", he yelled.

Powell did not understand what the Priest had screamed as he grasped Vikram by the kurta collar and dragged him up till his pink nose was stuck to the brown mustard oil smelling one of the Zamindar's. Jabbing the revolver barrel against Vikram's cheeks and gritting his teeth the officer hissed, "I could kill you for that".

Powell's pink nose was still stuck to Vikram's brown one when the officer felt something cold pressed against his own cheek. It was the muzzle of Vikram's pistol which he had fished out from the folds of his dhoti. Through gritted teeth and with equal venom the collar grasped Zamindar hissed back. "Arrest me Sahib, for assaulting an officer sahib of his Majesty's Government of India. Or I will not let you leave my compound alive".

Seeing the altercation the two policemen lifted their rifles and ran forward as Vikram lowered his pistol. He was handcuffed and arrested and his pistol was confiscated for assaulting an officer of his Majesties Government of India.

Powell glanced towards the verandah where the villagers had got up. The bearded Priest had fallen to the ground in his fright and was trembling and looking at the Englishman from where he was lying. Powell bent over and picked up his hat and dusting it he adjusted it on his head and walked over to the jeep where he seated himself on the front seat. The driver climbed in and Vikram was led into the rear of the vehicle to sit with the two policemen. As the jeep reversed, the villagers walked out shouting slogans against the English. "Angreji Raj Murdabad", they yelled, "Vikram Singh zindabad".

The jeep slowly moved towards the gates and some villagers rushed forward so the driver braked. Powell got off and lifted his baton as he turned around as a warning to stop. "You've got your freedom", he shouted, "so stop yelling. I'm taking him along because he asked for it".

Luckily for Vikram the villagers did not understand English. Powell climbed back into the jeep and the vehicle was soon trundling out of the double lioned gates and turning left it passed the smiling naked scarecrow. The jeep skipped and bounced over the rutted road and finally reached the thin narrow pot holed strip of tarmac that was the highway. The vehicle turned right and was soon passing the little town of Jamalpur. People scampered out of the jeep's path recognizing whom the vehicle belonged to. The little Union Jack that was perched proudly on the bonnet made it too obvious.

A boy called, "Angrez Kutta", and disappeared into an alley. Powell knew what that meant but stonily looked ahead through the windscreen with unflinching eyes. He was taken by surprise when he heard shuffling and muttering behind him. He turned around and saw Vikram Singh standing erect through the hole in the hood holding up his handcuffed hands for everyone to see and yelling while the two policemen were trying to pull him down. "Nehru Gandhi zindabad", he yelled, "Angrezi Raaj Murdabad. Gali-gali mein shore hai, Angrez gora chor hai".

Down with the Zamindar

It had been a hectic day for Sita, Rama's thin wife. She was actually a girl in her teens and was approximately five feet eight inches tall and wore a green coloured worn out sari which the new mistress had given her. She had been making tea and cooking food for the numerous visitors that visited her master through out the day. It was the spring of 1955 and the elections had been announced and Vikram was surrounded by visitors day and night. He had thrown open his kitchen to everyone who come and pledged their support to him. That's why his servants were overworked .

Sita was thin with a gaunt face and eyes embedded in deep sockets . She had long black hair which she prized and which Rama loved caressing when the two were alone in their musty smelling shack. She had been married when she was only four year's old and now worked as a maid in the master's house since her husband was the latter's servant or his Bandhua mazdoor. The master's slave.

It had become dark so Sita stole a candle from the mistresse's room and quietly walked out of the verandah and across the open ground to the line of shacks in which the second thatched house was her home. Entering between two mud walls she walked into a single mud walled room with a thatched roof. Groping in the dark she felt for the cot and under it found a box of matches. Lighting one, she lit the candle and made it stand in a corner of the room near the cot. There was no window but just the opening for the door. The room was around eight feet by eight feet with the roof only a foot above the woman's head. There wasn't any furniture except for the single cot along the eastern wall under which was a battered tin trunk which had been pilfered from the haveli. The cot itself was covered by a filthy mattress, half of which was draped under a filthy silk quilt. These two had once been the Zamindar's bedding and when a new set was bought, they were given away to the servants.

Sita was feeling extremely tired. She had been cooking from six AM to eight P.M, and felt as though she would faint. She opened the string that tied her hair into a bun and let the hair flow down her back. She sat on the cot and pulling the quilt over herself she lay down to sleep. Sita was exhausted and didn't notice her hair slip off the pillow and fall to the mud floor. Her mind was fuzzy as sleep overtook her and in her dream she mumbled. "I'll have to get up at five in the morning. I'd better not be late or the master will get angry".

The night drew on and the candle soon burnt out

Sita would never get up in the morning . As she slept she did not know of a race which was taking place in a field further on between gods creatures. Between the hunter and the hunted, between a snake and a mole. Fangs wasn't interested in politics or in India's Independence or whether the English should have left or not. He was interested in the mole that was trying to escape him. As he zipped across the field in the moonlight after it. Zig zagging through the harvested stubs, he realized to his horror that the little creature had run into a human's home. His forked tongue told him to cool it . It had picked up human molecules and the area was dangerous so he stopped. Rapidly shooting out his tongue he gathered his courage and moved slowly forward on his scutes. He soon reached the doorstep and scooted into the musty room. His tongue picked up the mole's scent so he cautiously moved forward and was soon passing under the cot. Moving on he touched the sleeping woman's hair, so he inspected it with his tongue. The information his sensory organ's gave him puzzled him since he did not know anything about human hair. In the dark he thought it was a vine leading up to a tree which he hadn't seen before. The Mole most probably would have escaped so he decided to climb up the hair and see what was up there.

In her sleep Sita saw a funny dream. The Zamindar who had a horrible ogre like face with large spider like eyes was twisting her hair and pulling at it. Feeling heavy in the head she lifted her hand and tried to brush the Zamindar off when she was bitten by Fangs who dug his poisonous teeth into her left palm. Feeling the sting the woman woke up and heard the loud "Khaa", just as she felt the weight on her hair. Panicked, she sat up and realized the snake was entangled halfway up her hair and was now on her back. She felt the bite on the back and screamed and tried to brush off the predator when she was bitten a third time. Screaming, she ran out of her room towards the the thatched roof where the master and a few people were sitting with Rama standing in waiting. "Master", she screamed, "master, help".

The villagers and the Zamindar looked towards the running woman who collapsed ten feet from the thatched roof. Fangs had got unentangled and had fallen midway due to the jolts he received from the bobbing head. He had been himself frightened, entangled in the hair as he was and had bitten in self defense. In one movement he pulled himself together and created his S shaped curves and zipped off back towards the row of shacks, past them and into the safety of the fields beyond as Rama and some of the villagers ran towards the stricken woman. "What is it?" shouted Rama.

"The shaitan bit me," replied the wailing woman.

"What shaitan?," asked Rama as he knelt over her.

"The one that bit the little girl and the three travelers".

"Run and get the Ojha," shouted a villager.

A couple of villagers took lathies and ran off into the dark while Rama made his wife lie down on her back. "My body feels as though it is on fire," she complained.

"Don't worry," replied a desperate Rama who was trying to control his emotions, "where did it bite you?"

"On both hands"

The Villagers had grouped around Sita and the lantern was brought over. Vikram knelt down and studied the puncture marks and realized that the woman was speaking in a nasal voice. "My body is burning," she complained, "my body is burning."

Sita passed away with her head cradled in a tearful Rama's arms. The Ojha soon arrived and as usual he pushed the people back and pulled out the photo of the bearded corps from a cloth bag that hung from his right arm. Making the photo stand on the ground ten feet away from the dead body he lit some incense sticks and stuck them on the ground before the photo. He did a hasty prayer after which he walked back to the dead body and sat cross legged near the stomach. A villager who had accompanied him was holding his broom and incense cup. Seeing the broom Vikram remembered what Powell had once told him and having his suspicions he quietly walked out of the crowd. He sat alone under the thatched roof. Half an hour passed and the answer he feared came. "The shaitan was too strong and the venom couldn't be drawn out." The Ojha packed his stuff back into his cloth bag and walked away followed by a couple of villagers. Vikram saw Rama walk out of the crowd."Rama", he called out.

"Yes master". Rama said as he walked up to Vikram.

"Is Sita dead?"

"Yes master".

"Then take the body back to your shack or the land behind it. I don't want it dirtying these grounds. Remind me to give you fifty rupees for the funeral.

"Yes master."

Rama walked over to the little group and with the help of his younger brother he carried his wife's body back to the shack where he lay her on the cot. He then went and sat cross legged at the door and waited for dawn to come. The younger brother brought back the fifty rupees.

The next day he and a couple of villagers entered a bamboo grove near the Mussahar village and bought a bamboo for two rupees. They brought the bamboo back and made a little seven foot long ladder. The corpse was placed on it and Rama went and chopped down two Banana tree's which had come up behind his shack. Hacking off the leaves he brought back the stumps and the little group of villagers lifted the ladder on to their shoulders and chanting "Rama naam satya hai", they left Vikram's campus traveling behind the line of shacks. They dared not cross Vikram's compound with the dead body. Reaching the dirt road they turned left and chanted as they walked on . After covering a little distance they left the road to make way for a big car. It was Vikram's Buick with himself sitting in the back seat on his way to Patna. He was going to request the Congress high command to give him the party ticket to fight the elections from Monghyr. After all he was the only freedom fighter who had slapped an English Superintendent of police on the face.

The mourners with the dead body crossed the highway and walked on straight across the road and the fields as the crow flies till they reached the banks of the river. They had to trudge over a kilometer of undulating white sand till they reached the broad stretch of glistening blue water that was the holy Ganges. Saying a silent prayer the people made the corpse lie on her side and tied her between the Banana stumps. They carried the sandwiched body and walked chest deep into the river and let the dead body and stumps float away. The group watched as the green stumps and the green colour of the saree merged and grew smaller and smaller till nothing could be seen. They had a bath in the holy waters and walked back from the river to Vikram Singh's compound.

Two days later Vikram's black Buick roared into the double lioned gates to stop in front of the thatched roof. Vikram Singh got off and entered under the roof and sat on the ground near the hole in the wall. He had bad news. The Congress high command had refused to give him a ticket. They were the very people who had applauded and welcomed him in Jail. "Better late than never", they had said. When he was released they had praised and pampered him so much that he had exultantly not cared to go and bid the Englishman farewell when the latter was leaving the country. "Let the English go to hell", he had thought. He was enjoying basking in the heaps of praises he was receiving. But now these very people had denied him the party ticket."People who had been fighting for years will be given first preference", they had said. "Not last minute converts".

"Who will get the ticket for Monghyr?," Vikram had asked.

"Shiva Rama", was the reply.

The Zamindar had flown into a rage. Shiva Ram was his own ryot, his semi servant. A person whom he had bullied many times and got him beaten up twice. Vikram had hollered and yelled at the politicians and challenged them that he would make their party eat dust in Monghyr."I promise you in the name of all the Gods" he had shouted, "if your party gets a single vote in Monghyr. You can chop off my nose and mustache."

Vikram had stomped out of the party office and got into his Buick and traveled all the way back to Ramnagar. He was adamant to hit the campaign trail the next day.

The next morning he sent Rama to fetch Shiva Ram from a near by village. Vikram had transformed himself from a pot bellied Zamindar to a pot bellied politician as he sat in the midst of a group of villagers under the thatched roof. "It was I who slapped the English S.P on the face", he boasted. "Have any of you heard of a Congressman in this area who did that ."

The listeners shook their heads.

"These Congressmen." Vikram continued," Never had the guts to fight the English face to face. They only did satyagrahas and what did they call Gandhi's movement. Non violence. I don't understand on what basis they want to fight the elections. It is people like us who slapped the English and kicked them out of the country. That's how we got our independence."

The listeners all nodded their heads.

"And what was Shiva Ram doing then?," Vikram asked and with a smile answered his own question. "Urinating in his dhoti with fright of course."

The listeners laughed at the Zamindar's joke.

"Did Shiva Ram ever have the guts to look an Englishman straight in the eye ?"

The listeners shook their heads.

"Off course not. He could never confront an English officer". Then thumping his chest with his right hand Vikram continued. "But it was I who slapped the English officer on the face".

The listeners nodded their heads. "Shiva Ram has gone mad", one of the villagers commented, "he doesn't know his limits."

"I've sent Rama to fetch him."

"I don't think he'll come," commented another villager, "after all he is fighting the elections against the master."

The little group fell silent as they saw two people walk into the double lioned gate. It was Rama and the person called Shiva Ram . The latter was short, dark, with curly hair and a face that was scarred by small pox. As a true Congressman he wore a Khadi dhoti and a khadi kurta and on his head balanced a little Khadi Gandhi cap. He was bare foot.

Coming close to the thatched roof he bent down low in a namastay and with bowed head walked in and sat in a corner under the roof.

Vikram glared at the ryot and his eyes reddened with anger. "You Pig," he roared, "You scum, you swine, you dirt of my feet. You're not even fit to touch may shoes and you have the temerity to file your nomination papers against me?."

Shiva Ram looked up. His face looked scared but not his eyes. The Zamindar did not notice this. "Master forgive me", he pleaded. "It was the Congress party high command in Patna that forced me to file my nomination papers. I told them I didn't want to contest against you, but they asked me to put up a token resistance. It would be a disgrace if the party did not field a candidate from here."

"Is that true?"

"As true as my mother married my father before I was born."

The anger seemed to vanish from Vikram's face.

"Why are you worried master?." continued Shiva Ram, "You

are the sure winner. I have travelled across the constituency and I have heard the people's voice."

"What do the people say?"

"Master, the people say that a poor person like me cannot help the people. What can I do ? I don't even have shoe under my feet."

"And what do they say about me ?"

"The people say the Zamindar has a lot of money and can use his power and influence to help the people. After all it was the master who slapped the English officer".

Vikram was visibly pleased. A little bit of tail wagging had sent him off the track. The slap across James Powell's face seemed to be paying dividends. Vikram didn't ever suspect the opposite, that the cowering head nodding people were making a fool out of him. They were all Shiva Ram's supporters and Vikram and his like all over India had failed to judge the definite undercurrent amongst the voters that was strongly against the Zamindar's.

"I will teach the Congress party a lesson for not giving me a ticket", Vikram stated as he got up to go towards the haveli. He would have his bath and get dressed splendidly to hit the campaign trail. "I hope all their candidates lose", he said as he went.

The villagers nodded their heads as Shiva Rama got up. "May I go master ," he asked," I have to make preparations for tomorrow's meeting. Some top officials of my party are coming from Patna."

"Wait till I come back", Vikram ordered as he walked on. Entering the haveli he suddenly remembered. It would be good to get divine blessings before he did something new. It would be an auspicious start. "Rama," he shouted as he walked on. The thin servant came running upto him. "Go and see if the Nagraj is anywhere around."

Rama nodded his head and turned to walk out of the verandah. He hated snakes especially cobras. One of them had taken his wife's life and this incident had changed his concept about reptiles. "They weren't Gods," he felt, "they were just horrible looking dirty, slimy creatures who were cursed by the almighty to be limbless and crawl on their stomachs,"

Rama passed the row of shacks and walked towards the giant Baobab tree. It still had the rope hanging from a branch. Looking up he saw her at once. The female cobra was sitting coiled with an open hood on the branch just next to the rope. Rama quietly retraced his steps and when he had reached a distance he ran back towards the shacks. He was soon breathing heavily outside Vikram's verandah. " Master," he shouted at the top of his voice.

"What is it?", Vikram shouted back from inside.

"Master the snake ," Rama shouted back, "On the giant tree".

It took some time for the Zamindar to come out. The latter had had a hasty bath and was dressed in his best. A silken

Kurta over a pair of expensive Churidar Pajama's and a pair of kolhapurie chappals. His pistol was snuggled safely in his kurta pocket. Accompanied by Rama he hastened towards the Baobab tree and passed the row of shacks with his right hand covering his nose. The two were fifty feet away from the tree when Rama stopped ." Master look at the rope," the servant said.

Vikram stopped as he noticed the rope. The snake was climbing down it and had nearly reached the ground. Vikram felt itchy at the base of his ankles and looked around for something high to stand on. There was nothing but the uneven ground.

"Rama", the Zamindar whispered.

"What is it master?," the servant asked as he walked upto him.

"Quick bend down on the ground like a horse."

The servant looked perplexed so Vikram caught his hair and shoved his head down. "On your hands and knees," he said.

Rama was now a horse and to his surprise the heavy Zamindar climbed onto his back. "Stay still", he ordered, "don't move or I'll fall."

Making the best of what was available and elevating himself as high as possible, Vikram stood balanced on Rama's back. He looked towards the rope and realized that the snake wasn't on it. It was lying on the ground with an upraised hood which looked at him. Pleased and scared Vikram folded his hands in prayer. "Oh lord", he said. "It has been with great difficulty that I have managed to search you out. You fulfilled my last request and got the English thrown out of this country. Oh how they used to fawn over us. I thank you most reverently for this. I have one more request to make. It is very small compared to the previous one. Please help me win the elections. If you bless me I am sure to win. I want to show these Congressmen what I am made of, and if I win I will make you a golden temple right on the spot where you are sitting on now."

"Master please get down," Rama groaned " I'm going to collapse"

"If you do I'll kill you." growled Vikram.

"But master."

"Shut up."

Vikram looked towards the tree and saw the rear half of the snake slither off in to the grass on the other side of the huge tree. "Now look at what you did," he said as he stepped down. "You caused the snake to go away."

Once on the ground he gave the servant a kick on the bottom and turned around to go back to the haveli where the Buick was waiting for him outside the verandah. Rama got up and followed his master back to the haveli where the latter climbed straight into the back seat of the big car. The hook beak nosed priest who was in his saffron best climbed into the front next to the driver's seat. The turbaned driver pushed the handle into the hole in the front fender and connected it to the crank pully. Yanking the handle he looked pleased as the engine roared to life. He threw the handle into the dickey and climbed into the car behind the steering wheel. Gunning the engine, he saw Shiva Rama and the villagers put their hands to their ears. The Buick had emanated an ear splitting roar. Vikram Singh's roar to the voters telling them that he was coming.

The heavy vehicle slowly trundled down the driveway as the villagers followed slowly from behind. Passing the double lioned gate the vehicle turned right and picked up speed on its way to the different villages where Vikram would warn the villagers of dire consequences if they did not vote for him.

"There goes the headache," commented Shiva Ram as he walked with the villagers who all nodded their heads, "Just let our party win," he said, "we will teach these Zamindars a lesson".

The group went on walking and when they were out of ear shot from the Haveli, Shiva Rama shouted. "We will abolish Zamindari and bring these cursed people to heel. Down with the Zamindars", he bellowed.

"Down with the Zamindars", the villagers yelled.

"Vikram Singh Murdabad," Shiva Ram yelled.

"Vikram Singh murdabad ," the villagers yelled back.

The roar of the Buicks silencer less engine was too loud for Vikram to hear the slogans as he sat in the rear seat of his comfortable big car feeling as happy as could be. The vehicle roared on as it bounced and bucked over the uneven rutted road. Reaching a village the car drove to the square where a group of villagers were assembled and sat cross legged on the ground in a group. Seeing him four of them got up and walked towards the vehicle and with folded hands greeted him. "Welcome master", they said, "we are honored by your arrival and were waiting for you. The whole village wants to meet you."

Vikram was visibly pleased as he stepped out of his car and followed the four back to the group of villagers who were all standing with folded hands in respect to him. "Are the free kitchens running?", he inquired. He had financed free kitchens in each village of his constituency and anyone who promised to vote for him could walk in and have a full meal of rice, dal and potato curry for free. "Is there enough food?," he asked.

"Yes master", replied the villagers, "There is plenty of food, we are very grateful. For the first time in our lives we are having a full meal not only once but twice a day."

"Good," replied Vikram as he turned to walk back to the Buick," What about the votes?"

"The votes are your's master. We are eating your food so who else will we give our votes to ?"

Pleased Vikram got into the rear seat of his car from where he gave his parting warning, "I'm feeding you all, remember that, if I don't get my votes you will have to pay. You know the consequences, don't you?"

The Villagers nodded their heads. "Yes master," they replied with their heads bent down low. " If we lie then cut off our heads"

Vikram made a sign to the driver and kicking up dust the Buick roared off on its way to the next village, the next kitchen and the next warning . The villagers who had been left behind looked at each other and smiled. "The fellow doesn't even know how to ask for votes", Some one commented. A tall gaunt looking man led them back to the spot where they had previously been seated, "The time has come for ourselves to get rid of these Zamindars," he stated, "the Congress party will win and Zamindari will be abolished. Down with the Zamindars," he yelled.

"Down with the Zamindars," the people yelled back.

"Shiva Ram zindabad," he bellowed.

"Shiva Ram Zindabad," the rest yelled back.

Vikram Singh could not hear the anti Vikram slogans. The Buick roared too loudly drowning the shouts as the driver steadily negotiated the vehicle across the uneven road. Vikram sat back in his big car. He was a happy man now. He was sure he would win and didn't expect what happened in the next village where he received a peculiar greeting. The village was under the Zamindari of a man who hated him .

The Buick roared upto a group of people who were discussing the elections. "It's Vikram Babu's car", shouted a lanky villager who immediately ran to the front of the vehicle and lifted his dhoti and urinated on the front fender, grill and radiator. Vikram Singh was surprised and angry. Nobody had the guts to look at him straight in the eye in these parts, forget urinating on the front grill and fender of his car right in front of him. The driver was also infuriated. He loved this car and didn't like the idea of washing urine dirtied vehicles. He would be the one who would have to do the washing so he swore and angrily opened the door . He took one step forward and stopped short. A short pucker faced boy had blocked his path and was urinating on him. The driver helplessly looked around as the boy stubbornly continued piddling on his dhoti. The former realized the villagers had surrounded the Buick and all of them were urinating on the body of the proud American car.

"What are you people doing?", yelled the priest from the front seat. He opened the door and stepped out adamant to give the people a dressing down and a lesson on ethics quoting liberally from the "Ramayana" and the "Mahabharata". Outside the car he realized his mistake as pee hit his dhoti and dribbled down his legs as though he was doing the job himself. "Chee, Chee, Chee", he said in disgust. "Ram Ram Ram "

"Vikram Singh murdabad", yelled a piddler.

"Vikram Singh murdabad", the piddlers yelled back.

"Ram, Ram, Ram", exclaimed the disgusted priest who was now in the safety of the car. "It seems like Kalyug has truly arrived".

This was too much for Vikram . He was red in the face as he looked around at the upraised dhoties and the urinators urinating on his beautiful big car, his status symbol as they shouted slogans against him. His driver was standing sheepishly outside and the bearded priest had slunk back into the vehicle with a scared and apologetic look on his face. So the Zamindar whipped out his little silver Colt and opened his pee wet door. Stepping out he raised the pistol above his head and fired two shots in the air. The urinators scampered off in different directions wetting their dhoties as they ran.

"Cheeee!," exclaimed Vikram in disgust as he saw the wet shades on the black body of the car as yellow liquid dripped to the ground.

"Chee, Chee!," said the disgusted driver.

"What chee chee!," scolded Vikram. "Get in and lets get out of here and remember to stay clear of villages that aren't in my Zamindari. I don't want any more of these experiences."

The Buick roared on its way to another village, a safe village that belonged to Vikram's Zamindari. Due to the loud roar of the engine Vikram did not hear the piddlers shouts and yells zindabading Shiva Ram and murdabading himself. Vikram reached the next village and received a warm welcome. The free kitchens were running and every one was well fed. The people would give him their votes. Vikram left them after giving a final warning of dire consequences if they did not vote for him after which the driver steered the roaring vehicle out of the village on it's way to the next one.

The great day came and Vikram had visited all the villages in his Zamindardom. He would rake in the votes today so he dressed up in his best. He wore white silk churidars and his paunch was hidden under a kurta which was made of the finest silk from Bhagalpur. Putting his pistol in his kurta pocket, he climbed into the Buick behind the steering wheel while the Brahmin priest, the two pehelwans and the driver climbed into the back. Rama yanked the handle yanking the six cylinders to life causing the engine to emanate a loud roar. Vikram Singh's roar. Telling the voters. "I am coming."

Vikram drove off steering the vehicle along the dirt track following ruts. jumping and skipping over obstacles, giving the people in the back a rough time. He drove fast not caring for the old American's well being or its bad health. He had to cover many villages in a very short time and rake in the votes.

At the first village he was greeted by the village head man who approached the vehicle with his hands folded in respect. He was short, dark and fat and wore a kurta over a white dhoti.

"How is the polling going?" asked Vikram.

"Perfect master," replied the head man, "don't worry about our village. Every one is voting for you."

"Good," said Vikram as he meshed the gears and drove on. The Buick kicked up dust on the headman's face as the vehicle roared out of the village .

"Okay," yelled the headman, "the headache's gone. Continue voting for Shiva Ram and make sure no one votes for the Zamindar."

The vehicle roared on and Vikram turned around for a glance at the four people sitting behind him. They all had excited looks on their faces so Vikram smiled and turned back to pay attention to the road along which he was driving the old American. "Punditjee" Vikram shouted over the Buick's roar as he honked the car's horns at a bullock cart. The bullocks panicked at the approaching noise and rushed into the wheat fields to the right with the cart jumping and bouncing behind the animals while the rider tried desperately to pull in the reigns. Vikram grinned. "Proper response to a car," he muttered. "Punditjee," he shouted again, "Do you think I will lose ?"

"Concentrate on your driving Judgemaan," the priest shouted back. He was having a tough time trying to sit straight in the madly bucking vehicle. "Your driving too fast," he yelled.

Vikram Singh grinned and increased speed causing the car to buck and bounce more . The vehicle soon arrived at the next village and drove upto the polling booth which was a simple white washed brick room with a tiled roof. "Panditjee", ordered Vikram, "Go into the booth and quietly see who they are voting."

The bearded priest opened his side of the vehicle's door and stepped out. Rubbing his bottom he slunk out towards the polling booth as seven villagers walked upto the car. All of them had their hands folded in respect and namastayed the Zamindar. " All the votes are being cast in your favour", they collectively told the master.

"And Shiva Ram?," asked Vikram.

"Not one vote has been cast in his favour."

"Good", said Vikram," If I win......" The Zamindar was cut short by a scream from the booth as the bearded priest poked his head out of the window. Judgemaan," he yelled," Not one vote has been cast in your favor. They are all voting for Shiva Ram".

"What ," retorted Vikram as he got out of the Buick and pulled out the pistol from his kurta pocket. The two Pehelwans had also got off and were behind him. "I will teach you a lesson", Vikram growled as he fired into the air and barged into the polling booth. The Pehelwans hit any one who came in their path, " Get out ," Vikram shouted, "Everyone of you get out,"

The villagers hastily slunk out.

"Two of you stay back," ordered Vikram and with the help of the Priest and the Pehelwans he hastily stamped his symbol on the ballot papers. The symbol was a goat, so goat after goat was stamped and the papers were hurriedly folded and put into the ballot box.

"Vinnay," Vikram shouted to a Pehelwan," You stay back here and make sure all the papers are stamped in my favor while I go with the others to the next village. They may be upto tricks there also,"

At the next village Vikram got a similar shock and fired his pistol at the crowd just above their heads. They had all been voting for Shiva Ram and most of the votes had been cast by the time the Zamindar arrived. Hearing the pistol shots the villagers scampered off as a furious Vikram took hold of a ballot box and dumped it into a nearby well. He saw the huge splash the box made and watched as it sank easily . "Panditjee bring the other box," he yelled.

The bearded priest obliged and came running out of the brick walled polling booth holding the box and threw it into the well. He watched grinning and showed his white teeth as the box sank. He was enjoying the whole episode.

Vikram was now desperate as he ran towards the Buick whose engine he had left running idle. Getting in he slammed the door closed behind him and meshed the gears, gunned the engine and released the clutch pedal causing the Buick to leap forward. The Priest and the remaining pehelwan dived into the moving vehicle and slammed the doors shut behind them.

"The scoundrels have made a fool out of me", Vikram shouted above the vehicles roar. "Let the election end and I will teach every one a lesson. " The furious Zamindar had his foot on the accelerator and the Buick sped down the dirt track jumping and bouncing on liberal coil springs like a bucking bronco. The Priest and the Pehelwan were thankful for the plush rear seats of the big car. Approaching a village the occupants of the Buick saw a bunch of horse and bullock carts blocking the road. Vikram honked on the cars horns and as the vehicle came closure, the Zamindar realized that none of the carts were hitched to animals. The Buick skidded to a halt five feet from the first cart.

Honking on the cars horns, Vikram saw a group of men get up from behind the carts. It was a road block. Getting out Vikram. shouted , "Remove the carts why are you blocking the road.?"

"Master," one of the villagers shouted, " go back we won't allow you to go further ."

" Remove the carts," yelled Vikram.

" No master," shouted back the villager, "we know you have come to rob our votes. We will not allow you to do that".

Word had spread like wildfire, faster than the Buick that the Zamindar was on the rampage. That he had gone berserk and was robbing votes or throwing ballot boxes into wells. This particular village had blocked the road and the residents were ready to fight for their rights."

"Remove the carts," Vikram yelled again .

"Over our dead bodies," was the reply.

"Then there will be dead bodies ," Vikram muttered as he climbed back into the Buick. Never before had any Ryot spoken back to him. Pink faced he rammed the gear into reverse and the Buick shot back sixty feet and stopped. Slamming the gear back to forward the Buick leapt and picked up speed till it crashed into the bullock carts turning one over. Reversing, the heavy vehicle shot back fifty feet and stopped and leapt forward again until it smashed into the Bullock cart and turned it over on its back.The Buick roared back and shot forward a third time, smashing the bullock cart and pushing away another as it dug itself deeper into the jumble.

"Marro salle ko," shouted a villager who saw his cart getting crushed. In response the other men picked up stones and pelted the reversing vehicle.

Slamming the gear to forward Vikram put his foot down on the throttle and let the clutch go. The vehicle shot forward and the Zamindar ducked and threw himself flat on the seat. A hail of stones hit the windscreen and a particularly big one smashed the glass infront of the steering wheel. The Buick barged on as the heavy engine forced the heavy vehicle to plough through the carts, upturning them, crushing them with the wheel's spinning over splintering bamboo and wood. The head light lamps got smashed and shards of glass fell to the ground. An iron rod from a cart pierced the grill and radiator and a particular clanging noise told the Zamindar that something had gone wrong with his vehicle as it stopped. The engine coughed and fell silent and died and the clanging stopped as the Buick stood still in the jumble of overturned carts.

"Throw stones," shouted the villagers as they pelted the stricken vehicle with stones. Glass shattered, the rear view mirror fell down and the side windows smashed to pieces. The priest and driver and the pehelwan lay on the floor board cursing themselves and the pelters while glass flew over them.

"Judgemaan," shouted the priest, "do something or be killed,"

Lying on the front seat with glass flying over him, Vikram pulled out the pistols' magazine, took out the used shells and put in fresh ones and slammed the magazine back into place. With his feet he unlocked the door and pushed against it causing it to open. Getting up he slipped out of the stricken vehicle and crouching behind the heavy door he fired two rounds at the crowd. The bullets luckily hit no one.

The villagers stopped and looked at the gun toting Zamindar who fired a third shot in the air. Getting cold feet they turned and scampered off through the fields. Getting up Vikram adjusted his dhoti and disheveled kurta and opening the rear door of the vehicle, he looked in. The driver, the pehelwan and the priest were piled over each other,

" Punditjee you can come out now ," Vikram announced.

The priest got up and brushed the glass from his clothes as the other two brushed theirs. "Judgemaan I thought we had it," he said.

The driver and Vikram walked to the front of the car and the former opened the bonnet. The driver peered in and shook his head. He knew it was futile to start the engine without getting the radiator repaired and the fan replaced. That was the end of Vikram's fight to rake in the votes. He realized he had been made a fool of by the lowly Shiva Ram and the cunning voters of the different villages. They had happily eaten from his kitchen and voted for the upstart.

Vikram and his group walked back to Ramnagar from where bullocks and men were sent to tow the Buick back to the haveli. The Zamindar did not bother to go to supervise the counting of the votes. He knew he had lost.

The Non Believer Dies

As usual Vikram got up early and did his morning ablutions. He had a refreshing bath sitting cross legged at the well with Rama pouring buckets of water over him. He prayed to the sun and then asked for a towel which Rama gave him. Wiping his body, he wore a fresh clean dhoti and walked over to the thatched roof under which the headman and a couple of villagers sat waiting for him. Acknowledging their namastays he sat down cross legged near the hole in the wall and made a sign to Rama which meant. "Bring me a cup of tea and my pistol."

Rama ran over to the haveli's verandah as Vikram turned towards the two bare backed Pehelwans who walked into the thatched roof with one of them holding a small steel cup which was half full of mustard oil. Smearing the oil over the Zamindar's body, they proceeded to massage his back.

"Any news?," Vikram asked the headman.

"Bad"

"What?"

"Shiva Ram won by one lakh votes."

Vikram turned pale and shrugged. "How many votes did I get?," he asked.

"Only twelve hundred."

Vikram raised a hand and the Pehelwans stopped massaging him.

"I told you not to contest the elections," continued the headman. "Now look at what you've done."

"They cheated me," replied Vikram.

"You failed to understand the voters,"

"They cheated me."

"How?"

"They ate from my kitchens and voted against me."

The headman fell silent. He did not have the courage to tell Vikram that it was he who had tried to cheat the voters. The latter had simply seen through his game and had made a fool out of him.

"I think you should leave this village for a couple of days", suggested the headman.

"Why?"

"There is going to be celebrations in this village and in the other villages in this area. I don't think you'll like it."

"Mukhiyaji you are wrong. The people will celebrate. But they will do it at a distance from this compound," replied Vikram.

"You are still wrong, you still haven't gauged the people's mood. Do you know the first thing the Congress party will do?"

"What?"

"They will abolish Zamindari. From now on government agencies will recover taxes directly from the land holder."

Vikram fell silent and looked at the ground. "The English shouldn't have left," he muttered.

"What did you say?"

"Nothing."

Rama arrived with a tray on which balanced five little steel glasses which were half full of tea. He gave the first cup to Vikram, the second to the headman and the rest to the villagers and then walked out from under the thatched roof and waited for further orders as he held the Zamindar's pistol in his right hand. He didn't have to wait long. As he stood in silence listening to the tea drinkers blowing into the hot liquid and sipping it noisily, he heard the distant sound of drums. The sound gradually grew louder and louder as the Zamindar grew paler and paler till it finally reached the double lioned gates where the procession stopped. A group of people were dancing to the rhythm of the drums as others threw red vermilion powder in the air.

"Down with the Zamindar," some one yelled,."

"Down with the Zamindar," the processionists yelled back.

The dancers went on jumping and prancing about in their weird dance.

"Abolish Zamindari, " the person yelled.

"Abolish Zamindari," the people yelled back.

Vikram was red faced with anger. His chin quivered and his hands shook as he watched the people openly shouting slogans against him in front of his gates.

"Open the Zamindar's dhoti," a person shouted.

"Open the Zamindar's dhoti," the processionists yelled back.

This was too much for the Zamindar. He yelled and got up and ordered his pehelwans to beat up the revelers.

"But there are thousands of them," replied the elder pehelwan," and only two of us".

Vikram looked at the two wrestlers standing foolishly behind him. He turned to Rama and asked for his pistol.

"Here it is master", said Rama as he handed the little weapon to Vikram who pulled the magazine out of the butte to see if it was loaded. It was, so he slammed the magazine back into place and pushed back the safety catch. "You'll pay for this," he yelled and fired into his own roof.

The revelers heard the pistol shot and stopped and looked towards the thatched roof. The Zamindar had lowered his weapon and was aiming it at them. Terrified they turned and ran into the wheat field that surrounded the smiling scare crow.

"Cowards," Vikram shouted. "Base cowards. That's what they are."

"You shouldn't have done that," the headman warned.

Vikram whirled around and glared at the headman. " I know what I should do and what I shouldn't", he growled.

The headman fell silent.

"It was you who instigated me against the English," the Zamindar continued, "It was you who instigated me to pull down the flag,"

"I did nothing wrong," replied the headman," I just helped you to take advantage of the situation as the country was getting its independence."

"Take advantage of the situation!," Vikram roared," and you saw the result."

"I told you not to contest the elections."

" Do you know what I now realise?"

"No"

"The English shouldn't have left this country. The English should not have left this country. It will now be ruled by uneducated people like those people who were dancing out there.

The headman and the villagers looked up as froth dribbled down a corner of Vikram's lips.

"Do you know who created the Zamindar?," Vikram yelled again. The onlookers nodded their heads.

"It was the English. They created the Zamindar so that they

could rule the land through them .And these idiots, these big headed fools, these morons ..."

"Who are you speaking of?," asked the headman.

"The Zamindar's who helped the Congress party. They were fools to help the Congress. They hacked off their own feet with their own axes. The country was prosperous and happy under the English. Why was it necessary to fight for independence? Independence from what?"

The villager's quietly looked on.

"Independence from what?," continued Vikram, "independence from a good strong law abiding government to that ruled by the rabble . By the commoners. Do you know what the Englishman once told me? He said that there was too much hatred amongst Hindus and Muslims, and amongst the Hindus themselves and the Muslims themselves for this country to be a good democracy. He said that the people were too illiterate to know what was right for them. It was the English who came to this land and fought many fractured kingdoms. They used their brains and conquered a country which had been divided into a thousand pieces by Raja's and Maharaja's and Nabob's on the basis of caste and religion. It was the English who united this country into one whole mass that it now is. It was they who called it India. It was they that brought the people under a single government . This task would have been impossible for Nehru and Gandhi to accomplish. If they had tried, Nehru would have been branded a Brahmin and Gandhi a Kayastha and the rest of the country would have aligned with a king of their caste or Nabob of their religion. I now think the English man was right."

"Are you against independence?",asked the headman.

"Of course I am," Vikram yelled back."Now who is going to collect land revenues? People like Shiva Ram? Do you expect the money to reach the government? The money will pass through his house and in a room it will fall off". Vikram laughed at his own joke. "Do you know Mukhiyaji. These people will turn out bigger crooks than we Zamindars were. They will rob this country to the last roti and the last glass of water and the the people will fight each other in the name of caste and religion. This is what the English officer told me . He made fun of me when I prayed to snakes." Vikram stopped and thought."Aaaha, the snake", he continued. "The Nagraj. The English officer was remarkable. He noticed many things we didn't. He told me that half of us Hindus kill the snakes while the other half pray to them. Did you ever realize that Mukhiyaji? And I prayed to the snake. To think of it. I prayed to the snake.I asked for a boy child and I got a girl. I asked for victory in the elections and I lost. Do you know 'Mukhiyaji what I think ?".

The headman shook his head.

"The snake isn't a god. It is a creation of god that travels at the level of our feet. Man was made to kill it and the snake was made to bite man. There never can be friendship between the two. And to think that I prayed to these creatures all these years, all my life. Rama." he yelled. "Take these two pehelwans and take sticks and kill all the snakes in this compound. I don't want to see any of these creatures alive on my lands. It is these creatures that have brought me misfortune. Go Rama and the two of you and bring back dead snakes by evening. I will pay you fifty rupees for every creature you kill."

Rama looked at the two pehelwans who looked back at him.

"What are you three looking at each other for?", asked the Zamindar. "Take a lathi each and go and remember. Don't come back empty handed."

The two pehelwans walked out from under the thatched roof and joined Rama and together the three trotted towards the line of shacks in which the peasants lived. On the way, near the lonely flagless flag pole they picked up a lathi each from the ground and trotted on till they were past the row of shacks,when they finally stopped on the boundary of a field. The two pehelwans put their sticks down and sat cross legged on the ground.

"Come on lets go to that big tree," said Rama as he pointed his right hand fore finger towards the Baobab tree.

"Are you going to kill the snakes?", asked the elder of the two pehelwans.

"Yes", replied Rama, "The master told us to".

"But we pray to them. They are a god".

"We pray to the photos of the snake around lord Shiva's

neck", replied Rama ,"not to any snake you see,"

"Don't you pray to the snakes?", asked the Pehelwan.

"No,"

The Pehelwan did not realize how much Rama hated the reptilian wo.ld after his wife had died. He did not believe in snake gods or in the powers of the Ojha.

"But we pray to them," replied the Pehelwan.

"Well I don't pray to them", Rama replied, "and we'd better do what was asked of us. That's if you want to retain your jobs and if I don't want to hang upside down from that tree."

Rama turned and walked towards the Baobab tree. The two Pehelwans got up and followed him.

"Rama can you do us a favour?" the younger of the Pehelwans asked,"we'll help you search for the snakes, but you must do the actual killing".

Rama nodded his head and the three walked on scanning the ground and wheat fields around them till they reached the Baobab tree. They took turns and one by one climbed up the rope to the branch from which it was tied. There was a flurry in the foliage above them as crows, Pied Mynahs, a black headed Oriole and some Redvented Bulbuls took to flight. Undaunted the three humans climbed higher into the foliage and scanned the branches They unfortunately saw no snake so they climbed back down to the ground.

"Now where?," asked the Pehelwans.

"Lets walk towards the Banyan tree on the other side of the

pond," suggested Rama.

The two pehelwans followed Rama towards the pond and as they passed it they disturbed three Water Hens that had been skulking amongst the reeds. The three took the air and seeing the water Hens fly, a couple of purple blue Moorhens who had been sauntering over floating weeds and Lotus leaves got disturbed.

"Hah", shouted Rama as he waved a hand and watched as the birds ran for cover and not finding any took to flight. They flapped their wings and flew laboriously and feebly with the long ungainly red legs dangling behind. Rama's loud `hah' and hand waving not only disturbed the birds. The dragon fly who owned the pond had flown back from the Banyan tree seeing the humans trespass over his property. Hearing the loud `hah' it shot up higher and turned around and flew back. In the water the Boatman and the Back swimmer hastily swam to the other side of the pond.

The three men skirted the pond and walked on till they reached the Banyan tree where each of then climbed up a thick prop root and were soon standing on different branches and were partly hidden by the leaves.

"Watch out for those Bees", Rama whispered pointing to a swarm covered Honey Comb which hung from a branch fifteen feet above him. "Do any of you see any snakes?."

"No," the Pehelwans replied as they scanned the foliage above and around them. A Money Spider traveled down to investigate the intrusion. Like an ascending mountaineer it let go a long strand of silk out of it's body from which it hung as it went down. Reaching the humans it stopped and studied them with its eight eyes. Realizing that they were dangerous it slid back up taking the silk strand along with it.

Rama heard a loud noise on the upper branches and looked up. It was a huge brown Pariah kite which was looking down at the intruders. It had just flown over and had landed on the top of the tree.

"Hah," shouted the elder pehelwan and swung his stick at the bird. The stick flew smashing into the leaves and the disturbed kite opened its wings and flapping them lifted itself up into the sky and flew off to find a safer perch.

"There aren't any snakes here," Rama commented, "lets go and search another tree."

The three climbed down the prop roots and Rama picked up the spade as the elder of the Pehelwan picked up his stick which had fallen to the ground after disturbing the Kite. "Lets go towards the Mussahar village", said Rama as he turned and walked towards the north.

The three had walked some distance when the younger pehelwan noticed a rat hole. It was pretty large and he felt confident that a snake would be in it. "let's dig up the hole," he said, "and see what's in there".

Taking the spade from Rama he started digging into the ground. He lifted the spade above his head and swung it down into the soft earth.After the third swing, when he had lifted the spade for a fourth go, he saw a rat scamper out and desperately scamper away.

"There goes your snake," Rama commented as the Pehelwan put down the spade.

The three continued walking as they scanned the ground around them. They disturbed a pair of Hoopoe birds that had been running around and pecking at the ground. Further on a green colored Chameleon watched them with its turret like eyes as they dug into two more rat holes but found them empty and watched them as they walked on. They were nearing the Mussahar Village and by-passed a couple of Neem trees and stopped under a Crepe tree. Looking up into the foliage they saw the usual Crows and Mynah's and Bulbul's but there wasn't any snake except for a funny green vine hanging from the lowest branch. The three turned to walk on when Rama noticed the Vine move. So he turned his face to have a proper look at it. The head of the vine moved to its right and Rama realized that it was the snout of a pencil thin three foot long green coloured vine snake. In one movement the servant swung his lathi up and hit the twig around which the tail was lapped. The twig snapped and fell with the snake to the ground where the reptile curled itself up in self defense. Three more swift blows from the lathi and the snake was lying senseless on the ground.

"Club the eyes," the elder Pehelwan goaded, "it could have

taken our pictures,"

It was a popular belief that the dying snakes eyes photographed the killer and if the reptiles mate saw the eye, he or she would see the photo of the killer and would hunt the person down and kill him. So Ram lifted the lathi and clubbed the face and eyes till the former was flattened and the eyes were completely destroyed.

"That's one snake for the master," commented the elder pehelwan.

"Isn't the master crazy," commented the younger pehelwan.

"He's half mad. Or is he fully mad? Just a few days ago he was praying to the Nagraj and was asking for his blessings. And now he want's them killed."

"He's eccentric," commented the elder Pehelwan.

"Lets carry on," said Rama who had the dead snake balanced on his stick, "we'll have to kill more snakes".

The three turned to the left and proceeded towards a distant clump of trees where they had previously hacked down a Jamun tree and dug up a huge pit. Reaching the grove they approached the pit and looked in . The bottom was covered in tall grass so the three prodded it with their sticks to see if there was any movement. There was. A Chameleon scurried to safety followed by a Centipede. Grasshoppers hopped to the middle of the pit and hid themselves in the grass as brightly colored Shield Bugs gave out a foul smell. Spiders scampered into the safety of the undergrowth as psychedalically colored Butterflies took to the air. A white Goliath Beetle with black shades on its back dug itself into the mud wall of the pit.

But there was no snake.

Rama had dropped the dead snake on the ground before he had prodded into the pit with his stick. He re-balanced the dead reptile on the stick and looked around at the other trees. "Look into those trees," he said as he himself moved forward. The three walked upto a couple of Amla trees and looked up into the foliage. They saw past the fine feathery small leaves into the upper branches. Small greenish flowers were borne in clusters and ripe yellowish green fleshy fruits hung from stems . There were a few Red whiskered Bulbuls and a green colored yellow breasted Iora gouging on the fruits but there was no snake.

Still balancing the dead snake on his lathi Rama walked and stood under a Gul Mohar tree and looked up into the light feathery leaves of the open-branched tree which looked like an umbrella. The thick cluster of leaves made it difficult to peer into the branches so the servant walked on and looked up another tree. It was a Rain tree this time with a spreading crown which formed a canopy over the ground. He looked up and saw clusters of pale white flowers but saw no snake so he put his snake holding lathi carefully on the ground and sat down cross legged himself. The two pehelwans walked upto him and sat down.

"Its weird", said Rama, "how you see things daily, and when

you need them you cant find them."

"Weird", replied the elder of the two pehelwans. "Snakes can be seen slithering around these areas daily, but when you want one, none shows up."

"Now what will we do? The master won't be pleased on seeing a single snake. He'll be furious," Commented the younger pehelwan.

"And hell hang me from that tree."

"What should we do?"

"I got it," said Rama. "The pond. I'm sure there will be some watersnakes in the water. Lets kill one of them.

The three got up and Rama picked up the snake balancing lathi. The younger Pehelwan took the spade and the three walked hastily towards the pond. The day had drawn on and it was afternoon with the sun directly overhead. The three reached the pond and Rama dropped the snake while the younger Pehelwan dropped his spade. Lifting their dhotis to their thighs the two wrestlers waded into the water and splashed and kicked around making a lot of noise. They jumped and pranced in the water while Rama kept a vigil on the banks. The pehelwans stopped and looked at Rama who shook his head. "Splash more," the servant said so the two pehelwans jumped and pranced about as Rama looked on. No snake slithered out of the waters and the two wrestlers soon got tired and waded out.

"Now what do we do?", asked the elder wrestler to the

younger one who simply shrugged his shoulder.

"Don't know," replied Rama, so the three sat down and thought.

"I'm feeling hungry", said the younger Pehelwan.

"Me too", said the elder one.,

Lets go and have lunch", suggested Rama ," we could come back and continue our search,"

The two wrestlers nodded their heads so the three got up and walked towards the Baobab tree and the line of shacks. Passing under the tree they looked up and saw nothing so they walked on with Rama still balancing the dead Vine snake on his Lathi. The three had crossed the tree when Rama saw him. The snake was on the fields embankment and was slithering towards the line of shacks. It was Fangs who was headed towards the Zamindar's compound where he was sure he would find something to eat.

Rama stopped and pointed towards the reptile. The pehelwans stopped and looked with awe at the snake. "Are you going to kill that," the elder Pehelwan asked. "That is the Nagraj himself. The snake that resides around lord Shiva's neck,"

"It's just a snake, whispered Rama as he let the green Vine snake slide off his lathi and fall to the ground. "I'm going to kill it."

"Don't," warned the younger Pehelwan. "It is the lord and it hasn't hurt anyone". The two wrestlers folded their hands in silent prayer so Rama shrugged and lifting his lathi he let out an ear splitting yell before he charged. Running towards the snake with uplifted lathi he screamed again. It was a shrill "Aieeee."

Fangs felt the vibration of the feet pounding on the earth as the human ran. He turned his head around and saw the charging man. The face looked horrible and dangerous and the uplifted lathi told the snake what would happen next so it zipped off.

"Wham," the lathi hit the ground where the snake had been. Rama saw the snake zip forward so he ran on and lifted the lathi above his head and swung it down a second time. "Wham", it hit the ground but there wasn't any snake. The reptile was zipping on and had turned to its left so Rama turned and swung three vicious blows at the snake which all missed. "Wham, wham, wham", and to the servants horror he saw the reptile suddenly swerve and bark a "Khaa" at him, and with an open mouth and shining Fangs it lunged for his legs which the servant parted with a hop. The hop confused the snake who was unable to decide which leg to bite. The head swerved from the right to the left giving Rama enough time to react and run. The servant hopped over the confused snake as he dropped his lathi and ran back towards the two pehelwans.

Fangs wasn't a coward. He was a cobra , a being which was known to be very aggressive when disturbed. He avoided humans but was too majestic a creature to be chased about no matter how big the assailant was. This human had attacked him and he had tried to escape.The human had persisted on chasing him so the snake had turned around and attacked. Rama didn't know that for the cobra, the best form of defense was to attack.

Fangs lowered his head and zipped off after the fleeing human. He was furious and was adamant to bite him. He saw two other humans further off. One ran to the right while the other scampered off to the left and the one he was chasing ran on towards the big tree with the rope hanging from it.

Fangs picked up speed and zipped on and realized he was closing ground with the running feet. The brown sole grew larger and larger and larger and the snake was readying itself for the final lunge when the sole disappeared. The snake stopped and looked around. He realized he was under the big tree so he looked up and saw the human climb onto the branch and hastily pull the rope up behind him. The reptile was exasperated as it looked up at the terrified human. It was furious and barked out a couple of loud "khaa's" at the man who was now flailing his hands at him.

"Shoo," shouted Rama, "run off, go away".

The snake continued looking up.

"Go away you shaitan", shouted Rama as he gesticulated with his hands. He had just had a lucky escape and had lost the courage and ardor he had had a few moments earlier. "Shoo," he shouted, "go away, push off."

The snake refused to move so Rama looked around. He had scared the birds and all the little creatures that lived in the tree. "Where are the two pehelwans?," he wondered. They were no where to be seen so the servant broke a thin leafy branch and waved it at the reptile.

The snake watched the human waving the branch so he barked a couple of more "khaas" at the person. How he wished the idiot would come down so that he could bite the feet. The idiot however refused to come down and after some waiting the snake lowered its hood and slithered off in the direction from where it had come . It soon disappeared amongst the green stalks of the wheat field. Rama however refused to give up his safe perch on the tree. It took some time for him to gather his courage and throw down the rope with the help of which he climbed down. Keeping a careful watch around himself he gingerly walked to the spot where the snake had turned and attacked him. Picking up his lathi he walked back to where he had dropped the dead Vine snake, and scooping it up on the stick he walked toward the row of shacks with his eyes darting around to make sure the snake wasn't any where around. Nervously looking back, and seeing nothing , he walked on and soon reached the row of shacks and walked past them to the other side where he saw the two pehelwans standing in front of the thatched roof saying something to the Zamindar.

He saw something else. The snake that had chased him was sliding across the grass twenty feet behind the row of troughs. It had disturbed the cows who were all pulling at their tethers while some of them belched. Rama looked around and saw a twenty five foot long bamboo pole lying on the ground. He decided that the pole was long enough for a second attempt so he dropped the dead Vine snake and the lathi and walked upto the bamboo pole and picked it up by the fat end. Lifting the pole over his head he hurried back to where he had last seen the snake. He saw it slithering on though it had covered some more distance.

Rama gathered his courage and walked past the row of cows with the Bamboo held over his head. He turned left and aligned himself with the snake." Aieeee " he screamed as he started his run.

Fangs slithered on. His target was the rat hole he had previously visited. The hole from which the scorpion had run out and had been killed by the humans. He wanted to relax and having been attacked by the human he did not feel safe outside. He wanted to be deep down in a rat hole and the closest one was the one near the thatched roof. It didn't matter if the hole was near human settlement. Once underground he would be safe so he slithered on sensing that the hole was nearby. He felt the soft thump of the humans feet on the ground. The thumping grew harder and harder as the latter increased speed till it seemed to be pounding on the ground. Fangs didn't know that it was the same idiot chasing him. He felt the thump, thump, thump and the wham as the thin end of the bamboo slammed into the grass six inches to the right of his tail. He turned around with a loud "Khaa" and saw the long pole. It was the same human with the ugly look on his face. This time he was holding a long pole and was at a safe distance. So the snake turned back and zipped forward. It felt the thump thump thump and the wham, this time six inches to the left of its tail. It zipped on and knew it was in danger.

Rama swung the pole down and missed and felt the thin end splinter. Undaunted he ran on after the snake and lifting the bamboo swung it down again, stopping for an instant as the pole made impact. One shot, two shots three shots. All missed and Rama realized he was loosing. The snake was heading straight for a hole in the ground.

Fangs saw the hole as he zipped towards it. His tongue rapidly flicked out as he picked up molecules for his sensory glands. Just three feet to safety and he was there. His head shot into the hole and his body straightened and scuted in.

Rama saw the snakes head enter the hole. It was his last chance. He had repeatedly missed five shots. The bamboo was too long and heavy and coupled with his running it was impossible to aim straight . So he stopped and looked at the fast disappearing body which was entering the hole in a straight line. He took a deep breath and looking at the moving body he swung the pole down. The tip of the bamboo hit the tail which flailed. Rama lifted the pole for a second shot and saw his target disappear. There wasn't any snake where it had been a second earlier. There was only green grass and a black hole.

Fangs had felt the bamboo hit his tail. The pain had shot up his body further infuriating him. He wanted to turn around and fight . He however knew it would be futile to turn around just now as the pole was too long for him to make an effective attempt at the human. He calculated the latter would be prodding the hole with the pole to flush him out. He also knew that the tunnel he was in had another exit on the other side of the cavern he was headed for. He decided to scute out of this exit and skirt around the thatched roof and attack the hole prodding human from the back. In his anger he had forgotten that humans sat in front of this second exit also.

Vikram Singh was sitting cross legged in his corner under the thatched roof with his back to the hole in the wall. The two pehelwans were standing outside and had just told him about their inability to kill snakes. The thin bearded Brahmin had arrived and had given the Zamindar the news of the revelers, and who were reveling the most. As the the Priest spoke Vikram got tired sitting cross legged and decided to change his position as his back was hurting. He put his right hand down on the ground for support just six inches infront of the hole, just as the snake was reaching the opening. Thinking it was an attack the reptile who was already in a nasty mood shot its head out and dug its Fangs deep into the palm.

Vikram felt the sting shoot up his hand. For a split second he was paralyzed as he squealed a painful "aaah". and desperately flicked his hand to brush off the marauder. Fangs felt the wild jerk and at once let go off the hand and withdrew his head back into the hole, from where he watched the reaction of his attack.

The bearded Priest and the headman saw the snake bite and at once recognized it. They realized the Zamindar's predicament. He had been bitten by a cobra. Very few people survived its bite.

Vikram Singh's face was twisted with pain as he rubbed the bitten palm with his other hand. " Some one tie my arm," he gasped, "I must stop the blood flow,"

The two pehelwans rushed over and one of them grabbed the bitten palm while the other tore a part of his dhoti and tide it tightly around the wrist.

"That won't do," said Vikram ,"get some rubber and tie it tightly behind the wrist".

The younger pehelwan got up and ran towards the garage and came running back holding long rubber strips which the driver had given him. The latter had torn an old tyre tube and cut the rubber into strips to use as a catapult. Two of the strips were tied tightly around Vikram's wrist.

"Where's Rama?,"Vikram asked the people who had surrounded him.

One of the villagers looked towards the south and saw the servant ramming the bamboo pole into the rat hole. "Rama", He shouted , "the master wants you. He's been bitten by a snake."

Rama looked up from what he was doing and dropped the pole. He didn't know it was the same snake he had been chasing that had bitten the master. "Did a snake bite him?", he asked.

"Yes".

Rama ran towards the thatched roof where the villagers were all over Vikram, while a person rammed a lathi into the hole in the wall. Rama rose on his toes and peeped in from the top and saw the masters contorted face.

"Call the Ojha," some one shouted.

"No, no,no," shouted Vikram as he pushed some of tne villagers and the priest and stood up. "Don't call an Ojha." The priest looked at Vikram. "But the poison must be broomed out", he said.

"I don't believe in the Ojha's broom", Vikram replied.

The bearded Priest looked at the headman as the headman looked back at him. The two rubbers were tied tightly behind the wrist and the middle of the arm. "Then what are you going to do?," asked the headman. "The poison cannot remain in the hand".

Vikram sat down and thought. He was in a predicament and a slow realization crept into him. Why people turned to the supernatural and the Ojha or the village Godman for help.? The worst thing that could happen to some one living in a rural village was to be bitten by a poisonous snake. The only cure for it was to take an injection of an anti snake serum.

This was what the English officer had told him. These injections were most of the time not available in hospitals. Even if it was, the village was most probably miles away from the town or hospital. It entailed a long and painful bullock cart or tractor ride to the clinic and the victim would most probably die on the way. It was this desperation and feeling of helplessness that made villagers both Hindus and muslims turn to the supernatural for help. They had to turn to something for hope and the Ojha and Godmen were the only ones available. Powell had opened Vikram's eyes and he had seen too many good strong men die because of the Ojha's failure. Vikram understood his predicament and had a simple answer. "Tie me with a rope and chop off my palm," he ordered.

The headman looked at the bearded Priest. They understood that Vikram had chosen the Mussahar's way out. The people of the Mussahar community, if bitten by a snake, would generally get the bitten limb chopped off. That was how they survived snake bites.

"Come on chop off my palm," Vikram ordered.

The people standing under the thatched roof looked at Vikram but did not move . All of them were vegetarians and had never chopped off a chicken's head, forget chopping off a human's palm. That also the Zamindar's.

"Come on, take a rope and tie me up," growled Vikram.

The people lowered their heads and looked at the ground.

"If necessary chop off my arm ."

"Judgemaan," said the bearded Priest, "by not calling the Ojha, You are playing with your life. You are making a big mistake. You ordered these people to kill the snakes. You shouldn't have done that. It was the snake gods revenge on you and your sacrilegious deed. He sent the shaitan to bite you."

"Shut up," Vikram growled," If you can't chop my palm off, then go and fetch my car . I'll go to the hospital that is in Monghyr.'

"What will happen if the medicine is not available there?," asked the headman.

"The doctor will make me unconscious and he will amputate my hand. That was the second option the Englishman told me of."

The headman understood,"But your car is damaged," he reminded Vikram.

"Then get the tractor and trolley and put a charpoy in the trolley."

Rama and the villagers ran off towards the garage and helped push start the blue Fordson Major tractor. The turbaned driver backed it and the villagers hitched the trailer to the tractors tail. Rama picked up the drivers charpoy and dumped it into the trailer. He then flushed some hay over the charpoy and shouted to the pundit," Punditjee, the tractor is ready."

Vikram walked towards the trailer followed by the headman. the bearded Priest and the other villagers. Precious time had been wasted arguing under the thatched roof and Vikram felt the dull pain in his right hand. He was helped onto the trolley and made to lie on the charpoy. The rest of the people piled in and the tractor lurched forward and was off. It chug-chugged down the supposed to be graveled driveway to the double lioned gate and turned left along the dirt track which led to the narrow strip of tarmac which was the highway which led to Monghyr.

Vikram was worried and was looking up at the sky. His was an emergency case and the tractor was lumbering on very slowly. The springless trailer jumped and bounced on the uneven road and each jerk hurt the Zamindar and seemed to increase the throbbing in his palm.

"You are in deep trouble," continued the bearded Priest, "You should be praying to the Gods and asking for their help. You shouldn't have ordered the people to kill the snakes. Now look what the Nagraj has done to you."

"It was the Englishman who has made him a non-believer," added the headman, "he infused his English ideas into him,"

"Don't be a non-believer," warned the Priest, "You are already in deep trouble, and you are purposely heading for more,"

"Then what am I to do?, asked Vikram as he winced from a violent lurch from the trolley.

"There's still time. Lets go back and get an Ojha," suggested the bearded Priest.

"He will cure you," added the headman.

Vikram shook his head. "No" , he said, "I'm going straight

to the hospital."

"That Englishman will kill you."

Vikram looked up at the blue sky and wondered where the Englishman could be? What would he be doing now. If he had been here, he would have been of great help. He had been a powerful officer and could have easily procured the injection.

"Your going to kill yourself Judgemaan," Continued the Priest.

"Will you all shut up," growled Vikram

The people chattering in the trailer fell silent as the tractor chugged on. It soon reached the thin strip of tarmac and turned left to travel down the pot holed road towards the town of Monghyr. On the way four more villagers climbed into the moving trailer when they heard what had happened. They were petty Zamindar's and Vikram was their leader . They respected the latter and didn't want him to die so had piled in to help. What they didn't understand was why the tractor was headed to Monghyr?

"Because he wants to go to the hospital there," said the Priest.

"Why"?, one of them asked.

"To take some English medicines."

"But we are approaching the temple", the person reminded the people in the trailer. He was a tall heavily built man with a round face and was wearing a white kurta over a dirty dhoti. The other three were shorter and thinner than him and were dressed shabbily in dhotis and kurtas.

The road ahead turned right and skirted a temple. The people sitting on the trailer remembered it. The shrine was renowned for its power to heal. Especially snake bite victims. This particular temple had been built precisely on the spot where a snake bite victim had been cured. The ground had been adjudged holy and the temple had been built. It was a Shiva temple.

"Aaah, we forgot about it", Commented the younger Pehelwan.

"The master is sure to be cured here", commented Rama "We completely forgot about the temple,"

"Lets stop at the temple," suggested the headman, "and take Vikramji there. The priest has cured hundreds of snake bite cases. He's sure to cure him too."

Vikram was scared now. Here was another hurdle. The temple was highly venerated in the area and the people were sure to stop him. He knew he was loosing time. He had once told the Englishman about this temple. The latter had pooh-pooed it's powers . "The fellow must have been bitten by a water snake", he had said, "and not a poisonous one". The Englishman always had simple answers to his complicated questions. "You must understand religion Mr Singh," he had once said, "you must understand the relationship mankind has with God. Don't expect instant remedies. This isn't an age of miracles though they sometimes do occur. But these are rare.

One in a thousand cases. If you are ever bitten by a snake, take the injection. If it's not available then get that limb amputated."

"I'm not going to the temple," Vikram retorted

"What!", asked the Priest, "and why won't you go to the temple?"

"I want to go to the hospital."

"But the temple –."

"I want to go to the hospital."

"But at least take the blessings of the Priest", intervened the village headman.

"Look here I've lost enough time arguing," said Vikram. He realized that the trolley had stopped and the tractor was standing silent with the driver looking back at him. "I have got very little time left."

"Have you become a Christian?," asked the headman.

"No"

"Then why wont you go to the temple for the lords blessings."

"I want to go to Monghyr."

"You will kill yourself Vikramji," the headman retorted, "at least take the blessings of the lord. We can carry on again.

Vikram realized he was stuck. He had lost more precious time arguing and the dull throb in his hand told him so. He had little time left, and to resist would mean more argument. It would be better to humor the villagers, do a hasty namastay and ask for the lords blessings and carry on." Okay I will go in one condition", he said, "we pray to the lord and carry on".

The others agreed and a now humbled Zamindar looked sheepish as he was helped down the trailer. He quietly walked towards the temple door. His blood pressure and the pain near the rubber bands gave him his latest position and as he reached the doorway, he realized the Priest had shut the door and was blocking his path. "Now what?", he thought.

"Now what?," the villagers thought.

The temple's Priest was shaking his head and stated that he wouldn't allow Vikram to enter the temple with his hands tied. This was an insult to the deity and an insult to the latter's powers. "If Vikramji wants to enter the temple", he announced, "he can do so only after opening the rubbers tied around his hand and arm. To enter the temple he must have full faith in the lord."

This was the last straw. Vikram turned to walk back to the tractor when a confused headman stopped him. The Zamindar was feeling faint. The villagers also feared opening the rubber straps and were now in an awkward situation. They knew what would happen if the rubber straps were opened. What should they do?, what could they do? Hesitantly they gave way to the Priests order."

"Punditji", the hook beak nosed Priest suggested. "Open the straps with your pure hands."

Vikram stepped back. He felt that he was living in a dream. The people around him had all gone mad, or was it possible that he himself was mad? At ordinary times he would have done what he wanted and would have barged out of the group of villagers. He was very weak now and was being treated like a child, a sick child who was shying away from on injection which the elders were forcing him to take. Vikram realized he was too sick to fight back and his silence was adjudged as acceptance.

The priest opened the rubber straps as Vikram gave a final plea. "Please chop off my hand".

The rubber bands were opened and Vikram felt the surge of blood into his arm carrying with it the venom he had so successfully blocked. He felt the cold sensation rush up his arm and spread to other parts of his body. This cold feeling quickly turned warm and then hot and the Zamindar felt nauseous. Two steps into the temple and he was pleading in a feeble nasal voice. "Chop off my arm someone. My body is burning."

Vikram was five steps into the temple when the people helping him felt him go limp. His legs gave way and the entire weight of the body fell on the people who were holding him. They lay him down on the floor and the priest hastily chanted prayers, sprinkled holy water over the body, blew incense smoke and ran a broom over him as the villagers anxiously watched.

The Priest finally shook his head. "He was a non-believer," he announced, "he came in here with a closed mind. He did not have faith in the lord who has refused to help him. I am sorry I cannot do any thing now."

The onlookers were shocked as they looked at the Priest and the dead body. They pulled themselves together and gently carried the body back to the trailer where it was laid on the charpoy. The rest pushed the tractor and trailer till the former coughed to life after which the villagers piled into the trailer. The driver turned the vehicle around and headed back for Ramnagar where Vikram's young wife wailed over his dead body and as a custom broke the glass bangles that had beatified her hands to show that she was now a widow. News of the Zamindar's death spread like fire and soon the compound was packed with curious villager's and ryots. The two Banana trees that had remained standing behind Rama's house were chopped down and the stumps were loaded onto the trailer next to the charpoy which still had the dead body lying on it. The tractor was unhitched from the trailer, push started and hitched back to the trailer. The pehelwans, Rama, the bearded Priest and Vikram's seven year old son climbed in and the tractor belched smoke and chugged out of the compound with the dead body in the trolley and the crowd following from behind.

"Ram Naam Satya Hai," the Priest yelled.

"Ram naam satya hai," the crowd yelled back.

The tractor slowly chugged on and the procession behind it swelled as more people joined it chanting "Ram naam satya hai". The procession soon reached the Ganga where the tractor was stopped and the body was carried to the banks of the river.

It was made to lie on its side and the two Banana stumps were tied to both the sides. The Bearded Priest took the dead bodies hand and chanted some prayers after which the child was made to sprinkle water on the sandwiched body. Some people took hold of the stumps and the body and carrying them they waded into the water till they were chest deep in where they pushed the three into the currents. The crowd stood silently and watched the dead sandwiched Zamindar float away till he merged with the waters and could not be seen any more. The crowd then waded into the river and had a holy bath after which they dispersed and went back to their homes.

That evening as villagers sat around fires warming themselves, the main topic of discussion was the dead Zamindar. His death had enhanced their belief in the supernatural. The English officer he had known had made him a non believer, and the Zamindar had challenged the snake god, the deities and the power of the Priest. He had been rash and had ordered all the Nagrajs to be killed and had been bitten by the Nagraj himself, and had chosen English medicines to those of the divine. The villagers had seen for themselves first hand the result of sacrilege.

Vikram Singh the non-believer had died.

Captured

The month of July ushered in the monsoons and the repeated showers changed the countryside which was now covered in different shades of green. There was a marked difference from the previous season when the world seemed to be parched and dry and heat and dust prevailed over natures sleeping bounty. Repeated showers caused dormant seeds to come to life while creepers crawled up anything they could get hold of. Like walls, dead wood, trunks of trees, mud mounds and even the remains of old discarded rusted motor cars. Trees echoed with the songs of birds who were delighted with the change in season as they shook off the water from their bodies. Humans prepared themselves for the sowing season as the paddy fields lay six inches deep in water where shoals of little fish made their appearance. Where did the fish come from? Nobody knew. It was believed that they fell from the skies with the rains. It was also believed that the frogs fell from the skies. Overnight the ground was full of them with their overworked larynxes' creating a din which was supposed to be a song. Huge yellow frogs were everywhere and they became a nuisance by hopping into human homes. They had to be broomed out, but they hopped right back in and hopped into bathrooms, kitchens, larders, bedrooms, on beds and even the prayer rooms making an appearance seated happily amongst the dieties.

The humans disliked the frog for two reasons. Firstly, they looked warty and ugly and secondly they attracted snakes. The reptiles greeted the monsoons with mixed feelings. They were first irritated when they were flooded out of their rat holes and had to search for a drier place to live in. Like on a branch of a tree or amongst the tiles of a tiled roof. After suitable lodgings were found, they made forays into the countryside where there was plenty of food. Frogs were everywhere. There were frogs to the left and frogs to the right. Frogs to the north and frogs to the south. Frogs in puddles and frogs in ponds. Frogs in bushes and frogs in human homes.

The old discarded rusting Buick did not like this season. It had caused the bamboo beams holding the tiled roof of the garage to rot, causing the latter to collapse onto the roof of the car. The vehicle had been lying in the ram-shackle garage for the last two years since the Zamindar had died. The tyres had deflated and the metal rims had dug into the ground causing the metal underbelly to change color to rust red. Inside the musty cabin, the seats, floor board and dashboard were covered in a layer of dust while some of the seat springs had sprung out through the upholstery. Cobwebs hung from the gear lever and amongst the spokes of the steering wheel while termites ate into the wood work that was once the proud dashboard. The wind screen was a haze of dust and bugs and mites had made the seats their home. Something else had made the car its home. It was the snake that bit the Zamindar two years ago.

Fangs had been flooded out of his rat hole and had made the Buick his home. He had found a hole on the floor of the trunk section and had slithered in to snuggle himself cozily on the spare tire of the vehicle. The dickey had been untouched by the humans since the Zamindar had died and Fangs found it a perfect place to hide from the outside world. Especially from the horrible Mongoose that he had seen lurking around. It was four days since he had last seen the female cobra's dead body. He had been traversing through the grass between the Baobab tree and the pond and had got the smell. The dead cobra's molecules had been picked up by his bifid tongue causing him to change direction and slither towards where she lay. Her body was bruised and the head had been chewed off. He realized that the Mongoose had eaten up her head. Frightened, he had slithered all the way back to the garage and had entered the trunk section where he remained holed for the last four days. He felt hungry now and wanted to eat. Gathering his courage he slipped out of the hole which was just above the differential. Sliding onto the round metal object he slid down to the floor and slithered towards the front of the car and stopped directly below the engine. Flicking his forked tongue, he slid out from under the car and out of the garage and turned left to slither past the discarded tractor which was partly hidden in a heap of tiles which was the caved in roof. Flicking his forked tongue he continued slithering over the ground and passed a hundred feet to the left of the thatched roof under which a lone figure sat on a cot. It was the bearded Priest who was perennially sucking at a chillum and puffing out smoke. Vikram Singh's death had proved a boon to him and since the late Zamindar's son was only nine years old, the widowed mistress had requested him to stay back and oversee the property. The Priest was now the spiritual adviser cum manager of the family and was incharge of the estate. By biting the fat Zamindar, the snake lord had virtually handed the property on a platter to him. That's why the Priest now paid extra respect to the snake. His silent pleading prayers to the former had born him fruit and the lord in one bight, had removed the Zamindar and made him the master.

Fangs slithered on past the thatched roof and turned right to slither past the row of empty troughs. The Priest had advised the mistress to sell all the cows and Fangs was thankful for that. Now he didn't have to pass a row of irritated animals who showed him their horns. Neither did he have to worry about getting trampled under their feet. That's why he sometimes dared to slither in and out of the line of troughs. This was previously unthinkable.

Fangs lifted his head and opened his hood to enjoy the fresh breeze that was blowing. He enjoyed the cool air and looked towards the north. "Hey there are frogs over there", he said and slid over the ground. Crossing a puddle he reached a dead log. Drawing his body along the dead wood he found a crack and peeped through it. There they were. A bunch of yellow Bull frogs were sitting around a puddle and were singing in a chorus to the sky. They seemed to be happy and relaxed and one of them shot out a long tongue, caught a fly and flicked it back into its mouth. Another frog shot out a tongue and captured a dragon fly and flicked it back into its mouth. This pleased Fangs who watched from the crack in the wood.

The bull frogs were actually calling out to attract a mate. One of them hopped from the other side of the puddle into the water and hopped out again and gave a couple of hops towards the dead log behind which the snake was hiding. Fangs waited expectantly and saw the frog give two more hops. He watched through the crack and drew his body behind it. He was tense as he calculated his next move. The log he was hiding behind was twelve feet long and if he traversed it, he would have to travel six feet to the right or six feet to the left. It would be futile to attack from such a distance as the frog would have enough time to hop away. The amphibian was just three feet away from the log and Fangs decided he would have to shoot over the dead wood to the other side and grab his prey.

The frog came closer and stopped. It gave a suspicious croak and hopped to face the right. Letting out another croak it gave two hops and was now facing the left. The dead wood usually teemed with bugs and termites and other minute creatures which had all disappeared. The amphibian found this queer and grew suspicious. It was sure that something dangerous was lurking behind the log.

Fangs saw the frog grow suspicious and knew the latter would hop away, so he tensed his muscles and shot his head over the wood to the other side. His long body scuted across the log with the head shooting towards the frog. The amphibian saw the attack and leapt. It sprang into the air as the snake's head shot up and caught its leg in mid air and fell to the ground. Fangs gave the frog a slight prick with his teeth, injecting two grams of venom into the creature after which he pulled away. The frog gave a couple of hops and lay still. Further on, near the puddle there was a commotion as the other frogs were desperately bounding away, splashing through water and squelching through slush to be as far away from the place as was possible.

Fangs drew his body up behind the paralyzed frog and with his snout he turned the head to face him. Opening his mouth wide, he took the snout in, and his bone teeth slowly walked the creature into his oesophagus after which he made a turn in his neck to push the frog into his stomach. "Aaah, that tasted nice", he thought as he lay there to relax as the frog settled down. An hour passed as he lay in the grass so he decided to go back to his new home. The dickey of the discarded Buick. Turning his head around he slithered down the length of his own body and slithered past the empty troughs. Turning left he slid past the thatched roof and slithered to the Buick. Slithering under the vehicle he travelled to the rear and wrapped himself around the axle from where his head entered the hole in the dickey through which he slipped into the trunk section to coil himself on the extra tyre. He would now relax for four days before he would venture out again.

The frogs had desperately hopped away across the field and had stopped near a clump of bushes "That snake is a nuisance", one of them croaked.

"It ate up my husband", said a female frog.

"What should we do?", asked a bull frog.

"Some one should do something about that snake", croaked another frog.

The frogs heard a squawk above them. It was a crow. "What is it?", the crow asked, "you frogs seem to be disturbed".

"It's that snake", croaked a Bull frog.

"It gobbled up my husband", complained a female frog.

"That snake is a pest", groaned another frog.

“Yes”, crowed the crow. “He is a thief. He stole and ate my eggs”.

“But your eggs are supposed to be on a tree?”, asked a frog, “how did he manage to reach them”.

“By the rope that Spiderman uses to hang from a branch”.

The frogs looked puzzled. “What is a Spiderman?”, they asked.

“It’s the human who likes hanging upside down from a rope from that big tree’s branch. Like how the spider does”.

The frogs were still puzzled. They did not know that the crow was referring to the regular hanging sessions Rama had to go through from one of the branches of the Baobab tree. The bearded Priest was now the master and was playing the master bit to the hilt. He was in fact overdoing it and had gone out of control. The late Zamindar’s cruelty seemed mild compared to the Priests harshness. Vikram Singh would pick a reason to hang Rama from the tree. But the Priest sometimes did it without any reason, especially when he was stoned after taking an extra dose of ganja.

“I still fail to understand what you mean”, replied the Bull frog, “please elucidate”.

“Go and see for yourself”, said the crow, “he is still hanging from the tree with the two fat humans sitting below him”.

“Forget the humans”, croaked a frog, “what do we do about the snake?”

The crow was startled by some harsh chattering and saw a

group of dirty untidy Jungle Babbler's fly over. "What is the meeting for?", they asked.

"That snake has just devoured a frog", replied the crow as he flew in circles.

"Don't worry", replied a Babbler, "I've got good news for you".

"What?", croaked a frog.

"The Mongoose has come".

"What?", asked the frogs in unison, "can you repeat what you just said".

"We just saw a Mongoose", replied the Babbler, "he was sniffing for the snake's trail near the pond".

"Yaaaay", croaked the Frogs as they happily hopped around.

The bearded Priest who was sitting under the thatched roof smoking his chillum wondered at the increase in the volume of the croaks. "The frogs are a pest", he thought, "they have nothing to do, but to croak and croak and croak".

"Can someone tell the Mongoose where the snake is hiding", croaked the female frog.

"It's not necessary", replied the Babbler, "the Mongoose has got the scent. He is heading towards where the humans live".

"Peelow, Peelow", called an Iora, "have you heard of the arrival of the Mongoose".

"We were just discussing it", replied the crow, "we hear he is headed for the human's homes".

"I think he will fight the egg thief", the Iora replied.

"Yaaay, it's a fight, it's a fight", croaked the frogs as they happily hopped around.

"Lets go and see what the Mongoose is doing just now", cawed the crow as he turned and flew towards the line of dilapidated roofless shacks where the Zamindar's peasants had once lived. The bearded Priest had asked the inhabitants to pay a rent which the peasants were unable to do. The furious Priest had got the shacks vacated. As time passed, the roofs had rotted and collapsed while some of the mud walls had crumbled.

The crow was closely followed by the Babblers and the Iora and on their way they were met by a dozen Bulbuls'. "Where are you all going?", cried the Bulbuls.

"There's going to be a fight", replied a Babbler.

"Between whom?"

"Between the Mongoose and the snake".

"Yippee", cried the Bulbuls as they flew along. "That snake thought that it was a king. The humans prayed to it thinking that it was a God. The snake had also started imagening that it was a God and had started behaving like one.

"Yes", replied the Babbler. "It had become very pompous recently. It had the habit of sitting on the round mud head of the bamboo man in the field opposite to those two lions. It behaved like a king and fawned over the flowing field below him".

"The Mongoose will teach him a lesson", replied the Iora,

"He will kill him and chew off the head."

"Like what he did to the other snake", added a Bulbul. "We saw the fight. It was ferocious. But the Mongoose finally won".

"Look the Mongoose is down there", cawed the crow.

Sure enough down below near one of the roofless shacks was a short brown colored creature, with a long shaggy body and long furry tail. It had a pink snout and sometimes stood on its hindlegs and sniffed at the air.

"Yaaay", the birds called, "the Mongoose is down there".

The Mongoose looked up at the sky and wondered at the noise the birds were making. He had important work to do and he felt hungry so he got down on all his four legs and scampered towards the row of empty troughs. He got the scent of the snake, and sniffing the ground he walked upto the dead log behind which the snake had hidden. Yes the smell was there and it was strong. He scampered over the log and reached the spot where the unequal fight had taken place between the frog and the snake. He got the whole story and sniffing the ground he doubled back to the line of empty troughs from where he scampered past the thatched roof with the lone smoke spewing human sitting under it. He continued sniffing the ground and passed the tractor whose driver the bearded Priest had given the marching orders.

"Yippee", cawed the crow, "the Mongoose has reached the iron horse".

"My nerves are all tense", replied a Bulbul.

"It's a fight, it's a fight", peelowed the Iora.

The Mongoose was now sniffing at the front deflated tyre of the Buick from where he cautiously scampered under the engine. Standing on his hind legs he peered into the rectangular iron bracket which once held the battery. Seeing nothing there he got down on all fours and crossed over to the section which had the steering rod sticking out. Seeing nothing there, he got down and crossed over to the differential. The smell was strong here and it led to the hole in the floor of the trunk section of the vehicle. The Mongoose realized his quarry was in there.

Inside the dickey Fangs got a fright and vomited the dead frog out. His forked tongue had picked up the Mongoose's molecules and he was scared. He remembered the female cobra's dead body and wondered what to do.

Outside the dickey the Mongoose realized that if he made too much noise the snake would remain inside the trunk section so he scampered out from under the car and hid behind the Garage wall where he waited and waited and waited.

Inside the dickey Fangs also waited and realized that his tongue did not receive any more dangerous molecules. He was scared, curious and hungry and so he peeped out of the hole. The ground beneath the car was empty so he poked his head out and looked towards the left and towards the right. There was no sign of the Mongoose so he slithered out to investigate. Not seeing anything, he slithered to his left and got a fright. The Mongoose was standing on its haunches behind the garage wall. Desperate, he zipped off between the tractors wheels to the rear wall of the garage and shot through a hole in the wall. He was soon out in the sunshine on the other side and was zipping towards a couple of Horse Radish trees which had recently come up in the fallow field.

The Mongoose had scampered under the tractor and realized the hole in the wall was too small for him to pass through, so he rushed out from under the tractor and skirted the garage wall and charged after the snake that was headed towards a couple of Horse Radish trees that had a thick bushy under growth at the base.

Fangs shot into the undergrowth and wrapping himself around the rough cork like bark of the tree he quickly climbed up by weaving in and out of the branches. He was soon on top of the young tree and had wrapped himself around the thin trunk which bent under his weight.

"There he is", cawed the crow.

"Where?", asked another crow.

"There on top of that tree with the fern like leaves".

Soon there was a swarm of crows flying in circles around the desperate snake.

"Where's the snake", asked the Babblers.

"There on the tree", squawked the crows.

"My God, what is it doing up there".

"It's on the run, its on the run", chirped a Bulbul".

"The coward", squawked a crow, "go down and fight".

"Thief, thief, thief", squawked the other crows.

"Come on. You thought you were strong", challenged another crow, "then go down and fight. Why are you cowering up there".

"It's a fight, It's a fight", called a Blue Jay who had been attracted by the commotion the crows were making.

Pandemonium prevailed in the tree. Scared grasshoppers leapt off the leaves into the underbrush and desperately hoped that they were camouflaged in the greenery. They dared not hop out since they were scared of being eaten by the birds that were circling the tree. A pair of green colored Chameleons scampered out of the undergrowth and looked with awe at the huge snake on top of the tree. Higher up in the fern like leaves green colored lynx spiders leapt nimbly from leaf to leaf to disappear into the underbrush. Bugs scampered away and beetle's took to flight while Money spider's slid down into the underbrush with the help of their silk threads as Tree Hoppers curled themselves up to resemble thorns.

"Where's the Mongoose?", asked a crow.

"There", replied another crow.

The Mongoose was sitting on a branch half way up the tree and was screeching at the reptile. Its senses told it that the stem of the young tree would not take the combined load of both the combatants. The Mongoose did not want to risk getting bitten in case the thin stem snapped and the two lost balance and fell to the ground.

High up, the cobra had lifted its head and had opened its hood. It was desperately looking around for an escape and was letting out vicious 'Khaas' at the circling crows that dared to come too close.

"Come on", squawked the crows, "You have got him, Mongoose."

"Give him a left", chattered a Babbler, "and give him a right. Batter him black blue and white".

"Come on climb the tree", called the Blue Jay, "and show him how strong you are".

"Fight, fight, fight", cawed the crows, "and show him your might. He is nothing but an egg thief".

"Khaa", screamed Fangs, "Khaa, Khaa, Khaa".

Unknown to the birds and the different creatures a man was walking towards the Horse Radish tree. Rama had just finished a stint of hanging from the Baobab tree and had returned with the two Pehelwans to the thatched roof. The bearded Priest had sent him to see what the commotion was about behind the Garage. The swarm of crows and other birds had made him curious.

Rama had skirted the garage and had walked towards the Horse Radish trees where he got a shock. The snake that was on top of the twelve feet tall tree, on the slightly bent stem looked horrible causing him to scream in fright. The scream scared the Mongoose who scampered down into the underbrush.

"Where's the Mongoose", called a Babbler.

"He's run away", replied a crow.

"Why?"

"The human scared him".

The crows crowed in unison. "Spoil sport, spoil sport. Humans are always a spoil sport".

For some unknown reason the human turned and walked away.

Fangs looked down and realized that the Mongoose had gone. His fright was too great for him to go down. He wasn't sure if the Mongoose had run away or lay hidden in the underbrush so he decided to wait and watch. For an hour he braved the circling crows and screamed 'Khaas' at them especially at the ones that tried to dive bomb and peck him.

"Come on Mongoose, where are you?", cawed a crow.

"The human has gone and you have nothing to fear", chattered a Babbler.

"Give him a left and give him a right. Batter him black blue and white", goaded a Blue Jay.

Fangs looked up and saw something which frightened him. He had been sitting wrapped on top of the tree braving the birds for more than an hour when he saw the big brown thing swoop down on him. The horrible face of a Pariah kite focussed into view. It had been attracted by the commotion and was now diving to capture the snake.

Fangs let out a couple of vicious 'Khaas' at the eagle who

swerved at the last moment and flew off. He knew he was trapped. It was a case of choosing between the frying pan and the fire. He decided to choose the fire since there were chances that the Mongoose had run away. Uncurling himself, his head slid down and he started his slow suspicious journey down. Leaf by slow leaf, branch by slow branch, twig by slow twig he travelled downwards with his head moving from the right and to the left trying to see what was in the underbrush.

The Mongoose was down there and lay hidden in the ferns and was watching the snake's slow progress down towards him.

The snake knew that the Mongoose could still be hidden in the underbrush. There was also a chance that it had scampered off frightened of the human. The eagle was flying around the tree in circles. He had to take the chance and he decided to crash into the foliage and zip out of it. He would surprise the Mongoose and try to escape.

The Mongoose was peeping through some fern like leaves when it got the surprise. It had seen the snakes tail portion wrapped around a branch while the head had slowly come down. The tail suddenly unwrapped itself and the heavy snake came crashing down into the undergrowth foliage. Startled, the Mongoose scampered out into the open while the snake zipped out and in the confusion was moving parallel to the Mongoose. Both the hunter and the hunted realized that they were running together in the same direction so they stopped and faced each other. The snake curled up and raised it's hood while the Mongoose reared up and stood on its hind legs. Both the creatures glared at each other.

"Shoo, hissed the snake.

"Not on your life", screeched the Mongoose.

"Shoo", Fangs hissed again.

"Only after I kill you".

"Then die", hissed the snake and let out a loud Khaa.

"Not so easy", screeched the Mongoose as it jumped back.

Fangs lunged again and drew back. The Mongoose scampered around him confusing him so he lunged again. He didn't realize that his adversary was tiring him out.

"Khaa", hissed Fangs as the Mongoose shot his head forward and pulled it back. He was teasing the snake.

"Your head looks delicious", screached the Mongoose as it moved forward offering itself as a bait and then jumped back out of the snake's reach.

"Khaa", screamed Fangs as he gave another lunge, "I'll get you if that's the last thing I'll do".

"You'll get nothing", replied the Mongoose as it scampered once more around the snake.

Fangs was feeling tired now. The tension and the repeated attempts at the Mongoose had tired him so he became desperate and shot his head forward again only to see the Mongoose jump back. He drew his head back and got a surprise. The Mongoose had a terrified look on his face and was looking behind the snake. It screeched, turned around and scampered away. Fangs was bewildered. "What had scared the Mongoose?", he wondered, "was the eagle attacking him?" He was about to turn around when he saw Rama walk up to a place twenty feet in front of him and stand with his legs apart and his hands on his hips.

"Now what's happening?", thought Fangs, "what's happened to the world. Even the humans aren't afraid of me. Khaa", he hissed.

Rama jumped back and moved forward. Fangs was looking at him when he felt something hit his hood causing his head to fall to the ground where it was pinned to the grass as he lashed his tail. "Khaa, Khaa, Khaa", he screamed. A long U shaped stick had his neck pinned to the ground.

"The humans have captured him", squawked a crow.

"Yaaay", the humans have captured him", chattered the Babblers.

"Now they will club him and kill him", the other crows squawked as they flew around in circles.

"Shoo", shouted Rama as he flailed his hands at the crows. "Shoo, go away".

Fangs was bewildered as he desperately lashed his tail and screamed out "Khaa's" at the grass. A hand caught his neck and the stick that had pinned him to the ground was lifted.

"The human has caught him", cawed the crows.

"Now he will rip him apart", chattered the Babblers.

"The snake is big", said the man who was holding the neck.

He was short, dark, and had a round face and a bald head. He wore a dirty white kurta over a filthy green lungi and was bare foot. The snake had curled it's body around his hand.

"Pull out the teeth?", said Rama, "and be quick. Panditji must not know that you caught this snake. He prays to it. He says that it is a God and was the one who made him the master".

The two humans walked towards the boundary wall where two cloth slings attached to a four foot long stick, lay. A little basket made out of dried reeds could be seen in one of the slings. The basket was round and had a little round lid. Fang's grew suspicious as the man holding him lifted him up in front of his face. His hand pressed hard forcing the cobra's mouth to open wide showing the projecting pair of milky white teeth.

Fangs suspicion grew. Only one person had treated him in that manner. His open mouth was at the level of the man's face who was smiling. Two of the humans teeth were missing and there was a gaping hole where they should have been. The man put his right hand into his kurta pocket and fished out a pair of pliers. Fangs recognized it. "My god", he thought, "I've been captured again. It's a snake charmer who is holding me".

The pliers' traveled upto the mouth as the beady eyes watched it. "Good heavens. He's going to pull out my Fangs.

No, please, no. Please not that. My Fangs, my Fangs, my dear little Fangs. I'm helpless without them".

The pliers' made contact, clasped a white teeth and wrenched it out. "Aaagh", yelled Fangs as his body tightened around the mans hand. The plier let the teeth fall to the ground and moved up to the second one, and wrenched it out. "Aaagh", yelled the snake. "That hurt bad. My mouth feels as though it's on fire. Oooh, Aaah, Ouch".

The snake çharmer peered into the mouth for the venom bags and the pliers wrenched them out. The man then took out a stick from his kurta pocket. It's tip was wrapped in cotton and was covered in a paste. The snake charmer looked at the two wounds he had caused and jabbed the paste into them. The paste tasted bitter and hurt the snake who showed its displeasure by tightening its body around the hand it was wrapped around and hissing helplessly.

The snake charmer then bent down and opened the lid of a Pitara. A cobra at once lifted its head and opened its hood. "Here is a friend for you", said the man as he caught Fangs tail and unwrapped him from around his hand and lowered the tail into the basket. Fangs body automatically adjusted itself by coiling up inside the basket, so the snake charmer let go of the head and pushed the lid down on the two snakes. Taking a string he tied it tightly around the Pitara and put it into the cloth sling. He lifted the stick and put it across his shoulder and stood up with the two slings hanging from the stick. The other sling also carried a Pitara which housed a couple of water snakes.

"Thank you", said the snake charmer.

"Hurry, and be off. The Priest might see you".

Inside the pitara Fangs was bewildered with the turn of events as he fought with the other snake for space to adjust himself. Just a short while ago he was a ferocious Cobra whom the world had feared and hated. The birds, insects and everything he saw feared him and now suddenly he was in a basket with his teeth tonsured out.

"Will you stop pushing", hissed the other snake.

"Shut up", hissed back Fangs.

"Stop shoving", hissed the other cobra.

"Shut up", hissed back Fangs as he pushed the other snake's head.

"Stop bullying me", wailed the smaller cobra.

High up in the skies. The birds were bewildered. They saw the human pull out the teeth and put the snake into the basket and close it. They saw him carry the stick with the sling's and walk out of the double lioned gate. What the humans intentions were, the birds did not know. They were happy that the snake was being taken away. They unanimously felt that it was good riddance to bad rubbish.

Inside the pitara the bewildered snake lay silent as he adjusted himself as comfortably as was possible by using his nourished healthy body to bully the undernourished unhealthy snake. He wondered how the snake charmer had arrived at the spot. He did not know that the person had been seen by Rama in the village that day. When the servant saw him wrapped on top of the tree, he had quietly run off and informed the snake charmer who had hurried back with him. They had seen the commotion and had waited for an hour for the snake to come down. When the snake did finally come down and slithered out of the undergrowth slithering parallel to the Mongoose, Rama shooed off the Mongoose and had stood in front of the snake to attract its attention. The tired creature had forgotten about it's behind and the snake charmer had pinned it's head to the ground with a U shaped stick.

The snake charmer walked as he blew into the odd looking flute that he was carrying. Fang's could not hear it but remembered the smell of the basket. "Yuck, yuck, yuck", he thought as he flicked out his forked tongue and remembered the slight bobbing of the Pitara as the snake charmer walked on.

"Stop shoving", complained the other snake.

"Behold, the snake Lord", the snake charmer shouted, "behold the Nagraj. He is the lord and he is the giver. Ask him for anything and he will grant it. Ask him for money, and you will become rich. Ask him for a wife and he will give you two. Ask him for a boy child and he will give you four".

"Yuck", thought Fangs as he pushed his head up against the Pitara's lid. "Open up. I don't belong here. My mouth hurts and I feel like vomiting. This basket smells bad. Yuck, yuck, yuck, yuck, yuck. Open up and let me out. I don't belong here".

Blowing the flute the snake charmer walked away into the evening.